I0551968

THE EXPANSION BOOK 3
CONFLICT

DEVON C. FORD

PRESS

VULPINE

P R E S S

Copyright © Devon C Ford 2020

The author's moral rights have been asserted.

All rights reserved. No part of this publication may be reproduced, stored in or introduced into a retrieval system or transmitted in any form or by any means, electronic, mechanical, photocopying, recording or otherwise without prior written permission from the publisher.

This novel is entirely a work of fiction. Names, characters, places and incidents are either the product of the author's imagination or are used fictitiously, and any resemblance to any person or persons, living or dead, is entirely coincidental. No affiliation is implied or intended to any organisation or recognisable body mentioned within.

First published by DHP Publishing in 2018
Published by Vulpine Press in the United Kingdom in 2020

Cover image by Jamie Glover at eruleanfuture.com
Cover by Claire Wood

ISBN: 978-1-83919-334-7

www.vulpine-press.com

"War does not determine who is right – only who is left."
Bertrand Russell

PROLOGUE

Mars Deep Orbit

"Comm, get me a fleet-wide channel," Admiral Elias Dassiova said confidently, almost happily. He leaned back into his throne-like command chair on the bridge of the carrier *Indomitable*.

"Channel ready, Admiral," the comm officer responsible for inter-fleet communications responded smoothly.

Dassiova looked at the console beside his seat, a larger screen than was on his last flagship, the *Venture*. He needed the larger screen so that he didn't have to squint at it or accept the laser eye-corrective surgery he would no doubt require soon.

Just like my father used to be, he thought with a sharp stab of loss and regret. *My eyes are fine, but my arms aren't long enough to read the datapads.* He stabbed a very deliberate finger onto the button to transmit.

"Members of the Ninth Fleet," he said, the sadness replaced with happy excitement. "This is the admiral." He paused for effect, imagining the multitude of people under his command over the thirteen ships, stopping and looking up at the speakers as his voice emanated from them. "We are about to set course for the Centauri system. Be under no illusion that we will be fighting to take control of it. Our enemy there, the Va'alen, is a formidable foe and will test the new capabilities of our ships, our technology and our very personal resolve before we win this fight. I know you will all do your duty to the best of your abilities, and each and every one of you will go down in Earth's history as the brave men and women who forged the way for humanity to expand into another system."

He paused again, cursing himself for having gone off-book already in the speech he had prepared. "We *will* succeed. Trust in your commanding officers, trust in your fellow seamen and soldiers, trust in *me*, and we will be victorious. Let's get this done; Dassiova out."

He hit the button to end the transmission, feeling a little foolish and embarrassed to be addressing everyone. He was still growing accustomed to leading so many. He rolled his shoulders before giving his next orders.

"Sound general quarters," he instructed. The lighting changed as all non-essential personnel scurried away to wait out the possible risks at the far end of their artificial wormhole jump. "Helm, plot us a course for beyond the Oort cloud. The rest of the fleet to follow at twenty-second intervals."

"Course laid in, sir," the helmsman of their massive carrier responded.

"Instructions relayed fleet-wide, Admiral," the comm officer reported.

A ripple of emotion ran through the bridge, setting hairs on end as people shuddered at their controls. Dassiova fought the urge to rub at his forearms where the exposed skin showed the raised fuzz covering his lower limbs and turned slowly to look at the newest addition to his bridge crew. The lone Kuldar, Asha, seemed swamped by the flight suit bearing the embossed name of the fleet's flagship. He had been assigned to the crew, much by his own insistence and that of his mate. The latter was their rather laid-back monarch and leader. Sensing that he was under scrutiny, Asha turned to see the admiral scowling at him.

"I am," he said in hissing and hesitant English, "sorry."

Dassiova said nothing, but his body reacted to the emotion of the moment. The nervous excitement was so extreme that it took the breath away from the younger members of his crew. He rolled his neck slightly rather than telling off their alien ambassador. He'd found himself doing this regularly. Asha was like a curious child who asked what a thing did by pushing buttons. He had done this once too often when looking at the tactical station where the ship's main weapons were controlled. Dassiova faced forward and was glad that his own strong emotions didn't radiate out like their new allies' did.

"Initiate jump on my mark… Let's make history. *Jump*."

Almost two light years from Earth, the black, empty space of an empty sector suddenly hosted a dull, soundless flash. The huge shape of the *Indomitable* rippled into appearance as if from nowhere. That was, as far as technical definitions went, pretty accurate. They *had* been nowhere—nowhere in conventional space and time—for a little over a minute. During that short minute, the fine-tuned device protruding ahead of their now quad-layered frontal shields resonated electromagnetic fields to fold space. This allowed for the gargantuan carrier and the eight heavily armed destroyers nestled into her huge hull to pass through the artificially created portal.

Dassiova sat still in his chair and waited for the reports to come back; first from the helm to report that their jump was accurate to within a thousand kilometers. That distance was a vast improvement given the extensive experiments over the last few months in the far reaches of their home solar system.

The next report was from the tactical officer watching the sector readouts, calling out the contact of another UN ship arriving a few thousand kilometers away. Dassiova nodded his understanding, waiting until all the names of the ships appeared on the sensor display, each name following his enormous contraption of interstellar war like ducklings behind their mother.

Hammer. Venture. Cortez. Anvil. Vengeance. Ichi.

"All fleet vessels present and accounted for, Admiral," the comm officer reported. He had received successful jump flash reports transmitted on the fleet comm band as soon as they arrived in the sector.

"Outstanding," Dassiova said. The entire fleet was on his display as a well-ordered and closely grouped array of symbols. "Order all vessels to run full diagnostic reports and check in when they have the all-clear."

"Aye aye."

Protocols, Dassiova thought. *Even this far out we all still have to follow goddamned protocols.*

He knew the ships would be fine and in full battle-ready order. They had all tested their Fold Drives close enough to Mars to be able to limp home under sub-light speeds if something went wrong. But, since this was their first operational fleet jump, the rules had to be followed.

"Sir," the comm officer called out. "Captain Halstead of the *Vengeance* reporting a surge in her Fold Drive emitter's power supply."

"Signal the fleet for an all-stop," he said. "Conduct a training scenario for instant defense positions and ask Captain Halstead to use the time for a thorough diagnostic."

The orders were given, and the hours of fleet training paid off as Dassiova watched his little flock adopt the positions that the theoretical scenario called for. His own flagship, the *Indomitable*, aptly named, surged ahead of the more vulnerable ships in the fleet, where the maneuvers of her eight limpet-like attachments were slick to the point of outright intimidating. The docked gun barges, four on each of the carrier's sides, shed their clamps and fired their maneuvering repulsers at maximum to push their squat, space-tank-like hulls away before fanning out to form a front perimeter defense.

Dassiova wasn't a fan of the term 'gun barge.' He felt it made those ships sound like little more than slow-moving tubs. Instead, the separately crewed ships allowed his carrier a much more impressive capability for violence. They weren't quite cruisers. They certainly weren't battleships like the *Venture* had been before she was retrofitted, and by no stretch of the imagination were they on a par with the agile and heavily armed frigates. Still, Dassiova supposed there was at least some accuracy to the term attached to them. They were mobile artillery platforms capable of operating independently of their mother ship for a few days at a time, and although they had no Fold Drive capability, they were practically dripping with ordnance and carried more shielding than the surface of their moon.

The carrier itself was bristling with the new alien technology cannons, mass-produced on Mars and fitted to every ship in threes where only one conventional weapon would have sat before. She took point in the defensive line with enough firepower alone to dominate the entire space-going fleet of Earth, even without the thick-hulled, grossly overpowered squad of gun barges that seemed to suckle from her teats.

The admiral's screen refreshed, and he saw that the *Ichi*, their space-fleet's version of a silent reconnaissance submarine, appeared farther ahead to extend the range of their sensors. That ship, small and fast but well-armed and shrouded to be invisible to the enemy, was the scalpel in comparison to his wrecking ball.

To the flanks of their formation, facing outward and slightly to the rear at the end of the line of the gun barges, came the two heavy frigates: the newly built *Norton's Vengeance* and the repaired and re-fitted *Hammer*. Captains Hayes and Halstead ran those ships and having seen their performances of their last foray into the Centauri system, nobody could doubt their bravery or abilities.

Nestled in the center at the point of safety were the two most vulnerable ships of their flotilla: the repurposed *Cortez* and the newly added *Anvil*. The *Cortez*, commanded by the ever-unhappy Captain Wright, carried their main supplies. The *Anvil* was their mobile forge ship under the command of their Russian captain, Novak. It had a vast section of its belly missing to allow for other ships to dock in deep space and for the bug shield arrays to encompass them for re-pairs.

At the rear, turned side-on to show a full broadside and plug the gap, was the fleet's former flagship, the *Venture*. She, like the *Cortez*, had been hastily but thoroughly repurposed to be a weapons plat-form to house the skeleton of a defensive space station. That repur-posing was one of Dassiova's primary stipulations. He wholly be-lieved that a series of more permanent bases was required to capture and hold the sector from the worryingly large number of Va'alen still stranded there.

Dassiova's gaze lingered on the *Ichi*, far out in front. Often over-looked in the fleet because of its size, the *Boken sha Ichi* captained by Kyle Torres was a fine instrument and was the sole reason he was there in charge of the biggest, and most expensive fleet ever put to-gether. The *Ichi* might be small, but her retrofitting had seen the addition of another, larger power source to feed the additional guns and increase the effectiveness of the shroud. This had been further refined since allowing them to creep undetected far behind the enemy lines of the Va'alen. Utilizing the shroud, the *Ichi* had provided the critical intelligence used to destroy the gateway device that, as Dassiova had often said, "represented an infinite number of superior enemy reinforcements." The constant ratification of his signing-off on that mission, one conducted and conceived by Torres and Halstead, was required. The paymasters on Earth were less than impressed at having a newly refurbished frigate used as a suicide bomber.

"All ships report in position," the comm officer said loudly, breaking the admiral's bubble of a daydream. "All shields at maximum and all weapons systems ready."

"Outstanding," Dassiova said again.

"And the *Vengeance* reports normal diagnostics; just a blip in their shield emitter, which is all fixed."

"Good," the admiral said, feeling that the new word he used seemed inadequate after his over-use of 'outstanding.' "Signal the exercise over, dock our birds and plot the next jump."

"Coordinates, Admiral?" asked the newly transferred chief pilot. He had been taken from the demoted *Cortez* where a man of his talent wouldn't be required, since the ship was non-combatant.

"Edge of the Centauri system, Mister Moon," Dassiova said. "As soon as the destroyers are docked, punch it."

HYPeR facility, Mars

Six Months Earlier

"I'm sorry, Doctor Paterson," the black-uniformed private military contractor said woodenly as he barred the door to the research lab. "I can't allow you access at this time."

7

"What time *can* you allow me access?" Paterson snapped back, reverting to aggressive sarcasm when all other avenues had failed him.

"I'm afraid I don't have that information."

"What information do you have?"

"I'm afraid I don't have that information," the guard repeated robotically.

"You don't know that you don't know, mall cop?" Paterson goaded.

"I know that I can't allow you access at this time, sir." Paterson threw his arms up and walked away a few steps in

exasperation. It was the third time that day he had tried to gain access to the Hyper labs where Specter had been taken as soon as they had docked after returning from the Centauri system. The damage Specter had sustained on their mission wasn't catastrophic, but it had triggered either some kind of psycho logical disassociation or had scrambled whatever reprogramming they had done.

Jake, or Specter—depending on who he woke up as—had saved their mission, as well as the lives of some very key personnel. The secretive company that had invested in the almost dead trooper and rebuilt him to make him the incredible weapon he was now had since erected an information blackout about the cyborg's wellbeing.

The door behind Paterson hissed open, making him drop his hands from his face and spin back around to face the open aperture. His expression dropped when he saw the short man who walked out. Ryan Levenstein, the company administrator who found himself swept up on the wild ride of their previous mission, walked out wearing a shirt and pants that seemed tailored and expensive.

"Paterson," he said dismissively in arrogant greeting. His voice alone repulsed the scientist.

"He in there?" Paterson asked angrily.

"I can't confirm that," Levenstein answered annoyingly.

"Cut the shit," Paterson snapped. "What *can* you confirm?" "I can confirm that our company asset is functioning properly, and *if* said asset was deployed again, it would be under more strict control measures by the company."

"So, *he* is okay, but you want to send one of your hacks with him next time?" Paterson demanded, his anger taking the credibility from his words.

"However you want to interpret that, Paterson," Levenstein answered with a corporate smirk.

⁓

"The reason I have called you here is to remain between *us* only," Admiral Dassiova said as he glared at the assembled ships' captains to be certain that his point was understood.

"What I am about to say is, and will remain, classified."

A ripple of affirmations ran around the assembled officers, prompting him to go on.

"Over the last month, we have found unauthorized communications from here to Earth," he said. Before him a collection of eyebrows rose. "Whoever is doing it is smart; they're re-routing their transmissions through two or three of the ships remotely and sending encrypted data-burst only. As you all know, that makes it goddammed hard to pinpoint their origins. We've tracked the origins," he nodded to indicate Suranne Massey, his flight officer, "of these signals as far as possible, rotated out all of the encryption codes required to use the subspace comm arrays, and still are none the wiser as to who is sending home postcards without authority."

The room took on a fidgety feel, as though everyone present was shifting on the spot, in case it was any of their crew who was responsible. Finding the culprit among thousands was an almost impossible task.

"Do we know where the signals are being received?" Captain Halstead asked.

"No," Massey answered for the admiral, "only that the burst transmissions have been directed at both the Lunar base and Earth. The trajectories aren't recorded in the comm data logs—intentionally it seems—and every terminal that they have been run through is unmanned at the times they've been remotely hacked. Like the admiral said, whoever is doing this is *smart*."

"Who have you had working on it?" Torres asked. He thought they should use one of the best scientists they had, who just happened to be his friend and was now part of the *Ichi*'s crew after he had been dragged along when they were attacked at their Lunar base.

"Very few people for now," Dassiova said, "and all of those have been personally vetted by me." His words brooked no recourse to investigate anyone already in the know. The admiral's word was incontestable. "So, the plan is to create a new software protocol to actively monitor the arrays and record anything sent. Sure, it may be encrypted, but I bet that's nothing we can't break once we actually have some hard evidence."

"Sir," Captain Hayes interjected, "we sure it's UN? I mean, there are plenty of those Hyper assho– *people* here and their PMCs aren't exactly team players."

"I'm well aware of the fact that the private military detachments with the fleet aren't to your personal liking, Captain Hayes," Dassiova said coldly, "but I have it on high authority that our corporate friends aren't in play on this. In fact, they're the ones who are helping with the new software. They have just as much of a vested interest in keeping their prototype tech out of the hands of everyone who isn't paying a million credits for a new armor or gun design."

Silence filled the room once more after the obvious concerns had been raised, until Massey spoke again.

"We've used the new software patch to shut down the subspace comm array of every ship except the *Indomitable*. Unfortunately, that just means that this ship ends up being the one to send the messages, and we're still no closer to figuring it out."

"What do you need from us, Admiral?" Captain Novak of the forge ship *Anvil* asked. Their Russian UNID man who had done so much to ensure the rapid building of the new ships had gone smoothly was beyond suspicion, given how he had been so tireless in ensuring their readiness.

He was also infectiously happy and, like many Russians the assembled captains had met, was obsessed with everything from the American Territory. The Russians, after formally distancing themselves from the inter-territory squabbles that had threatened war on Earth, had firmly allied themselves with the British and the Americans.

"I need you to start from scratch," Dassiova said. "Wipe all comm protocols and authorities from every one of your personnel and limit that access to a rolling encryption accessible via the bridge rotations. If we get another transmission, we'll have a smaller pool to fish in." Dassiova stood and smoothed down the body of his flight suit. "Now, if you wouldn't mind making your ships ready, we'll be heading out to sea at oh-six-hundred tomorrow. Dismissed."

CHAPTER 1

Proxima Centauri Present Day

The subspace sensor array left behind on their last visit to the Centauri system—the one hastily jury-rigged and dumped as they jumped from the system—had been sending back a steady stream of intel. That intel, as sporadic as it had become over the last few months, showed that at least their jump entry point was safe and free of the swarms of alien ships that had forced them to flee the system.

Nobody considered that by destroying their enemy's portal to get reinforcements, they had also destroyed the remaining Va'alen's only way of leaving the system. They had condemned every Va'alen left stranded to fight for another way home.

When the Ninth Fleet first arrived, desperately underpowered and under-gunned, they had no clue that there were other races already there. They were unaware that one of those races was a warlike species, just one Va'alen capable of fighting with all the destructive power of an entire squad of human troops equipped with the latest weapons tech Earth had to offer. The footage of Brandt's small team engaging the pair of Va'alen on the eerily dark surface of Proxima had been classified to begin with. After it had been studied, enhanced and picked over by experts, that footage had been clipped and sanitized, with extracts being made available to the fighting strength of each ship's complement for educational and training purposes.

Quickly, Zero and the others had become legends among the fleet—every bit of footage containing Specter had been painstakingly removed—and that sense of celebrity spread like wildfire.

None of them liked that, especially since the two special operators—Brandt and Zero—had an ingrained need for anonymity. Brandt couldn't avoid people knowing who she was, not when she was the ground commander of the fleet's recon ship, but Zero had enjoyed walking around in his plain flight suit with no badge of rank or name tape. Even if he had worn his rank and name, that of Master Petty Officer James Conrad, he doubted anyone but a few of the crew would have known who he was.

Now they were off-base and out in deep space— 'at sea' as they called it in an archaic throwback to their naval origins—it was far less of an issue. The last few months on the Mars base and on the floating shipyards in orbit, Zero had been annoyed by every other person wanting to high-five him or slap him on the back for simply doing his job.

"Why do they have to be like that about it?" Zero had asked Brandt when they were alone after a briefing.

"Just relax," Brandt told him. She knew that it was really the attention he disliked, as though it painted a target on his back. "Them seeing you makes them feel like we have super soldiers on our side. People are scared of the Va'alen and they need something to get behind. Something to believe in."

"We *have* a super soldier, only people outside of this crew don't know he exists," Zero grumbled back.

Brandt, of all people, didn't need reminding of that fact. Jake Santana, or at least the parts of him that hadn't died and had been remade into Specter, had been kept from them almost the entire time they were resupplying and refitting on Mars. Zero hadn't known him before, but as Specter was one of his team, he felt an affinity and a responsibility toward the cyborg. Specter had returned only for the last stages of their build-up training and Brandt was so busy with her duties as a commander that she barely had time to acknowledge him. She ignored Zero's complaints about their classified teammate and changed the subject.

"How are you feeling about staying on the *Ichi*?" she asked.

After the mission reports from Proxima and his initiative in finding out more of the story between the Kuldar and the Va'alen, Zero had been offered promotion to Command Chief and the lead of his own CP team. He'd kept his face neutral and his voice stoic as he'd politely asked if it was an offer or an order, and then turned it down. He was resolute in his choice to remain on the crew of the *Ichi* under Brandt's command.

"Fine," he drawled, drawing the word out. "The way I see it, if they want to pin another shiny on my chest and give me my own team for just doin' my job, then that offer's just as likely to be on the table when we get back after this trip. If it ain't? Well, at least I'm where I wanna be right now. I've already made Master off the back of this, and some publicity stunt making me Chief half a dozen years ahead of the curve just smells like propaganda to me. No, ma'am; that dog won't hunt."

Brandt nodded, accepting his stilted compliment even if he didn't know he'd given it to her. Before anything else could be said, the ship's intercom buzzed.

"Commander Brandt to the bridge."

Brandt stood, recognizing Torres's clipped tones. She suspected that he had used the intercom because it was faster than hitting the additional commands on his console to get her comm directly. She told Zero to get to his gun position and left the soldier's ready room,

14

which had become a kind of duty team crash deck, to walk the short distance past the armory toward the bridge. The doors hissed as they slid open and Brandt walked onto the revamped bridge with the additional tactical station to manage the uprated shielding and weapons arrays. She nodded to Torres, who had glanced up as she entered, and she sat in the seat beside him.

"Fully charged and ready to go, Captain," Rogers called out confidently from the helm.

"Signal from the *Indomitable*," the comm officer said. "We're to jump last again after the *Vengeance*."

Torres nodded and gave the string of orders that would see them ready for action on their arrival in the Centauri system.

"Shields to maximum," he said confidently in a voice that demanded immediate compliance. "Helm, plot the course and stand by for my mark. Commander? Are your gunners in position?"

Brandt looked down at the console to her right, and saw the four readouts all showing green lights across the board as her troops signaled their readiness.

"Good to go, sir," she answered.

"The *Vengeance* has jumped," the ensign at the tactical station said.

"Lieutenant Rogers, you can go now."

Tense minutes passed as they traveled through the curious nowhere of the Fold Drive's effect. Very few of them under stood exactly how they worked, but the commonly accepted explanation was that the emitters folded space and time so that two places impossibly far apart could be manipulated to be closer together. Instead of the journey between their entry and exit points of this nowhere being thousands of years' travel apart, it reduced the time to mere minutes. Various terms were used when talking about it: wormhole, FTL,

Fold Space, jump. They seemed to collectively settle on each activation being referred to as a 'jump' as it seemed the most natural terminology to explain the science in very simple terms.

"We have the rest of the fleet," the tactical officer confirmed after their re-emergence into the galaxy.

"Everyone where they're supposed to be?" Torres asked.

"The *Anvil* is slightly off, but the formation is within limits," the report came back. This satisfied the captain that their jump accuracy problems had been almost solved.

"Sensors?" Brandt asked, checking if there was any trace of the enemy.

"Nothing on active sweeps," tactical responded. "Nothing from the sensor buoy or the rest of the fleet."

"Understood," Torres said. "Hail the *Indomitable*."

"Incoming comm from the admiral, sir," the comm officer said as she half-turned, smirking.

"On screen," Torres said. Dassiova's bridge blinked into existence on their large display that gave the impression of their ship having a giant windshield.

"Captain," the admiral growled. This was actually his good mood, though he gave the impression that he was perpetually annoyed with everyone.

"Admiral," Torres answered before pre-empting the orders. "You want us to jump ahead?"

"Yes," Dassiova said. "Push out a light year and go dark. *Indomitable* out."

Torres, accustomed to their fleet commander's brusque style, took no offense at the brevity of the orders and gave his own.

"Rogers, plot the jump and go when ready," he said. He caught Brandt's eye and got the nod from her that she still had her gunners ready. "Prepare the Shroud device and activate as soon as we drop."

The *Ichi* jumped, appearing in empty space and shimmering out of existence as soon as the ship emerged. It set off at three-quarters sublight speed on a heading toward the twin suns farther into the system. They maintained passive sensor sweeps as they slid along in their invisibility. The *Ichi* could act as fleet recon far more effectively now that the ship had been given the device that masked their visible signature from the prying eyes and devastating weapons of the Va'alen.

They saw nothing. Their protocol of waiting to see if their jump signature was answered with an incoming squadron of enemy ships yielded nothing. None came, and instead of the lack of response giving the *Ichi*'s crew a sense of bravery and reassurance, it made them all the more nervous.

"Tac, don't you take your eyes off the scanners, not even for a second," Torres said, betraying his nerves while he reminded his crew what was required of them.

"Yes, sir," the young ensign manning that station answered. He seemed energized by his captain's words instead of unsettled.

~

"Set a course for Proxima," Dassiova ordered. "Signal the fleet to follow in formation. A stereo response of 'aye aye,' came from ahead of him as his pilot and fleet-comm officer acknowledged their orders. The plan, which was all going as expected, was to secure the closest end of the system where the dull, red sun gave an eerie glow to the shadowy exoplanet locked in its orbit. That planet, the former temporary home to the rescued Kuldar, was to be secured and retaken before the rest of the fleet pressed closer to the twin suns. This all had to be done before they pursued the ultimate goal of eradicating the enemy in the system and harvesting the Earth-like planet.

The problem, at least in Dassiova's mind, was that when plans went so well, there was always a monumental setback locked and loaded, ready to fire at him.

The *Venture*, the repurposed colony ship which had set the UN back a few billion credits, now held the deployable space station that they planned to drop in deep orbit of Proxima Centauri to be their base in the system; it would be their toe-hold, their beachhead. From there, with their supplies on the *Cortez* and mobile forge ship, the *Anvil*, able to rebuild and repair any damage to their fighting ships, they could utilize their Fold Drives to send the fighting elements of the fleet to any part of the system in minutes.

That was the plan, anyway, but Dassiova knew from hard-earned experience that no plan survived contact with the enemy.

"Still nothing on sensors?" he growled at the tactical station.

"Nothing, sir," came the response, "active or passive."

"And the array?" the admiral asked. The automated and shrouded buoy they had left behind should be collecting data.

"No, sir. We detected the *Ichi* jump signature on its long-range sweep but nothing since. Skies are clear, Admiral."

Dassiova said nothing but frowned.

Where the hell are you, you bug bastards? he thought.

He wasn't surprised that they'd detected the *Ichi* jumping in. No matter what they tried, no matter how they recalibrated and regardless of whatever tests they conducted to attempt different ways of dropping out of the artificial wormholes they created, their ships reemerging into normal space set off a flare on sensors visible for close to a light year. The smaller the ship meant only a slight reduction in the signal spike, so for the massive *Indomitable* to jump into a system meant that anyone with sensors within two hundred and fifty million kilometers would know about it.

As much as they sought to avoid it, there was no way to mask their arrival in the system. But that didn't mean that they had to hang around and wait for the Va'alen to turn up and start ripping into them again. Dassiova was both apprehensive and excited about the prospect of meeting their enemy again; mostly to prove that the redesigns and upgrades he had insisted on—at astronomical cost—would be up to the task of defeating the aliens who had torn their ships to shreds during their last conflict.

"Take us in, Mister Moon," he ordered the chief pilot of the huge carrier flagship.

"Aye aye," Moon answered, fingers dancing over his console like a first chair violinist performing a solo recital in front of an audience of thousands.

"Signal the *Venture* to start pitching her tent," he instructed one of the bridge's comm officers, eager to get their stall set out and their defense array in place so he could go to work.

So he could start hunting.

CHAPTER 2

Alpha Centauri A Orbit

The Va'alen supreme commander, Muq Da'kath, stalked from his headquarters in a foul temper. All around him other Va'alen, all of them smaller, scattered to avoid his wrath. Each hoped that they weren't the cause of his evident bad mood. He was the Do-Ch'aal; the First Warrior and leader of the expedition, and he was deeply concerned.

It's too soon, he thought angrily to himself, *how can the humans be back already?*

He knew that his anger was just a reflex. He knew that it served no good purpose and wasted valuable energy on emotion instead of action. Whether he knew this or not made no difference, because the humans were back and his engineers had yet to manufacture enough of the new devices to get his legions out of the system. Even if they had managed it, it would mean the Va'alen abandoning not only the system and the resources they had found, but it would also mean scuttling much of their hardware and leaving behind many non-essential personnel to the mercy of the humans.

Muq Da'kath didn't know if the other species had any mercy, but he knew for certain that any humans left behind when his forces had run them out of the system would have found no mercy in his treatment. They would have been tortured for every scrap of information they possessed, taken apart piece by piece until they had nothing left to say, before being fed into the biological recyclers to feed his legions.

He stormed toward the empty bay where the team was building and fitting the device they had reversed-engineered into the single ship.

On seeing him approach, his fearful entourage scurrying along in his wake, the lead engineer broke away from the production line and ran to kneel before the head of their race.

"Supreme Commander," he hissed, his head bowing and the two right arms resting on his right knee as his left hit the floor with a chitinous thump. The supreme commander paused as he walked past but didn't break his step, allowing himself a feeling of smug power as the lead engineer rose quickly to his feet and ran to catch up.

"Tell me when you will finish," he snarled at the underling.

"We still need thirty rotations to fit what we have made to the ship. Twice that to test it and make refinements…"

"Too long," the commander said, without looking down at the engineer. He kept his face blank, scanning the workers assembling the devices. He suspected that his presence alone had taken a day off the estimate he had been given. He ignored the engineer, turning partway to address a Va'alen half his intimidating size to pose a question he didn't want the answer to.

"How many did they bring?"

The aide hesitated, but only briefly. She had no desire to be the second member of the entourage to have an arm ripped clean off their carapace for failing to answer a question. Though the limb would grow back, she had no desire to spend painful days needed for that if it could be avoided. The supreme commander turned a little more to look at her, prompting half an involuntary step back before her mate held out the arms on his right side to stop her, reminding her that she was a warrior.

"Almost twice what they had the first time," she guessed, given the size and number of the sensor spikes they had detected. "Maybe slightly more."

"So, I am faced with fighting more than twice the humans who came before, with no supply chain? With no reinforcements?"

Silence answered him. He glanced at the others around him, seeing them turn their faces down to the deck in fear.

"Why don't we just destroy these new humans and complete our work?" one of them asked.

The supreme commander looked at him. There was no averting of his gaze. The commander noticed the high sheen and rich brown color of the speaker's carapace that indicated his young age, but the status evident in his size and overt strength was on display.

Arrogant youth, he thought. *He still thinks that attitude can over come insurmountable odds.*

The commander didn't voice those opinions; showing weakness in front of any of his underlings was tantamount to suicide, but this one was even more dangerous. He was one of dozens of Va'alen from other clans who had been attached to the mission as either an opportunity to gain honor or as some inter-clan bartering to strengthen bonds or repay debts. This one was only there to earn glory, and the commander suspected that the glory would be to seize control of the mission and lead them to victory. The arrival of the aliens, foolishly broadcasting their planet's history along with the detailed information about their physiology, had sparked panic initially. Not panic among his ranks of warriors, not among those who had volunteered for the mission, but among the weak and pathetic.

Among those who were in this system distant from their home world without choice.

It was the reluctant ones he now had to inspire to work hard to achieve new mission goals, and this upstart from another clan, who almost matched his size but boasted less than half of his age, was spreading his poison at every opportunity.

"Because, Aq Qa'shal, we have fewer than a thousand ships left at our disposal," he began carefully. He spoke almost quietly to signal to the youth that he was speaking directly for his benefit alone. "Because we are stranded without reinforcements until this device can be made to work and we can send a ship back to our own system, so that it can be replicated and the clans can send ten thousand ships back to wipe out the humans, to eradicate them from the galaxy, to invade their home world and take all of their resources in punishment for the brave Va'alen they have killed here."

His voice had risen with each sentence he spoke. That made the rest of his entourage who were all of his own clan cower in submission with their blank faces turned down. The challenger did not cower. He did not adopt a pose of submission. Instead he stayed tall and resolute. But just as he made no show of deference to the supreme commander, he was also very careful to offer no confrontation. His behavior, which he knew would not go unnoticed, pushed the limits of their social interactions as far as they could possibly be pushed without either being forced to lay down a challenge.

The would-be challenger broke the deadlock with an insincere bow, which was automatically mimicked by his mate, who stood three paces behind him.

"Supreme Commander," Qa'shal said acidly without investing any reverence of respect in his tone, "I am certain that if any Va'alen

23

was equal to the challenges we face here, it is *you* who would triumph."

Da'kath, frustratingly disarmed by the words, was power less to challenge him without provocation. If they ever got back, the *Borka*, their assembly of clan elders under guidance of their Hive Lords, would hold him responsible for the challenge and find it unwarranted. He would be forced to pay the price of the young Va'alen to his clan, and that price would be exorbitantly high enough to ruin him.

That was if the Hive Lords didn't tear his limbs from his body beforehand.

And that's if I even won the challenge, he thought sourly as he again considered challenging the warrior. Although young and inexperienced, he couldn't deny the power and ability in the youth. He decided to play it politically.

"And what would you suggest as a strategy, Aq Qa'shal?" the commander asked carefully, emphasizing his underling rank of Aq to his superior rank of Muq.

A ripple of unease went through his entourage. They knew the question was as much of a challenge as the false compliments he had received. The younger Va'alen from another clan was faced with an impossible choice: back down and defer to the supreme commander, which was to openly accept his leadership and make any subsequent challenge harder to explain, or else suggest a strategy and risk death if that strategy failed.

To his credit, or at least in testimony to his youthful arrogance, he didn't hesitate.

"If I had the honor of being made supreme commander," he began dangerously, "I would send the hive farther away into the system and avoid conflict with the humans… *yet*… I would scatter our forces and hide them, order them to bide their time until called to fight, and when the device was ready to send back to our world, I would launch our offensive—send wave after wave at them until they were destroyed, and we could take the system again and return bathed in glory."

The supreme commander realized too late what had just happened. Far from manipulating the youth, he saw that it was in fact he who had been played so expertly into a corner. The rash statement prompting action had been designed to make the supreme commander consider a challenge, and his supplication invited the political play for a suggestion to be made. Now the commander had to dismiss the proposed strategy, which would be very damaging if his own plan were less than perfectly successful, or follow it and risk the political challenge that an underling was responsible for any success.

The supreme commander had been played, and it was all he could do to not tear the arms from the entitled brat. He didn't because it would be politically unwise, but also because he couldn't be totally sure that he would win the physical contest.

"*If* you had the honor…" the supreme commander mused icily. "Perhaps one day you will have the honor, but for now you do not. I will consider your strategy." With that, he turned back to the chief engineer, who had been watching the interaction as though either of the powerful Va'alen would launch an attack on the other at any moment. The engineer dropped into a kneeling position of subservience.

"Finish your work," Da'kath ordered, "or I will replace you with someone who can, and personally recycle your worthless carcasses."

He turned and stalked away, his entourage scurrying after him in their pairs, with the exception of the clan challengers who walked tall and proud. As he strode away, he considered the impossible choice he faced.

Returning to his headquarters he leant heavily on the reflective expanse showing the system, claws clacking on the surface over the icon indicating the entry jump points for the humans. Another, closer icon showed a second sensor reading, where just one of the human ships had emerged into normal space too close to them for comfort. He had only a few thousand Va'alen, belonging predominantly to his own clan and well over half of them warriors, but they were stranded in the system. They now faced the arrival of more humans just over a light year away. Those numbers, he mused angrily, were almost twenty percent lower than what he had come with because of his recent losses.

His clawed hands contracted, sharp ends scratching on the glass surface in angry frustration. He couldn't think of a better way than the suggestion he had been manipulated into asking for. His anger abated slightly as he considered how he could manipulate the situation; he could blame the challenger if the plan failed, but if it succeeded he could claim he had inspired creativity through leadership. That way, whatever the upstart from their allied clan would say should carry no less weight than his own reports.

Allied! he scoffed to himself. *Perhaps 'allied' wasn't the right term; he was more of an enemy at a truce for the sake of a joint venture.*

The four main clans had always operated like that, at least as far back as the stories passed down through generations of his family.

At various points in their species' history, two of the main clans would always be at war with one another. Some of the lesser clans would be brought in as proxy soldiers but usually the major clans fought for honor and position among their own. Missions such as this one saw him given the title of supreme commander. Other clans had sworn fealty to him and his clan leadership for just so long as he commanded the combined forces. Such collaborations weren't uncommon, not when the prize was too large for any one clan to fund the expedition, but the politics were what the commander hated the most.

Heavy footsteps behind him made his back stiffen, his finely honed senses shooting the alert across his brain like a ship's main cannon. The sensation of completeness came to him and he relaxed. That feeling only ever occurred when his mate was close to his side. He stood erect and turned to face her, looking down on a tall and strong Va'alen warrior with a lighter carapace than his own. She was smaller than him, but nearly every other Va'alen was. He trusted above all else the fealty of those sworn to him.

All with the exception of Aq Qa'shal, that was.

"You have decided, Supreme Commander?" she enquired. Her tone suggested he should have decided by that point, and if he had not, he should decide now and accept that choice.

"I have," he responded in their hissing, sibilant tongue. "Let the upstart have his plan, and if we suffer any losses, it will be he who answers for them. I will make sure of it."

"It is not the Va'alen way," she said simply. She stopped and ducked her head slightly, bowing her shoulders in a small but noticeable gesture of submission when her mate had reared up to tower over her as he issued a low growl. She closed her mouth to render the face of her carapace featureless, hiding her pointed teeth so no sign of challenge could be misconstrued by her mate.

"I will *not* be undermined," he snarled. "Not by some clan-challenger upstart and *never* by you." His anger held him in place for a moment until she spoke.

"I do not challenge you, my mate," she said firmly. "I only wish for your command to be clear and recognized."

"It is," he snapped with less anger than before, "and it will remain so. Give the orders; our forces are to divide into squadrons and lie in wait—*not hide, make that clear*—until I signal for action. The Hive Lords are to be removed from the hive, with their permission of course, and spread out in the sector for their protection."

She bowed deeper and walked away to give the orders. They would scatter their forces, they would hide their hive and they would destroy the humans. Then he would lead a fleet of ships to their home world and take it.

"Ensure that sufficient supplies are sent to the moon base with a strong escort," he threw over his shoulder at her. If nothing else, he hoped to salvage the invaluable precious metals. This would not only elevate his family's standing in the clan, but also strengthen the entire clan's position as the strongest of the leading houses.

"I mean it," he added. "I want at least half a squadron there and I want them well equipped. I doubt the humans would find them anyway." He hoped that his guess was accurate before adding, "And make sure they come from Qa'shal's clan. That way the upstart can't cause trouble."

~

Aq Qa'shal stalked into his own quarters and finally allowed himself to pour out his frustration. He pounded the supporting pillar of the chamber with double blows from the clawed fists of his right and left arms in turn before spinning away in rage and letting out a muted snarl in place of a battle roar.

His mate followed him, but the sense of completeness her presence brought served to calm him only slightly.

"Old fool," he spat at her, as though it was her fault in some way. "Dull-hided, weak, crusty old *fool*."

"He is a fool," Qa'shal's mate agreed in a tranquil voice, which he knew was an attempt to manipulate him into settling, "but he has played into your hands. You will strike a fearsome blow to the humans and all Va'alen will know that you are the better leader. They will turn from Da'kath and you will be named supreme commander. He will order our forces to run and hide, but your squadrons will destroy the human fleet and make this system safe for our forces once more."

"But without their portal technology I am *still* at the mercy of the old fool. I should challenge him. I'll rip the limbs from his dusty corpse." He turned and slammed two more salvos of vicious punches into the inanimate structure, until dust rained down on him from the ceiling of the chamber.

His mate bowed in supplication, her body language and words showing deep respect and reverence for his mastery.

"Powerful Qa'shal," she crooned softly as she kept her head bowed and raised the upper limbs of both sides to him, "your plan is good. It is destined to be successful and when it is—"

"*If* it is," Qa'shal interrupted petulantly.

"*When* it is," his mate corrected him gently, "you will be able to take control of all Va'alen forces here and return victorious. We will have our pick of the galaxy for a ruling seat, and I would expect to see us on the Sovereign Assembly soon."

Her words sobered him. They stifled his anger and smothered it with a blanket of ambition and hope.

"Very well," Qa'shal agreed as he stood tall. "The old fool can wait for his demise. Order my squadrons to mobilize so we can crush the humans."

CHAPTER 3

Deep Space Near the Twin Suns

"Still nothing?" Torres asked, with a hint of annoyance in his voice. He had kept the crew of the *Ichi* at battle stations for close to half a day and knew that if *he* was feeling the strain, the people rotating on the tactical stations and gun positions would be worse off.

"Nothing, sir. Not a peep," replied the young officer at the tactical station.

"Alright," Torres responded. "Signal the crew to stand down but remain at general quarters."

He stood, nodding to Sarvanto to take the chair as he walked to the captain's quarters set just off the main bridge. He sat at his terminal, entered the newly encrypted details to access the subspace comm array and completed the final security check to make the ultra-long-distance call by scanning his bio-implant chip. The screen came to life to inform him that his access was granted, when the door gave a whistle like an old ship's pipe.

"Yeah?" he inquired as the door hissed aside. He smiled as Amare Eze walked in. She was wearing her ship's uniform of the same dark blue flight suit, but from her tousled hair he guessed she had just stood down from a gun position and removed her armor.

"Hi," she said, returning his smile in an unprofessionally intimate manner.

"Hi, yourself," Torres said, returning the smirk as though they both shared a secret.

"Calling the admiral to tell him it's a ghost town out here?" she asked, leaning around his terminal to look at the screen.

Torres fought the urge to kill the display and risk offending her by showing a lack of trust.

"Yeah, it's eerie. Like they've packed up and left or some thing," he answered.

"How could they?" Eze asked, her curious and smooth accent, a mixture of African and English, washing over him as she perched one cheek on the corner of his desk. "You destroyed their ticket home, didn't you?"

"I *think* we did," Torres responded with a frown, "but who knows? They might have had another device, or built one, in the time we've been gone…"

"And they might've just abandoned the system and set off home. They might have cryo-technology or be in sub-light speed reach of another gateway device. They might be hiding ready to jump out on us for a surprise party."

Torres's brow wrinkled into deeper lines. The thought that their enemy could be lying low somewhere was not lost on him, but unless they had managed to mask their signatures in the few months the fleet had been back on Mars rebuilding and refitting, he saw no way that the Va'alen could be hiding from their sensors.

"No," he said. "They're here somewhere. It's our job to find them."

Eze leaned closer, opening her mouth to say more, when her comm device pinged and a voice emanated from her left forearm.

"Viper, Grip," Brandt's voice said confidently. Eze leaned back with a playful look at her captain and secret lover to activate the comm.

"Go ahead, Commander," she said, not taking her eyes off Torres.

"Combat crash deck in five," Brandt ordered with her casual ease of authority. She always managed to give a brusque order in such a way that nobody took offense.

"Aye aye," she said back, killing the comm link and standing with a sigh and a last wistful look at Torres. She turned and walked away without another word, pausing at the door to fire a deadly accurate wink at him.

Torres shook it off and straightened his expression. It didn't serve to contact the fleet admiral wearing a look like an excited teenager. The call went through, connecting and going immediately on hold as he imagined Dassiova walking from the bridge to his own cabin, where he sat and activated the terminal. The admiral's gruff and un-impressed face filled the view in front of Torres.

"Report, Captain," Dassiova said as he leaned back to sip on a steel mug of something hot. He looked at it, confused briefly. He had expected coffee and instead found himself drinking a kind of soup that he didn't recognize.

"No trace of the enemy, sir," Torres told him in a tone more confident than he truly was. "They didn't react to us jumping in. No sign of any search or pursuit."

"Good," Dassiova said, not sharing the young captain's unease. "Maybe the bastards have packed up and gone home?" He sipped his soup again, the look of confusion gone and replaced by unexpected satisfaction.

"Perhaps, Admiral…" Torres said, allowing a note of trepidation to creep into his voice.

"Spit it out, son," Dassiova said. "Just say what's on your mind."

"I don't like it," Torres began, "if something seems too easy…" He hesitated, knowing that his old commanding officer would be finishing the idea inside his own thoughts.

"Yeah, maybe," Dassiova replied. "Just stay sharp and report when and if you see anything. The plan remains until such time as you report something that throws a wrench in the gears; conduct a deep recon and keep me posted. We'll send more firepower deeper into the system after the station is unpacked. Anything else?"

"Any more unauthorized comms?" Torres asked, more out of curiosity than any operation need. He could tell that there hadn't been from the look on the admiral's face even before the other man shook his head.

"If there is, I'll notify you and take the bridge crew manifest for investigation. Believe me, anyone coming under suspicion will find their ass strapped to a chair and enjoying a little private one-on-one time with Chief. I'm sure you remember how he's a real people guy."

Torres smiled, signing off from the conversation. He allowed his thoughts to drift back to when he'd first met the newly appointed ground commander of the *Indomitable*. Command Chief Onyilogwu, the unnaturally malevolent Nigerian who had been the senior NCO in Torres's first unit under Dassiova's command, had been brought out to Mars on personal invitation from the admiral and despite the ruffled feathers of a few career officers, had been put in overall command of the troops. The fact that he had even risen to the very top of the NCO ladder and still refused a commission directly to lieutenant on more than a few occasions spoke volumes of his character and abilities, not to mention his luck. But as he had also gone on to command CP teams and still retained enough years left in service to be on the front line elevated him to something nearing legendary.

Torres could only begin to imagine how uncomfortable that particular conversation would be. His thoughts were interrupted by the ship-wide comm channel breaking into sound.

"Captain to the bridge."

Torres rose and strode from the room, pausing for the door to slide open with a pneumatic hiss, before walking onto the bridge and calling for a report.

"A pair of Va'alen ships on long-range sensors," his tactical officer said excitedly, "but the energy readings are different; there's something strange about them."

"Strange how? Are they damaged? Are they venting atmosphere?" Torres asked as he tapped at the console beside his chair to look at the sensor data himself.

"Not sure, sir. They appear to be connected to a third power source but this one is… *different* somehow," the ensign tried and failed to explain.

"Can we get them on screen?" Sarvanto asked from the chair beside the captain.

"Negative, too far away."

"Are they shrouded?" Torres asked. "And are they sending out active sensor pulses?"

"Negative," the tactical officer responded.

"To which question, Ensign?" Torres asked, carefully enunciating the words, indicating he was leaning toward having the young man's ass removed from the station for a second time. It had the desired effect, and the ensign took a steadying breath.

"No fluctuation in the power signatures, which makes me think that they aren't shrouded. I'm reading no incoming sensor spikes but at this distance I can't say for sure that they aren't using active sensors in localized space," he said, mastering his youthful enthusiasm.

"Very good, Ensign. Lieutenant Rogers, come about and loop in toward their signatures from their stern. Three-quarter speed." An acknowledgement of the orders from the pilot was drowned out by the tactical officer's high-pitched voice calling out again.

"Sir, I have to caution that there may be shrouded signatures out there that we can't detect at this distance. I'd recommend sens—"

"Thank you, Ensign," Torres interrupted. "I'm well aware that I can't see what I can't see."

Red-faced and clearly embarrassed, the ensign acknowledged the reproof and kept his eyes on the scanner. Off to his left and seated lower down was the helm where Lieutenant Nathan Rogers, young and justifiably cocky with a natural gift for flying, piloted their sleek and unique reconnaissance ship.

Rogers knew his job well, knew it almost on an instinctive level. This combined with his joker attitude made people believe that he didn't try hard. In reality, he tried hard every day to make his natural skills look easy, but it was the way he carried it off that gave people the wrong impression as to just how difficult it was to be a fly-boy with that amount of ability.

Rogers called out the bearing and percentage of engine power in use, sticking to the safety guidelines and maintaining less than sixty-six percent propulsion to lower the risk factor of being detected behind their Shroud.

He recalled a conversation with their resident marksman on commander Brandt's detail; the guy went by the name of *Zero* like some kind of mystical SpecOps ninja, but after a single conversation with him, he left as a converted believer.

He explained the concepts of concealment and camouflage as they applied to him as a trained sniper, and Rogers applied as many of those principles as he could to the *Ichi* and the *Tanto* when he got to go joyriding in the miniature version of their one-of-a-kind warship.

"Shape, shine, shadow, silhouette, signal and spacing," Zero had said to him, his southern accent drawing out the words as though crooning a lullaby. He sipped his drink, no doubt smuggled aboard from an illicit stash on the Mars facility, and drew his lips back from his teeth as he let the fiery liquid burn the inside of his mouth before swallowing it. He didn't throw it back in a shot like others did, but savored each mouthful as though he was preparing to remember how it tasted before they went dry for as long as the mission took.

"Don't reflect any light, disguise your shape at all times because nature don't make straight lines, put yourself in a position where you'll be in shadow wherever possible," he explained slowly, taking another pull on the appropriately named Bulleit whiskey. "Never silhouette yourself on high ground with light behind you, watch what signals you put out because an errant transmission is as easy to DF as waving a flashlight—"

"DF?" Rogers interrupted before logic caught up and he answered his own question. "Oh, direction finding. Sorry, go on."

"—and keep your spacing between you and your squad buddies. That last one's *real* important, because if there's another like me out there lookin' down his barrel atcha, you can bet your ass he's waiting for you to do something dumb like stand in front of your CO and salute. *Pop*: two for one sale."

Rogers listened intently, converting the marksman's rules into his own rules for moving their ship through space. The reflection and shape elements were covered by the Shroud device. He would use the cover of planets wherever possible to put physical barriers between them and any potential enemy, and be sure to stay apart from the other fleet ships and be wary of where he positioned them in relation to the sun.

Suns, he thought, *plural.* It was hard to adjust from the habit of a lifetime when he had only ever known one sun in the sky. Now he had two sources of light to contend with, and he plotted his approach accordingly to come up behind the abnormal readings, without silhouetting their hidden form against the powerful light of the two burning orbs.

It took him under two hours to plot them within a few hundred thousand kilometers of the enemy ships.

"I have them now, sir," the tactical officer reported. "Confirm two enemy ships, not shrouded, and they appear... they appear to be *towing* something."

"On screen," Torres said as he sat forward. The large display blinked into life and showed them the most curious thing they had seen the Va'alen doing so far.

~

"Oh," Brandt said in slight surprise. She hadn't expected her lieutenant and second-in-command to walk into the team's private crash deck near the armory so soon.

"Yeah," Eze said as she went straight to the coffee pot and poured herself a cup. "I was on the bridge checking in when you called me."

Brandt smirked to herself but turned away to bring it under control as she heard the sound of the sugar tablet container being popped open. She kept her eyes on her reflection in the mirror of her locker as she twisted the strands of her hair into braids running the length of her skull. She had been forced to find a way to keep her hair from getting trapped in the new armor ever since she'd decided to abandon the short style she had been living with for years and grow it long. There was something about being so far removed from Earth and the constant bureaucracy that came with the tight constraints of regular service that made her feel a little more free than she had done for years.

Free, but under near-constant pressure.

As far as the other commanders in her position went, she had by far the easiest job in administrative terms. The *Venture* and the *Indomitable* both had entire units to command and organize. The *Cortez*, the *Anvil* and the two frigates had two or three squads on board to rotate on guard duty and provide rapid response teams. In contrast, she, on board the small reconnaissance ship, had a small mixture of regular seaman—ground pounders all—attached to her detail which was backboned by her hand-picked CP special operators.

She finished twisting the last braid into place and pinned it back. "Everything alright on your gun rotation?"

"If by 'alright' you mean boring as hell with nothing to do, then yeah; it was perfect," Eze replied as she turned and gave an 'okay' hand gesture. Like Brandt, she too had grown bored with training exercises in the empty shield domes on Mars.

"I hear that, Lieutenant," Brandt replied as she swung her locker door shut and turned to face the younger woman.

Both of them had their flight suits unzipped, had pistols holstered on their right thighs and their sleeves rolled up to above the elbow.

Both of them were trying to stay cool, which almost looked like some kind of uniform in itself. The environ mental controls in the adopted soldier's ready room had been unable to maintain a steady temperature for some unknown reason. Both the ship's chief engineer, a constantly smiling but harassed guy named Harris, and Jamie Paterson, had run over the diagnostics of the control software and found nothing amiss. It had to be a hardware issue, he had told them, and short of ripping all of the wiring out of the bulkheads to find the fault, they had little choice but to accept that the room they had to hang around in was ten degrees higher than was comfortable.

"You needed me?" Eze asked.

"Yeah, the captain asked me to put together a ground team ready for a couple hours' time," Brandt said, earning a furrowed brow on the otherwise flawlessly smooth skin of Eze's face. Brandt saw it, and let it go without her own face registering a response. If Eze thought that she and Torres were a secret, then she was kidding herself. Of the four people on board who had been trained in covert operations, two of them were involved with each other and the other two saw their subtle interactions. They saw it a mile away as clearly as if they were looking through the sights of Zero's heavily customized DMR, his cherished dedicated marksman rifle that would probably breach a few UN convention restrictions back on Earth.

Eze recovered quickly, forcing away the reaction to blurt out that she hadn't been told, and asked the question she should be asking.

"What do you need?"

"I'll take the mission, if it happens that is, and I'll need you to take over on board as ranking officer of the ground troops," Brandt told her.

Eze was unhappy not to get her hands dirty, not to be included at the sharp end, but her formal acknowledgement as the troop commander would go a long way to support her claim to be promoted to lieutenant commander when they got back; the difference between undertaking the role and being awarded the title still counted in the bureaucratic systems of the UN. She kept her face straight and asked the next logical question.

"Who are you taking?"

"I'll take Zero as my *Two*," Brandt said. It didn't surprise Eze at all that she would use the capable and dependable sniper as her second-in-command on the ground. "I want Specter, obviously, as long as the Hyper assholes will let him out to play."

Eze made a huffing noise, agreeing with Brandt's annoyance at how tightly they had the cyborg locked up. Only Paterson had seen him much, and that was because they needed his expertise with shield harmonics, among other things. Paterson, the former grunt of a ground-pounder who had been the friend of Brandt, and Specter when he was Jake Santana, way back when, had only served his tour to earn the credits to get his degree. When events conspired to give him that opportunity, along with all the well-funded research he could get his teeth into, his true colors shone through and showcased his brilliant problem-solving mind.

"They'll send at least one of their PMCs to make sure we aren't messing with his head again," Eze offered.

"Hmm," Brandt grunted in agreement, suspecting something more sinister in the fact that Specter was escorted everywhere he went. "That leaves me five or six spare seats."

Eze shot her a look, the questioning expression fading into mild excitement.

"You're taking one of the new mech rigs?" she asked, figuring out the available space on the *Tanto* with a squad of ten on board.

"Two," Brandt said with a smile. "I'm pretty sure I can squeeze them in."

CHAPTER 4

Proxima B Orbit

"Deployment at four percent, Admiral," the comm officer on the bridge of the *Indomitable* answered Dassiova's nagging. He had asked for an estimated time of completion an hour previously, which now equated to an entire one percent progress. The admiral ground his teeth and gave no response. He was apprehensive about having the fleet so exposed while the big sections of their flat-packed floating base were expanded in painfully slow motion. He decided that action was better than nervous tension.

"Signal the destroyers to push out another fifty thousand clicks and get me Hayes on comm," he ordered. His words were acknowledged as both comm officers spoke in their calm and commanding radio voices. Moments later, Hayes's face appeared on the display screen with the bridge of the *Hammer* providing a very war-like backdrop.

"Admiral," he said in gruff greeting. He was often a man of even fewer words than the taciturn fleet commander.

"Captain," Dassiova acknowledged. "My compliments—if you would push out a half light-year and conduct an active sensor sweep to relay, I'd be obliged."

"Understood, sir," Hayes said, clicking off the active link between the two ships.

Dassiova looked down at his personal console and watched as the icon for the *Hammer* blinked out of existence. He used two fingers on the screen to widen the field and as the icons for the majority of the fleet shrank down to become one instead of the cluster of individual readings, he saw the *Hammer* reappear far ahead of their location. He zoomed out further, watching in an awe that never got old as the single icon for the fleet sat almost directly behind that of the newly jumped *Hammer*, and he marveled at just how far the *Ichi* was from them. He imagined that one-off recon ship with its crew of misfits drifting silently in the deep waters of open space, just waiting and watching for prey to swim by unaware.

"Sensor readings incoming," the tactical officer reported as he began to receive the relayed data from the distant frigate. He paused, double-checking the information before he spoke. "Nothing, sir. Clear skies as far as we can see."

"Signal the *Hammer* to remain on point and maintain active sensor sweeps," the admiral replied, glancing down at his personal console. There was a sudden and urgent flashing of an icon. He hit it, seeing the boxed message show up in large text.

UNAUTHORIZED SUBSPACE COMMUNICATION

"Massey, on me," he ordered his flight officer as he practically leapt from his chair. She didn't respond. He looked around for his executive officer and saw her walking out of the briefing room wearing a look of concerned confusion at seeing the admiral on his feet in earnest.

He was struck by an immediate sensation of curiosity mixed with fear and shot a warning glance at Asha. The alien hurriedly looked away and brought his emotions under control to prevent him being forced to take another walk and return when he could stop projecting everything he felt.

Dassiova switched his glare to Massey, somehow conveying that their covert computer fishing program had caught a bite and that he needed to see what was on the other end. She understood, nodding toward his office and the two of them walked rapidly to the door. She threw herself into his seat and began hitting the glass surface to input the commands faster than he could type.

"Authority," she muttered to him, pausing as he scanned his left forearm over the reader on the side of the screen. "I'm in." She peered closer. "Data burst transmission, less than a second long, from us to Earth by the look of it…" Her eyes scanned quickly over the data on the display as she interpreted it. "Came from further ahead of our position…"

"How much further ahead?" he asked her impatiently. He needed to know if his suspicions should fall on the *Ichi* or the *Hammer*.

"Checking," she answered. "Calculating the time the transmission took… it's the *Ichi*," she concluded confidently. "It has to be. The signal took too long to re-route to be the *Hammer*."

"And it *had* to originate there?"

"No way to tell," she said with evident annoyance. "The tracer algorithm can't see it."

"Goddammit," Dassiova growled. "Alright, give me a minute and I'll call Torres."

"Is that wise, Admiral?" she asked carefully, earning a hard glare from him.

"Speak your mind," he told her after a pause. He wanted it straight, not suggested cryptically.

"I mean, what if it has something to do with him or his friends? They're a small, tight crew after all…"

Dassiova considered her words, not to give them more time to soak in but to better slap down her accusation so that she wouldn't make it again.

"Massey," he said in a voice like ice, "feel free to come to me with evidence of treason at any time but be *damn* sure of yourself before you accuse anyone."

"Understood, Admiral," she said, her eyes cast down as she dropped the train of thought.

Dassiova gestured for her to move aside as he worked the controls himself; his fingers dancing less deftly over the icons than hers did but still fast and efficient in contrast to his gruff manner. He worked more slowly than she did, but he trawled through the data to the end of the trail of breadcrumbs, finding that she was right and the trail did go cold at the *Ichi*.

"Ahh, shi-it," he said, dragging out the curse word. He was frustrated. "Alright, I'll have Torres look through his crew manifest." He looked up at her expectantly. When she raised her eyebrows in question as to what was expected of her, her spoke gruffly to make his silent point clear.

"Go see if you can encourage the space station op to move quicker. Dismissed."

⁓

"Sir, incoming hail on subspace from the *Indomitable*. It's the admiral and is marked for your attention only," the comm officer cut in.

"My compliments to the admiral," Torres answered distractedly as he looked at the sensor data from the enemy ships. "I'll get back to him just as soon as I have the time. Advise him that we're currently monitoring unusual enemy activity."

"Aye aye, sir," the comm officer responded as she tapped at her console and spoke quietly into the boom-mic attached to her earpiece.

"Talk to me, tactical," Torres said loudly.

"Captain, the two at the front are the same type of standard fighter we encountered last time but the third is different. It looks like a transport container and doesn't appear to have its own propulsion and… *All ahead stop! Power down to dark mode!*"

The tone of his voice, the panicked higher octave of the orders in particular, were met with instant reaction from Rogers at the helm. He killed the lights, so to speak.

Stationary, emitting as little power as possible, the *Ichi* hung in enemy-controlled space and held its breath just like the crew did.

"Care to tell me why, Ensign?" Torres asked, careful to keep his raging pulse from affecting his words.

"They… they *responded* to us, sir. Somehow," the tactical officer whispered, lending an air of conspiracy to the darkened bridge, "when we sent the last subspace comm."

Torres watched the display, seeing the unmoving icons of the three enemy ships hanging in space as they did. Tense seconds ticked by until the passive sensors refreshed and provided an updated set of data. To the captain's relief, the enemy hadn't moved.

"Another signature detected," came the whispered report from tactical. "Shrouded but definitely there; fifteen thousand kilometers off our starboard."

"Hold position, crew to battle stations," Torres instructed carefully and quietly, not whispering just because another person was doing so. "Gunners to make ready."

The flurry of quiet activity as the orders were issued calmed him slightly, as though action was safer than doing nothing.

"Four ships now on sensors," the bridge heard, "conducting active search pattern."

"Hold position," Torres said again. He was reminded of watching old films, in which the submarine commander ordered the ship to sit in the depths in total silence, hoping that the vessels above passed them by without noticing. He tapped at the console beside him to open a channel directly to Brandt's comm.

"Go ahead," she said in short, efficient syllables that rolled into a single sound.

"Sitrep: we may have been detected by four enemy ships. Two others appear to be towing a non-combat vessel and I want to know where and why. Get your ground team ready," he told her in a quiet voice. "Prepare to slip out if this goes noisy and follow the anomaly."

"Understood," she replied, cutting the link.

"Sir, permission to join the mission?" Rogers asked the captain.

"Lieutenant, you've been at the helm for what? Six hours already?"

"Almost, sir," the pilot answered. "But with respect, if you're thinking what I think you're thinking, then the *Tanto* needs the best wheelman available, whereas this tub," he lovingly ran a single finger along the edge of the helm console in a manner that was almost sensual, "just needs to turn her nose and jump away."

Torres paused, considering the words of his cocky chief pilot and knowing it to be entirely truthful.

"Granted," he said, waiting for the young man to be relieved by the standby crewmember and walk past his chair. "Nathan?" he added quietly, getting his full attention.

"Sir?"

"Armor, weapon, and be careful," he told him. "Do whatever Brandt tells you, when she tells you. You got that, kid?"

Rogers nodded seriously and left the bridge at a jog.

Brandt, already in the team's overly warm crash deck, slipped down her sleeves and zipped up her flight suit before attaching the pistol and comm device to her armor. She smiled as it opened up ready to accept her form, liking the modifications she had managed to have done without official authorization— just another one of the perks of being temporarily outside of the big UN machine. She stepped inside, feeling the cool air begin to circulate around her as the suit's systems instantly recognized her elevated body heat and cooled her down. Her HUD came online, rapidly running the startup diagnostics and giving her the all-clear before she had even stepped down from the charging plate.

With her hands, the tiny servo motors working as fast as she could move her own limbs, she ran through the holographic projection of the suit's menu subsystems with her eyes and opened the comm channel. She tapped on the names of the people she needed by blinking as she focused on them, hand-picking Zero and Specter before taking the first four names off the deployment list of her few available soldiers. When all the names were added to the active comm channel, she hailed them all.

"Report to shuttle bay in full deployment gear," she ordered, excitement and confidence in every word. "Prepare for immediate dust-off."

Protocol dictated no need for verbal acknowledgement in a rapid deployment scenario. They simply had to signal ready, which would highlight their names on the commander's display. But a storm of very gung-ho *aye ayes* came back to her. She came off the channel, opening another to the hangar where the *Tanto* was powering up.

"Shuttle bay from Commander Brandt," she said and waited. She was about to repeat herself when the channel came back with a lot of background noise.

"Yeah, Burrows here, go on…"

"Load up two mechs into the *Tanto*, RFN," she ordered before cutting the channel.

The door to the crash deck hissed open. She bumped a careful fist with Zero, conscious not to shatter the man's shooting hand with her own armored gauntlet. She walked out without a word, striding the short distance to the armory, where she took extra ammunition for her weapons and mag-locked her newly uprated submachine gun to her main chest plate. She shot a look at the single battle rifle on a rack by itself, glad that she would be accompanied by the modified weapon and the weaponized human that wielded it.

Torres had told her to be ready for a ground mission. Their intention was to conduct more thorough reconnaissance of the Earth-like planet, but the unexpected discovery of the alien activity promised work for her in some form. In her mind it never hurt to be prepared, so taking the loadout she had planned on for a ground mission stayed on the docket.

If we stay in space and trail them, so be it, she told herself.

Her attention was drawn to the door hissing open and an excited Lieutenant Rogers jogging in to scramble into one of the ready-suits, the lightweight armor not designated and customized to one specific user. He moved his limbs about awkwardly until he found the HUD controls to retract the gauntlets and helmet. He caught Brandt's eye, her own helmet retracted after she had finished with the comm channel, and he smiled.

"Better fine motor control," he explained, waggling jazz hands at her comically.

She laughed. "You're not on rotation," she observed, guessing the pilot would have somehow convinced their captain to allow him out to play past his bedtime.

"Who needs sleep?" he responded playfully.

"Pilots do, Lieutenant," Brandt said sternly.

"Yes, ma'am," Rogers answered, standing a little straighter

and pulling a face that he hoped appeared appropriately chastised and sensible.

Brandt sighed and gave up, stepping toward the drop tubes leading to the shuttle bay. Rogers stepped onto the aperture beside her and shot her a look as he tapped at the comm device on his left forearm.

"Superhero landing?" he asked hopefully.

Brandt gave him a withering look and turned her face away as the helmet reactivated to cover her head. Rogers did the same, his head and hands covering in the lightweight metal as the deck beneath them literally opened up.

They landed in the shuttle bay, Rogers dropping to one knee with his right hand planted flat on the deck in a mimic of all the superhero movies he had watched as a kid. A few chuckles ran around the crew getting the *Tanto* ready to fly out if ordered. Rogers grinned and decided to take the laughter as appreciative and not mocking.

One face stared straight at them, registering no mirth. It registered nothing, in fact, but simply stared at Brandt when her face was exposed once more. His matte-black armor was unique among them despite the modifications they had made. He had two large pistols, one on each leg, of a design and caliber not made available to the UN or the CP troops on the recon team of the Ninth Fleet.

"Specter," she greeted him, "good to have you here."

Specter, glowing green optical implants and scarred face looking down at her sharp features implacably, responded flatly without any trace of their former squadmate and all his Latino charisma.

"Commander," he said in acknowledgment.

"And you brought your dogs!" Brandt exclaimed sarcastically, firing a dismissive glance at the Hyper private military contractors beside him.

Horne, no first name apparently, sneered back at her and barely resisted the urge to give a full commander the finger.

The two had first met long ago. She had been a lowly petty officer class 1 and the cyborg beside the PMC had been the remains of her friend in a box being kept alive until they could rebuild him. Brandt had leveraged the situation and exacted the cost of her silence about the incident and enrolled for life on the fast track promotion program. Being a track, especially a female track with no political or family connections, usually meant that Brandt would have made commander and been sent to the worst, most boring postings in the solar system that no real soldier would be forced to take unless they were being punished.

"Still lettin' your mouth do the fightin', chief?" Horne asked her goadingly. He had fallen out with her after their return from the first foray into the Centauri system when she had refused to allow him on her ground teams, instead consigning him to turret defense duty.

"Who said that?" Brandt said comically as she looked around in mock confusion. She looked down at Horne and gave a start like she hadn't seen him down there. "Still getting paid to guard a real warrior who'd eat you for a light snack?" she shot back.

He sneered harder at her and turned away. Specter, who Brandt still thought of as Jake Santana, was guarded by a member of Hyper's private army around the clock. It galled her that they saw him as property, a deployable resource representing a significant investment instead of a person.

"Just one of you," she ordered. "I don't have room for two tourists."

Horne shifted uneasily but didn't respond other than to nod to the other PMC who he must have outranked, sending him slinking off and trying to hide his relief.

"Load up," Brandt said to her small group, watching as they hefted gear and weapons to shuffle onto the *Tanto*. She noticed another person working on an exposed circuit panel beneath the stubby delta wing on the right side of the little ship. She challenged him.

"Paterson, what the hell are you tinkering with?" she asked.

Jamie Paterson, unnaturally tall and naturally strong, gave her a strained look of annoyance.

"The hell does it look like I'm doing?" he grumbled. "Goddamned shield emitter's wobbling like Jell-O on a spin dryer. Those Va'alen would have to be blind to miss it."

"You're kidding me, right?" she asked incredulously. "We've got probably a half-dozen of those cockroaches out there right now, we're preparing to launch and *now* you're telling me the shield emitter is on the goddamn fritz?"

"Hey," he said as he plugged something back in and slapped shut the access panel before sealing it. "I just work here, okay?"

Brandt opened her mouth to berate him, to berate the shuttle bay crew, to cancel the mission and report the technical failure to the bridge when all hell broke loose. Two huge explosions shook the entire ship, sounding to those in the shuttle bay like they were on the inside of a bass drum.

"Bridge to shuttle bay," came Torres's voice urgently from the loudspeakers on every suit of armor and every speaker on the entire deck as the emergency ship wide channel activated, "Launch the *Tanto* immediately. Go now!"

No time for argument, Brandt stepped aboard the tail ramp and watched as the deck workers ran for the far hangar doors. As two massive percussive impacts rattled the entire ship, she locked eyes with Paterson and saw them reflected back at her like main beams on a ground transport. The klaxon sounded for the shuttle bay to decompress, ready for launch. Unthinkingly, she grabbed the material at the chest of his flight suit and practically threw him bodily up the open ramp into the ship with her augmented strength, courtesy of the powered armor.

"Go!" she roared, her suit automatically sealing up as the atmosphere began to rush out into empty space.

CHAPTER 5

Deep Space Near the Twin Suns

All was quiet on the bridge of the *Boken sha Ichi*. The crew waited with bated breath for the searching pairs of Va'alen fighters to inch closer to their position. Thoughts ran riot through their minds, wondering how they could have been so invisible to the enemy on their last excursion this deep into the system, when now they had somehow caused a ripple that was worthy of investigation.

"Sir," the comm officer announced, "incoming from the admiral on subspace. He says," she hesitated and cleared her throat. "He says you're to put your little dick away and answer the goddamn call…"

"I'll take it in m—" Torres began before the near-squeal from the tactical officer cut the air.

"Incoming weapons fire—" He hardly had time to get it out. The twin impacts hit them before he had even finished speaking. Torres, remembering Rogers's last words about the pilot of the *Ichi* only needing to be able to turn the ship and jump away, hit the ship-wide intercom and yelled for the *Tanto* to launch. He hoped their jump would mask the launch of the little shuttle, but also hoped that the smaller ship would be invisible to the Va'alen in the chaos. He told himself he'd be able to fill Brandt and Rogers in on the sudden and unwelcome developments just as soon as they got clear, but his logic assaulted him. He linked the incoming subspace communication with their detection and connected the dots.

"Helm," he yelled as he righted himself in his chair, "one half light-year back toward the fleet. Go as soon as the *Tanto* is away. Gun positions, buy them enough time to launch —*weapons free!*"

A thudding chatter filled the ship as the bulkheads and decks vibrated from the upgraded weapons pods' immediate firing. Outside—not that any of them but the gunners could see it and where none of them could hear it, thanks to the soundless vacuum they occupied—two Va'alen fighters shone in pulsating brilliance as their shields absorbed as much punishment as they could take before overloading and degrading to nothing. Almost simultaneously, in testimony to the gunners' skill, the two alien fighters erupted into furious sparks as they disintegrated.

The *Tanto*, already shrouded before Rogers piloted her expertly out into the void, rippled the space around its big sister as the *Ichi* spun on the spot to turn her nose about, and slipped away undetected.

~

"Admiral, incoming hail from the *Ichi*," the comm officer said. "Captain Torres sounds pissed, sir."

"In my office," Dassiova said as he rose and stomped away. Sitting down at the terminal in private he opened the channel icon blinking on his screen and started in.

"When I call, *Captain*," he said acidly, "*you* answer!"

Torres ignored the start of his ass-chewing and changed the subject.

"Subspace communications were detected," he said. The admiral was taken aback until he gathered himself.

"I know, that's why I was calling you," he said.

"What? You knew the Va'alen could detect our subspace comms and… and *you called us anyway?*" Torres snarled.

"No, goddammit, we detected a subspace call back to Earth originating from the *Ichi*, which is why I called you! What are you talking about?"

"We were shrouded and sitting in the dark with a squad of Va'alen ships looking for us," Torres snapped. "But when the subspace comm was received from you, they somehow pinpointed our location. We've suffered no real damage to speak of, but I've jettisoned an away team in the *Tanto* to follow anomalous enemy behavior."

"Do they know they can't use subspace comms?" Dassiova asked after the briefest of pauses.

"No," Torres said, "and we can't exactly tell them now, can we?"

~

"Rogers, report?" Brandt barked as she held Paterson down into a vacant seat using the power of her armor against the physical forces in play. He strapped himself in and nodded up to her in thanks, seeing only his own face reflected in her visor.

"The *Ichi* has jumped away. Two enemy fighters are floating scrap and two others are forming a close escort on the pair towing… whatever that thing is they're towing."

"Are we clear?" the commander asked the pilot, prompting a second's pause as he double-checked his readouts.

"We're clear. Shields are holding steady and Shroud is showing in the green."

Thank God for Paterson, Brandt thought, looking at the man himself and seeing only annoyed concern on his features. "Sound off," she barked into the open channel, reaching out and thrusting a head-set at Paterson.

"Zero."

"Horne."

"Specter," the robotic twang answered.

"Rogers."

"Payne," a female voice said.

"McMarrow," the large figure beside Specter, clasping a squad support gun to his chest like it was loot.

"Perez," another male voice.

"Turner, medic," the last armored man said as he glanced up at the commander.

"Paterson," the confused scientist added after a pause.

Brandt nodded to him, placing a gauntleted hand on his shoulder to try and reassure him.

"Rogers," she said as she turned and walked to the cockpit. There she pulled herself into the co-pilot's seat and hit the buttons to give her virtual control of the quad cannon atop the small shuttle. "Take us away at one-third speed."

The pilot complied and deftly manipulated the controls to move them away from the conflict area in the hope that they wouldn't be noticed. Brandt, detached from the real world inside the ship, watched the outside space through her HUD as her eyes controlled the direction of the gun turret.

"Nothing," Rogers muttered, earning a shush from Brandt.

"They're moving away," she said. The two vessels towing the ungainly lump between them grew smaller.

"Yeah," Rogers said after checking the passive sensor data. "Moving slow—slow for them at least—and the last pair of fighters are shrouding again to follow."

"They haven't seen us," Brandt said on the crew channel. "They must think the *Ichi* was all we had here, and they know it's gone now. We follow them; see what's what."

"Aye aye," Rogers said as he moved the small, shrouded ship off after their slow-moving quarry.

"Everyone else okay?" Brandt asked. She expected to hear positive affirmations and she received them until the line reached Paterson in the chair farthest away and nearest the ramp.

"Paterson," she snapped efficiently. "You good?"

"Aw maaan…" Paterson moaned. "My wife's gonna kill me!"

"Your *wife*?" Brandt let out involuntarily.

"Yeah, she made me promise not to do anything dangerous or stupid again. I was supposed to stay with the fleet or on the space station. Figured she'd never know if I stayed with the ship…"

"Yeah, well," Brandt said as she clutched at straws for positive comment when she didn't even know her friend was married. "She ain't gonna find out from your obituary that I dragged you onboard to save having your ass vented into space at least. Get a grip, dude." With that comment she reminded him of their shared past like a live electricity wire being touched to a circuit. At her words, Specter gave a small start, glancing around as though something had woken him from a power nap behind his mirrored visor. Paterson watched as Horne tapped at the device inside his left forearm. He glanced at the cyborg as he relaxed.

The hell did you just do, asshole? he thought to himself as his eyes narrowed involuntarily. He knew he shared an acidic dislike of the man with Brandt, guessing that she wanted any excuse to jettison the PMC into space, but what he thought he had just witnessed troubled him. *Some kind of sedative? An increase in dopamine levels?* He had no time to dwell on that, as the mission and his survival came first.

Paterson dug deep inside himself, thinking back to the four years he had spent as a trained recon trooper. He had been a good one at that with two confirmed terrorist kills adorning his official service record. He tried to summon that mindset from before he had earned his degree. After that, he had forgotten the military life and gone straight into prototype systems development research on behalf of the shady underbelly of the United Nations, the UN Intelligence Directorate. He searched himself to find an echo of the capable soldier he had once been.

"Aye aye, Commander," he said with sudden gravity in his voice that seemed stronger than the artificial gravity of their ship.

"Targets heading toward the exoplanet," Rogers cut in. "Matching speed and course at a five-thousand click distance."

"Keep on the sensors to make sure they don't make us," Brandt said.

"On it," the pilot snapped back, suddenly all game and no jokes. "Taking us in on a new heading to avoid outlining us against the smaller sun."

Impressive, Brandt noted privately.

The next hour went slowly, tensely, as they all expected to be detected at any point. Their protocol was to stay dark on comms unless contacted by the fleet, so the silence on the sub-space comm array was expected. After an hour, Brandt called for Zero to take over gun control via the software patch in his suit, which he did unquestioningly. An hour spent looking down the sights with your metaphorical finger on the trigger was an insane amount of mental pressure to bear; worse when combined with the added burden of command.

When relieved, Brandt unstrapped from the cockpit chair and walked back into the cramped cargo area where her tiny crew was squashed into the small seats. The rest of the cargo area was taken up with the compressed forms of the two battle mechs she had luckily ordered loaded into the *Tanto* well ahead of time. Strong and worrying memories—memories that kept a commander awake all night—stung her from the last time she had set foot on the surface of an alien planet. That time, she couldn't forget, she had had her ass gift-wrapped and handed back to her complete with a bow on top.

Only the working wireless link to the *Tanto's* cannons had saved the entire team from being ripped apart by just a single pair of Va'alen—'roaches' as the crew had started calling them —and she was adamant that the next time she met one of them, she would be the one standing victorious over the body of her enemy. At least their weapons were more powerful now than the last time they had tangled.

Jesus, she thought, *when did you get so morbid?*

"Change of heading," Rogers called out, snapping her of her reverie.

"Direction?" she asked.

"Small moon orbiting the planet," he said, indicating with a pointed finger on the holo-display.

The probe data on the system had been downloaded and the archive image showed a satellite not unlike their own moon, though this was densely forested and with obvious surface water; it seemed almost like the hilly wooded areas around the Canadian lakes where the mountain ranges jutted out into the dark water like fungal fingers capped with white snow.

"Nicer than ours," she quipped, earning a scoff and a chuckle from Rogers, who agreed wholeheartedly.

Their moon was just a gray lump of dust that kept their oceans from going haywire, whereas this one seemed like a habitable planet.

"Anything on sensors?" she asked.

"Escorts are breaking away," he told her. "Direct heading toward the last known location of their ring device thingamajig…"

"The gateway device," Brandt educated him unnecessarily.

Rogers gave a shrug and made a noise, which she took as a 'meh'.

"Stay with the cargo… *thingamajig*," she told him.

They did, and when they got closer to the moon, the sensors picked up massive electrical activity in the upper reaches of the atmosphere.

"What the hell is that?" Rogers asked.

"What the hell is what?" Paterson asked from way in the back.

"We're reading major electrical storms in the atmosphere of the moon," Brandt told him. "Sensors can't penetrate it."

"Is it natural or manmade?" Paterson asked, earning a moment of silence as nobody knew how to answer. "Well, not *man*made, obviously…"

"Can't tell," Brandt said. "Going to burst a sitrep back to fleet before we go further."

She tapped at the ship's console to send the brief text report via sub-space before hitting send. Almost instantly, the sensors lit up as the two escort ships they were following stopped and powered up their shields and weapons, the process lighting up the board with threat warnings.

Rogers yelled something that she couldn't hear. The oppressive vibration of their shields being pounded shook her brain inside her armor.

"Get us out of here!" she yelled, ignoring the shouts of protest and alarm coming from a few of those in the passenger compartment.

Rogers did. He rammed the manual controls hard and tore through space at a speed that implied he no longer cared if they could detect their ship. He didn't know how they already had, but he had a suspicion based on the coincidental timing of Brandt sending the subspace message.

"One ship in pursuit." Brandt dropped back into the weapon control sub-menu. "Zero?" she called out, dragging out the marksman's name. "I have the guns."

"Handing back control," he answered simply, his voice radiating calm under extreme pressure.

The hull vibrated with Brandt's barrage of fire; she began lighting up the black expanse with bright orange bolts of directed energy. The enemy ship zigged and zagged as it varied its forward momentum randomly, making it impossible for her to send accurate fire. She settled on filling the void with a barrage of full auto in the hope that something would land a hit.

In contrast, their initial flight away from the contact gave the pursuing Va'alen a line on their speed and heading which Rogers had timed only fractionally wrong. He pulled out of the dive too late and the *Tanto* suffered five more direct hits to its shields.

"One, no *two* more contacts inbound," he shouted.

Brandt took her eyes off the targeting reticule for just long enough to see how the new signal converged on their beleaguered ship. She made the only sensible call available to them.

"Jump us out of here," she ordered.

Rogers didn't acknowledge her, simply hit icons on the display as he hauled on the manual controls, then reached out a triumphant finger to activate the Fold Drive.

Just as another series of impacts rattled them hard.

"Fold Drive's offline," their pilot yelled in panic, getting both hands back on the controls. He hauled for all he was worth to try and keep them out of harm's way. "So are the forward and port shields!"

"Shit," Brandt cursed in a hiss as she worked the gun turret as hard as she could. She knew they couldn't mix it with four enemy ships, even if the new sensor readings were in fact single vessels and not pods of two and four like they had seen before. She was stuck between guaranteed destruction, which would result in mission failure along with the death of some of her favorite people, or the uncertainty of the moon's surface.

"Get us down there," she said in a low voice through gritted teeth.

"Where?" Rogers asked, his own voice higher than usual. "The surface. Put us on the deck. Do it now!"

CHAPTER 6

Proxima Centauri B Orbit

"I asked for a private conversation," Dassiova complained, "and he jumps back from his recon mission instead?"

"Sir, the *Ichi* is reporting enemy contact," the comm officer said sternly. "Captain Torres is requesting face-to-face comm."

The admiral stood and walked to his office without another word, knowing that the communications officer would connect the call to his terminal in a few seconds. He sat, put on his unimpressed face, which came to him naturally, and activated the link.

"Okay, son," Dassiova said. "From the beginning."

"Admiral, enemy contact near the twin suns," Torres answered with a wild look in his eyes. "They appear to be able to detect us when shrouded, sir, it happened when we used the subspace comm."

"That's what I wanted you for earlier," Dassiova said in annoyance. "*Someone* used the array on your ship without authorization. They got around our security protocols a little too easily and sent the transmission a few minutes ago."

"No, sir," Torres insisted with a resolute shake of his head. "The Va'alen detected the subspace comm *you* sent. They pinpointed the ship and fired on us."

"…Oh…" Dassiova began, unsure of what to say for a brief moment.

"We managed to deploy the *Tanto* with a recon team onboard before we jumped," Torres continued, "transmitting the data to you now on what we were following before they detected us."

"Hold up, Captain," Dassiova interrupted. "Just to be clear: you're telling me that the enemy can detect us when we're shrouded if we use subspace communications?"

"Yes, sir.".

"And you were covertly trailing the enemy *before* I hailed you?" the admiral asked carefully.

"Yes, sir."

"God*dammit*," Dassiova cursed, slamming a flat palm into the desk. "So the unauthorized transmission back home can't have originated from the *Ichi*."

"Unless it was pre-programmed and already transmitted back to the *Indomitable* before we jumped ahead," Torres answered, not even believing his own logic. His trust in his crew was absolute.

The admiral paused before admitting, "Hadn't thought of that. I'll look into it. Now, tell me what you found before you had to evac from the sector."

~

Their entry to the atmosphere of the moon was nothing short of a gut-churning, terrifying death ride. It was worse than any theme park ride or Earth re-entry or combat dropship deployment any of them had ever suffered.

"It's not my fault," Rogers complained over the ship channel. "It's the ion storms in the upper atmosphere; we're hitting pockets of electrically charged air everywhere."

Nobody answered. Nobody could do much except hold their breath and try to keep the contents of their stomachs inside their bodies as the pilot slammed them bouncing through the fierce electrical storm like a ball thrown down a tight stairwell.

The ship groaned and lurched, complaining at the treatment it sustained until it seemed as though it could endure no more. Brandt, gauntlets gripping the arms of the co-pilot's chair so tightly she left grooves in the smooth polymer from the force of her servo-powered fingers, closed her eyes. It was the only way to cope with the flashing imagery that threatened to overload her brain. She hadn't had time to disconnect the remote targeting program from her suit, so whatever the exposed quad cannons saw was projected straight into her HUD, giving her the unfortunate virtual reality experience of riding the storm from atop the *Tanto* as though she was surfing it.

It was too much to bear. It was too much for any mere human to endure and it was being beamed directly into her brain. She squeezed her eyes shut. She tried to block out the swirling vortex of bright slices of sky corresponding with the lurching movements of their vessel as they were pounded by the charged particles.

"Shields at thirty percent!" Rogers yelled into the channel. "And I can't see an end to this shit any time soon."

"Take us straight down," Brandt ordered through her grinding teeth.

"You want me to *nosedive*?" Rogers responded in a near shriek.

"Do whatever the hell you have to do," she growled, eyes still screwed tightly shut. "Just get us on the deck."

"Oh, that'll happen, don't you worry. You know… *gravity*?" Rogers quipped breathlessly as he fought the controls. "Don't think you'll like the state we're in when we get there, though…" he added, not quite under his breath.

Brandt had no answer. She couldn't manage another word, especially not as the sound of choking and vomiting sounded over the channel from someone in the rear. She tried to open her eyes, to blink on the squad icons and check the health status of the other people onboard, but the disorientating light show filling her field of vision threatened to make her throw up too.

"Can you…" she gasped, "can you shut off the turret link to my suit?"

A pause filled the ship with only the choking sounds of labored breathing and vomiting dominating the channel.

"Got it," Rogers snapped.

She opened her eyes and blink rapidly to try and clear the confusion that had assaulted her brain. She checked the team, seeing elevated heart rates everywhere except on Specter's readout. Even his showed a spike in neural activity, indicating at least some form of human response to the life-threatening peril they were in.

"Perez," she shouted as soon as she saw his vital signs peaking dangerously high. "Open your visor."

No response.

"Turner," she tried, calling their medic. The chances of her making it back there in one piece if she unstrapped were slim. "*Turner*," she tried again with more urgency, "can you reach Perez? I think he's choking."

"Can't… reach him… Commander…" Turner responded.

In desperation, she looked at the squad readouts on her HUD again. Paterson, the only one not in a protective suit, seemed to have passed out. Perez was spiking dangerously, and the others weren't far behind on pulse and blood pressure readings. Any one of them, herself included, was at risk of losing consciousness at any point.

If Rogers succumbed, they were guaranteed a sudden and savagely brutal death. Without Rogers in control, the *Tanto* would inevitably find the surface at a speed fast enough to atomize them all and leave a crater the size of a large building.

"I can reach him," said a familiar but vaguely robotic-edged Latino voice.

Specter, she thought, as she recalled the scene behind her where they were strapped in. *But he can't reach Perez without—*

"Negative, stand down. Do not unstrap!" she barked, but it was too late.

A thud sounded, so loud that it came to her over the comm channel as well as through the sound receivers built into the armor. Her mind conjured all manner of horrendous scenarios, each one of them flashing into her brain as an unforgettable image with blood and broken bodies strewn about the cargo deck of the ship. She looked at the vitals and saw Perez's reading lower. A hard, metallic slapping sound came to her as a massive, gasping intake of breath ruled the air for a moment, replaced by more desperate coughing.

"That's right, buddy," Turner's voice said. "Get it all out."

"Specter, sitrep," Brandt ordered, her concern evident in her voice.

"I am undamaged, Commander," he said smoothly. "I have caused minor structural damage to the deck of the ship, but I think it's only cosmetic."

Brandt let out an audible sigh of relief. "Strap in," she ordered. "This ain't over."

"Er, Commander…?" Rogers said, in a tone of voice that was preparing to deliver bad news. "I think we're clear of the stor—"

An enormous impact rocked their little ship; it seemed to have come from the ground and not from any lucky shot of a pursuing ship. The knock was so hard that the pilot thought for a second that he has misread all of the instruments and had hit the ground hundreds of feet before he expected to. With a huge lurch of downward pressure to match the pilot's desperate haul on the controls, and an impossibly hard smash to the belly of the ship, the lights went out and Brandt's brain lost its tenuous grip on consciousness.

"Have we received any word from the *Tanto*?" Dassiova asked impatiently. "Anything at all?"

"No, sir," Torres answered stiffly, trying to cover the concern he felt so keenly. "But as they deployed, I tried to inform Commander Brandt that the enemy appeared to have the capacity to detect our use of subspace comms."

"And they haven't jumped again, and we don't have them on long-range sensors?" the admiral asked.

"No, sir," Torres said. He kept his eyes fixed on an empty spot on the bulkhead in Dassiova's office onboard the *Indomitable*. He had been summoned there on their return to the sector containing the red dwarf star.

The admiral stared for a second, giving the few people in the room the impression that he might explode at any point, then relaxed and turned to address the live comm channel on the big screen.

"Captain Halstead, Captain Hayes?" he said, addressing the two frigate commanders.

"You are to jump to the edge of the sector where the *Ichi* has just come from and conduct a search for our recon team. I'll have the *Indomitable*'s gun barges deploy further ahead as a combat screen until you return, and the *Ichi* can deploy ahead of that under Shroud to give us early warning of any attack."

"Sir," Hayes began. The look on his face promised to offer his due respect to the admiral before he wholeheartedly disagreed with his orders.

"Save it, Hayes," Dassiova growled to cut him off. "It's happening; you can either bitch about it or you can bite the pillow and take it like a big boy. Only use the subspace comm if you're in dire need, but otherwise check in at…" He paused to look at his forearm comm device. "Oh-nine-forty tomorrow. Twenty-four hours. Dassiova out." The admiral hit the icon to cut the comm and turned back to Torres.

"Happy?" he asked the younger man. Torres shifted slightly.

"Not happy, sir, no. I'd rather jump back in and look for them myself, bu—"

"But you don't have the firepower," Dassiova interrupted with an upheld hand, "and those two do. Deal with it: do your job and put me out a defensive recon screen. Dismissed."

CHAPTER 7

Unnamed Moon Surface

Brandt opened her eyes, blinking into consciousness as the screaming whine in her ears rose in undulating intensity. Her stomach woke up before her limbs and roiled uncomfortably with the bubbling threat of expelling its contents. She heaved involuntarily, her whole body convulsing but restrained by the tight straps of the cockpit chair. She clamped her mouth tightly shut as her cheeks instantly ballooned with acidic mush that burned the back of her nose and made her eyes water. She reached for the forearm device to hit the emergency release icon and free herself from the imprisoning armor, but stopped herself. Choking to death on her own vomit was a sudden and unexpected choice, given that the potential alternative would be burning up or suffocating in an atmosphere that could be toxic to humans.

She heaved again, the slightest squirt of bile forcing its way between her lips to splash the inside of her visor. Brandt tried to concentrate on the display of her HUD and tried to make out the atmospheric readings in the likely event that the ship's hull had lost integrity. In the end the sheer panic of the inability to breathe won through. She hit the emergency release to make the helmet and visor retract before fountaining the foul contents of her stomach and mouth over the controls in three huge expulsions.

She gasped a massive breath in, replacing the lost oxygen extravagantly and realizing that she wasn't dying from the intake of air. She spat to try and clear the last of the stomach debris before reactivating her helmet.

The smell inside intensified, threatening a repeat of the last few seconds, but she screwed her nose up at the bile an inch from her face. She activated the drinking tube to swill her mouth out and spit a stream of water against the inside of the visor to try and wash the stench away. She had no choice but to allow the suit's reclamation protocols to wick away the fluid and filter it; she'd just have to deal with the smell in the meantime.

Brandt's HUD cleared, showing the information she sought as her eyes flickered through the sub-menus. Her team, nine other suits, all showed up in the green except one.

"McMarrow," she croaked, her throat burning so badly that she was forced to sip more of the water supply in her suit before trying again. "McMarrow, sound off!"

Nothing.

"Commander," said a weak voice over the channel. Her HUD flashed the name of Turner as the radio went live. "McMarrow is dead."

"Dead how?" she retorted, unstrapping her restraints with disorientated difficulty.

"Stand by," the medic answered. He accessed the deceased trooper's suit software and scrolled through the recorded activity log. "Commander, it looks like he suffered a massive stroke during our descent. He went before we crashed. He shows no physiological reaction to crashing. Existing medical condition by my best guess; must've been an undetected blood clot."

Goddammit, she cursed internally. *Haven't even set foot on a new planet and I've already lost a team member.*

"She said sound off," another voice ordered. That voice took her back to a place very, very far away as she sat in her best dress uniform and waited for judgment to be passed on her.

"That's a maybe," Zero answered equably from the depths of her memory. "Part of the responsibility of what went down is on you, because it was your team and you were in charge. We all have to live with shit and I imagine that weighs heavy on your soul, but you aren't to blame. Remember that difference, Grip."

The echo of his words spoken long ago reverberated around her head for a second before her senses came back to her with a jolt.

Get a grip, she told herself.

"Zero," he stated, clear and confident.

"Rogers," mumbled the pilot as he sluggishly hit the controls before him to no avail.

"Horne," groggy, but still as aggressive as ever.

"Specter," robotic and implacable.

"Payne," the other female voice groaned, sounding pained.

"Perez," a choking, coughing response.

"Turner," subdued.

"Paterson?" Brandt asked in sudden worry, unable to see her friend's vital signs.

"He's alive," Turner said. "The crash seat collapsed like it was designed to and he's unconscious, but as far as I can tell, he's uninjured."

Brandt visibly relaxed at the news; two deaths in one crash landing would mean twenty percent losses, and already her mind was racing ahead to consider how long they would be stuck there before a rescue came.

"Alright, everyone," she began as she struggled out of her chair. The deck was at an angle, forcing her to hold on as she went to walk back to see the carnage in the cargo area.

A voice, filled with panic and fear, lanced through the channel to her brain.

"Singularity containment failing!" Rogers shrieked. "Everyone out, now! *Now!*"

No further orders were needed.

A collapsing singularity was not a thing anyone wanted to witness, not if they wanted to ever recount the event. The blast radius of the ship's power source would be almost that of one of the warheads on the larger ship's missiles.

"Go!" Brandt yelled, stumbling as she lost her footing on the oily liquid sloshing around in the cockpit. "Rogers, eject the emergency crate. Everyone else, grab what you can and get out!"

Her orders were hardly the epitome of calm command, but setting an example was just as relevant in her current situation; her people needed that burst of urgency if they were going to live.

She hit the emergency release for the back ramp and tried to climb over the wreckage of one mech rig, which had fallen out of its moorings on impact. The rig's compressed form, folded in on itself like a puzzle, made for easier transportation but also made it effectively a solid block of reinforced polymer-metal alloy blocking their exit.

The ramp stuck, showing a darkening skyline ahead with one sun higher than another. Brant paused, reaching out to hit the release button again in case the controls had jammed. Her arm was knocked aside by what felt like a freight train. Behind her, looking over the mech to see the jammed ramp, Specter saw the problem and took immediate action.

He sank low, his powerful cybernetic limbs augmented by his unique suit with a near-infinite power source, courtesy of the tiny singularity embedded inside him. He braced his gauntlets against the mech. Specter pushed like a pro footballer, feeling the resistance disappear quickly, and barged the rig past Brandt like a battering ram to smash it into the blocked exit.

The ramp crumpled outward. The makeshift battering ram fell out onto the rocky ground and flattened the few tufts of tall, spiky grass growing in the soft patches between the jagged points. Specter turned, his mirrored visor locking onto Brandt's for the briefest of moments, before he jumped back onboard and began almost throwing the others out. Brandt turned back, watching her staggering pilot reach the exit uncertainly and pause, as if setting foot on an alien planet was outside of his job description. She helped him, snatching up a weapon case that had somehow come to rest near her feet during the crash. She thrust it into his chest before she launched him out into the air above the rocks.

Other than the commander and her ruthlessly efficient cyborg, three people remained on the ship. McMarrow was dead inside his armor and wouldn't be moving anywhere under his own power. Turner was administering something to the unconscious Paterson with a hydro-syringe to the soft flesh of his neck. He came to with eyes wider that the twin suns, sucked in a breath and screamed like an enraged animal.

"Adrenaline," Turner said quoting the stim's marketing slogan. "Guaranteed to motivate."

Brandt ignored the quip and reached out to help Paterson up. He rounded on her, eyes still wide and with a look of belligerent rage as though the adrenaline had awoken his inner-animal. She was reminded that Paterson, despite his jokes and claims to be just a

76

scientist, was a big guy who had been in active service for years along-side her. She stepped clear, pointed with her left gauntlet to show him the way out. She watched as he rolled his shoulders, then ran and jumped down from the wrecked ship to follow the others already making for higher ground.

Guaranteed to motivate, she thought to herself.

"Activating the emergency gear launch." Rogers's voice cut through on the channel just as a *crump* and a percussive shockwave rippled through the wrecked fuselage. High above them and unseen, the emergency kit rocketed up into the sky where it would descend slowly, steered toward the controlling pilot automatically with thrusters. Brandt opened her mouth to tell Turner to get the hell out of there but saw that he was already jumping down with as much of his medical gear as he could grab. She switched her attention to Spec-ter, who was tapping at the control panel on the compressed mech.

"No time," she said to him, a desperate edge creeping into her voice. The thought of being crushed into nothing by a collapsing singularity weighed heavily on her mind.

Specter ignored her, his fingers moving impossibly fast on the activation controls. He stepped back and allowed the automated function to unpack the battle mech. They watched as it righted itself, doubling in size to stand and wait for a pilot.

"Get in," Specter ordered.

She knew there was no chivalry involved. This was no dumb male sense of looking after a woman as though she was delicate or inferior; it was just pure, simple logic. He could move faster than she could, and the mech could move faster too. She had to drive the mech out of there so that both of them could escape the impending blast and rescue at least some of the heavy equipment they'd brought to com-bat the Va'alen.

Brandt's pause of hesitation lasted a microsecond too long, and she found herself being picked up and launched upward to place one armored boot into the footrest. The rest of her metal body followed and spun to land heavily in the seat. As she moved, the option to link with the mech came, a flashing icon hovering over it on her HUD, and she blinked on it to wirelessly connect her suit to it. Before she had even shifted position, the armor began to fold in around her and the HUD flashed out to be replaced with a wider view. She ignored all of the start-up protocols and launched the thing into a clumsy, long-gaited run after the others.

Movement came into her peripheral field of view, morphing into Specter bounding ahead of her with long, soaring bounds that would be impossible for a human to replicate without being in low gravity or augmented by technology. He carried a large burden, the limp and lifeless body of McMorrow still with his squad support gun and boxes of spare ammo mag locked to his sagging form. Her own footfalls from within the rig sounded heavy and metallic as the wide feet crushed rocks and flattened the sparse, tough foliage.

"Run!" she yelled unnecessarily, watching as the remnants of her scattered detail picked their way recklessly over the jagged boulder field. She found that the easiest footing for her large mech was through the long, shallow trench caused by their crashing ship, and she followed that as fast as she could to the low rise of a crest ahead.

She was the last one to reach it, just as a sonic boom from far behind her sucked the air from the surface of the moon.

"Come on!" yelled Rogers over the channel.

"Move it!" Zero snapped at her, uttering the first words since he had called for the squad to sound off. She reached the lip of the landscape, moving as fast as a freight train and under far less control.

"Get down," she told them.

The reflective visors ducked down as she jumped, sailed through the air, and landed to drop to one huge artificial knee and steady herself with a massive pulse cannon-arm slamming into the rocky dust.

"Superhero... landing..." Rogers's voice sounded softly as he fought for breath.

The outer shockwave of the detonating ship rushed over them, blowing a cloud of dark red-brown dust and debris over their heads and blocking out the fading light of the suns for a long, mostly silent moment.

"Sound off," Zero said again.

"Brandt."

"Horne."

"Specter."

"Rogers."

"Payne."

"Perez," rasping and weak.

"Turner."

Paterson, Brandt thought. *Where the hell is Paterson?*

She rose, HUD scanning the landscape until she located him. He had run another three hundred yards further than the crest, not stopping where everyone else had and nobody noticing his adrenaline-fueled sprint.

"Ah crap," Turner said as his own HUD picked up his patient. He rose to his feet and set down his burden of medical equipment cases to set off after the wired scientist.

"Stay here," Specter's robotic-sounding voice cut in. "I'll get him, you save your battery power."

Brandt watched as the cyborg began to sprint ahead, instantly cutting the distance between himself and Paterson. Something in his words rang a dull echo in her mind.

Save your battery power.

It hit her then, and a quick glance at her HUD showed ninety-seven percent on the mech and ninety-nine on her own, customized suit. She saw similar numbers on the other squad members. They wouldn't be able to recharge any time soon, given the loss of the *Tanto.* She faced the risk that eventually they would all be without power with the exception of Specter. The thought heavy on her mind, she stood tall, well over head-height for a normal person in the rig she was driving, and asked Rogers where the supply crate was. He looked at his forearm device, tapping at the display with awkward and unfamiliar gauntleted hands, telling her that it was still a few thousand feet up, according to his readings.

"In the storm?" she asked

He nodded, silently acknowledging the potential issue. "Yeah, it's being thrown all over the place," the pilot admitted.

"Well, bring it to us if you can, and if not, we'll have to go fetch it."

"I have Doctor Paterson," Specter's voice said over the channel; he was not the slightest bit out of breath, despite having sprinted almost half a mile over rough terrain faster than a professional athlete could cover a hundred meters. "He has lost consciousness again."

"I'm not surprised," Turner said. "Commander, he'll probably be out for a while. I need to get him somewhere I can monitor him. I... er... I gave him a little more than was *strictly* safe to get him moving—"

"Understood, Turner," she interrupted the medic, not judging even a little. "Zero? Got anything for us?"

"Ridgeline, five clicks southwest," her marksman and second-in-command replied stoically. "Probably caves and cover there, plus hard to assault without air superiority, which in these storms is unlikely."

"Good. Take point," she told him. "Everyone else stack up, fifteen-meter-intervals an—"

"Whoa there, chief," Horne's gravelly voice interrupted. "We need to prioritize the recovery of the emergency kit and get a subspace beacon set up to call down a rescue bird."

Everyone stopped, waiting to see how the ominous challenge of Brandt's command would be received.

The battle mech rig turned to face the mercenary and looked down at him. Brandt was cautious to keep her hands down and not raise the massive cannons.

"No," she said in a calm and steady voice. "We find a defensive position, we consolidate, and *then* I decide when we go for the supply crate. Staying in the open and using subspace is likely to bring down a storm of Va'alen on us, so why don't you leave the thinking to me?"

She turned away without waiting for any response. "Move out," she ordered.

CHAPTER 8

Proxima Centauri B Orbit

"*Hammer* to *Vengeance*," the captain of the lead frigate said confidently into the comm.

"*Vengeance* actual, go ahead," came Halstead's quick response. She was never far from the controls.

"*Vengeance*," he asked in a serious tone, despite his excitement, "can you tell me what time the little hand says it is?"

"*Hammer*, I do believe the little hand says it's time to rock. See you on the other side, out."

A casual onlooker peering from one of the few portholes on her home ship, gazing out into the deep, black expanse of space, saw the two squat and square-edged ships bristling with quad-cannons and dimly lit by the light of a nearby red dwarf star. Those two ships, seemingly so close together when viewed from one angle, were in reality so far apart that it would take a person almost six hours to walk the relative gap between them without stopping; such were the distances in play when humanity left the comfort and safety of Earth's surface.

That same onlooker, marveling at how small the two vessels seemed, each as long as a twenty-floor apartment building was tall, also saw the dimly lit hulls shimmer as though looking at them through a heat haze.

That's not possible, she told herself. *You have to have atmosphere to have heat haze. You have to have* heat.

The shimmering hulls wobbled out of existence with the dullest of flashes, making the watcher imagine a muted pop. She was almost disappointed with the feeling of anti-climax. She turned away. There was a small sense of achievement like a bucket list item had just been crossed off, but it had left her feeling empty and let down by the display. It was as though the reality were less impressive than the concept. She walked through the corridors and stepped through the sealed compartment doors as they hissed open. After settling herself at a terminal in an empty section of the ship, she typed in a complex sequence of instructions to access the subspace communications array.

The message to Earth, to her true employers, was buried inside the transmission data burst and thrice encrypted using a protocol not favored by the United Nations. She doubted anyone in the Ninth Fleet would be able to crack it, even if her hidden words were discovered. The transmission was a sitrep, an update on what was happening in the fleet, as well as further schematics gleaned from the unsuspecting mainframe. Plans and technical specifications were downloaded, encrypted, and sent to their competitors.

The woman completed the task and inputted another long coding sequence. The terminal would then re-route the data through other ships before finally using the *Indomitable*'s array to send the burst. Once finished, she wiped down first the electronic evidence and then the physical evidence of her use of the terminal.

Standing and smoothing her uniform, she went to get some food and carry on as though she wasn't betraying every man and woman risking their lives alongside her.

"Shields to maximum," Hayes barked from his command chair. "Active sensor sweep in all directions; talk to me, tac."

"Two signatures on long-range sensors, sir," the tactical officer answered. "Heading away at the very limit of our sight... they're gone."

"Runnin' scared," Hayes crowed, managing to leave off a near-involuntary whoop. He feigned a simple satisfaction with the enemy's unwillingness to engage them, intending to reassure and stiffen the resolve of his crew. He was no fool, far from it, and he was painfully aware that both his and Halstead's original surviving crew from their last mission to the system had left a lot of good people dead and even more apprehensive to return. He had done everything he could to show confidence in their new upgrades: the shields, which were four times more powerful, and the new weapons.

The shields were running at seventy-five percent above their original maximum through a stupidly simple new design—they installed three new shield generators in empty cargo holds with additional power sources and layered them over one another with non-conflicting resonating harmonics. This upgrade gave them four protective skins over their reinforced hulls against the savage power of the Va'alen weapons.

They had their own weapon upgrades too, courtesy of the rescued Kuldar. The alien race was mostly back on Mars, where a dome had been set up for their particular environmental needs. Not all of them had stayed behind. In fact, a dozen were onboard the *Indomitable* as advisors and even more were on the *Venture* and the *Anvil* as part of the engineering teams. They had been tasked with repairing and constructing, as well as hastily connecting the collapsed prefabricated sections of the small space station to provide a semi-permanent float-ing base in the system.

Both frigate captains had been formally asked to welcome a Kul-dar representative on their crew, but the matter hadn't been pressed. When the ships' departures had been moved up, the captains never got around to taking the representatives on.

The ship's new weapons, essentially the same technology as the ones which had nearly destroyed both ships, were powered and in-stalled under what Hayes called 'P for Plenty'. Where their original cannons sat, now three of the new quad-guns bristled the surface of the ship in eager anticipation of conflict with their enemy. The sting of their near-defeat was still sharp in their sides; more so for Halstead, who was forced to abandon her original ship and use it as a Trojan horse suicide bomber before they fled back home. She had, at least, dealt a crippling blow to the Va'alen.

None of them was so naïve as to think that the enemy would forget that.

"Skies are clear," the tactical officer reported smugly.

"Stay on the sensors," Hayes ordered. "Comm, hail the *Venge-ance.*"

"On screen," the comm officer answered after a brief pause.

Hayes smiled up at the face of Halstead displayed on the screen.

"Captain," she said.

"Captain," he replied, trying to keep the smirk from his face.

"Sit tight and wait to see if we get a reception committee? Then spread out one light year apart and scan?" she ordered in the subtle form of a suggestion.

"Sounds like a plan. Keep the line free. *Hammer* out."

After an hour with no response to their arrival the ships moved apart, each performing a very short jump to allow sufficient distance to maximize their combined sensor reach. They began searching the sector for enemy activity. Both ships ran at battle stations, and both had almost no personnel onboard who weren't operationally vital. They were warships, plain and simple, stripped down and modified for one purpose alone.

Their scans yielded no signs of the *Tanto*, and Hayes's restlessness prompted him to rise from his chair to hand over control to his flight officer. He instructed the communications officer to request the other ship's captain to connect on private comm.

He walked to the captain's quarters, much smaller and less grand than the equivalent quarters on every other ship in their fleet, and he sat at the simple terminal beside the regular cot. The screen came alive, showing Halstead.

"Nicola," he said in greeting.

"Craig," she replied, mirroring his smile easily now that their entire bridge crews weren't watching their interactions.

"We got nothing over here," he said as he tried not to show his impatience. "What do you say we just drop in to their last known coordinates?"

"I'm in," she replied as she pushed an errant strand of hair behind her right ear. "On your mark."

Hayes stifled his smile at her actions. "Weapons hot," he said. He felt instantly childish and embarrassed, as though one of the Kuldar were in the room with him and had forced the emotions on his brain and body.

She smiled back at him, saying nothing but cutting the comm link.

"Weapons hot?" Hayes asked himself out loud. "Dammit, Craig, you're such a dick…" He rose, walking back to the bridge wearing his captain's expression again.

"Helm, lay in a course for the last known location of the *Ichi*," he said. "The *Vengeance* will follow our lead… on my mark…" The pilot turned and nodded to him in readiness. "Hit it."

"Break here," Brandt ordered. "Find cover. Specter? Can you take a look ahead?"

He didn't acknowledge his orders, just stepped onto the arid plain from the small depression they occupied and scanned his visor left and right. Brandt looked at the more in-depth atmospheric report her suit had taken and checked the important facts.

"Atmosphere is breathable," she told the team. "Nitrogen levels are a little high and Oh-two a little low, but it's essentially all good. Think prehistoric Earth and you're there. Stay closed down in your armor unless you have to."

"Cave," Specter said as he stood stock-still and stared ahead. "Just over one kilometer. Single approach, high ground."

Brandt looked down at him from her higher vantage point. The unconscious Paterson was being carried limply in his arms and transported with as much effort as she would carry an empty paper bag.

"Zero," she said as she pointed to a small outcrop off to her left. "Overwatch. Payne, watch his back."

Both of them jogged away to carry out their orders as Brandt turned to instruct the others. Turner was marching beside Perez who still struggled to move and coughed so horribly that the medic made him mute his link to the team channel and kept a private one open between them.

The main hood of Brandt's mech was open, and the way Turner's visor stayed glued to her prompted her to open a private channel to connect with the medic.

"What's up?" she asked.

"Perez isn't doing great," he said. "He's aspirated his own vomit. I need to work on him or he'll end up with pneumonitis and probably die within forty-eight hours." *That* got her attention. "I need to check Paterson over, too."

Brandt nodded. She was too aware of the deadweight burden attached to the back of her mech. They had to bury McMarrow before his armor became unusable for anyone else. If they had any luck at all, it was that their dead man and their un-armored scientist were both well-above average height. The thought of Paterson back in armor beside her and Jake once more gave her a strange feeling in the pit of her stomach; it was something between excitement and sadness at how much they had changed and lost since they'd first became inseparable a decade before.

"Commander?" Turner prompted.

"What? Sorry, I was on another channel at the same time," Brandt lied smoothly. "You were saying?"

"I was saying that Perez is in a bad way and I need to get to work on him before his situation becomes critical. Paterson might have some side-effects too, seeing as how I gave him enough stims to make an elephant do a Zumba class…"

"Understood," Brandt said in her most commander-like voice. "Stay here with the others." She switched back to the team channel and hit the eject sequence for the mech. "Specter, on me. Horne, provide cover for Turner and the rest. Use the mech."

"Listen, chief." Horne stepped forward and began his rebuttal in a tone that made almost palpable his unhappiness at her ordering him around. She could feel the other visors turning to face the two of them expectantly.

"No, civilian, *you* listen. First off, asshole, it's Commander." She jabbed an armored finger into his chest plate. "Not chief." Another jab. "Not darlin'. *Commander.* You got that?" She paused for a heartbeat but carried on as though she didn't expect an answer. "Secondly, in case your dumb ass hasn't noticed, we are stranded on a hostile planet with next to no supplies and little chance of a rescue any time soon. We have one dead, one potentially critical and one unconscious. Our situation, *Mister* Horne, is tenuous to say the least. Now what I need is for you to climb your short ass up into that mech and provide cover for the others while we go and clear a defensible position where we can consolidate. Questions?" The last word rang out like a gong and challenged him; *dared* him to push back. Her faceless visor showed no features, but anyone who knew her—Zero listened with amusement while jogging over the rocky ground to his overwatch position—knew that her eyebrows would be meeting in the middle and her mouth would be pursed tight to stop her saying anything else. Anything… *unprofessional.*

"Not at this time… *Commander*," Horne finally said with an amused tone.

"Good," she replied curtly. "Specter?"

"Ready to move," the cyborg answered flatly.

"I'll come," Rogers offered in a voice that made him sound far younger than he was.

Brandt stifled the loud sigh that threatened to transmit over the team channel.

"Lieutenant," she responded formally, "you stay and cover Turner. Assist him with the casualties if he needs your help, okay?"

Somehow, even through a mirrored visor, she could sense his face falling in disappointment. He slowly holstered the pistol by mag-locking it against his right thigh and squared his shoulders to do what was asked of him. Truth was, their only pilot was what the SpecOps community called PC: precious cargo. If there was any settlement on the surface, any vehicle capable of taking them out of the atmosphere, then Rogers would become their principal and not just a team member.

"You got it, Commander," he said, keeping the disappointment out of his words well.

They moved. Fast at first, then more tactically when the available cover left them potentially exposed to anyone or anything on the high ground. Regular reports of clear skies and no movement came from Zero in his implacable voice.

"Defilade, three hundred meters to your eleven o'clock," he called out, alerting them to the slim possibility of an ambush ahead and to the left of their approach.

"Gotcha," Brandt replied. She was breathing a little harder than normal thanks to the uneven, rocky surface.

"Maintain comm discipline," Zero said back to her in a flat and businesslike tone, which masked the heavy sarcasm she alone heard. It took a while to get to know the marksman, to understand his unique brand of humor. Brandt doubted that the others heard the mockery; it went back long enough to their shared past before either of them had made the cut of the harsh CP training program.

"Understood, overwatch," she crooned in her imitation of a dropship pilot's voice. "Adjusting approach vector to clear defilade. Specter?"

"I'll take left, you take right," he said, cutting across her path with ease.

She let him go, seeing how he moved with far more ease and grace than her own legs managed. The powered armor made rough terrain much easier to cover, especially when the driver was as practiced and experienced as she was. The balance and strength, although heavily augmented, still came from the person inside the high-tech shell. Specter, with his endless power supply and cybernetic arms and legs, made it look like he was floating. Everything about him, about how he moved and the effort he used, was different. He was graceful.

They paused at the lip of the dead ground hidden from their approach until Brandt counted them down from three. On the command to go, both soldiers popped their heads up over the rocky ledge and leveled their weapons.

Brandt tucked her submachine gun in tightly to her right shoulder with the short barrel gripped hard in her left gauntlet. Her HUD scanned the ground faster than her eyes, locking onto the movement on the far side of the small crater.

"Animal," Specter's voice said. "Didn't get a good read on it."

"Predatory?" Brandt asked, keeping the worry out of her words as they still transmitted on the team channel.

"Insufficient data," he said.

"Break right, I'll cover," Brandt ordered. Specter gave no answer. He merely holstered one of the two pistols he carried to give himself a free hand and crossed the ground fast to reach the approach to the cave. Brandt followed as soon as he had adopted a defensive position and trained a weapon on the black maw of the cave's entrance. Dropping in beside him, she asked his opinion on the best way to approach it.

"Suit lights?" she suggested.

"Stand by," he told her as he stared directly ahead intensely. "Nothing on thermal imaging. Optical intensifiers show some sign of animal tracks... but they appear to be old. I think."

She heard his voice, his accent, which had been marred by the addition of the metallic, robotic edge where they had repaired his scorched vocal chords. She could still imagine the younger face saying those words, the face of Jake Santana before the glowing green eyes that showed no emotion and the scars were added. She shook the thoughts away and got a grip of the mission.

"Move out," she told him.

CHAPTER 9

Deep Space Near Alpha Centauri

"Nothing?" Captain Halstead demanded of her bridge officer manning the tactical station.

"No, ma'am," the nervous lieutenant responded as his eyes darted over the screens before him. "Haven't detected a single trace since we jumped in."

Halstead chewed her lip and rested her hands on her hips, which only made the young officer more nervous. It was as though the lack of enemy activity would somehow be construed as his doing.

"Comm, give me a ship-to-ship subspace with the *Hammer*," the captain instructed. The acknowledgement came only slightly before the activation of the viewscreen showing the similar bridge layout of their sister ship. Halstead allowed herself a smirk that hers was newer and better, then lost it as she recalled the pain of sacrificing her old ship.

"Anything your end, Captain Hayes?" she asked.

"Negative," Hayes answered sullenly from where he sat still in his command chair. "Recommend we move to planetoids and drop into orbit for closer looks in case they went down anywhere."

"Agreed," Halstead said.

They jumped again in tandem, this time only for a few seconds to save themselves half a day of steaming and scanning as they advanced toward the last known coordinates of the *Ichi*. Neither of the frigates, even if caught on their own, would be forced to turn and flee under those circumstances, but then both were heavily armed and reinforced space tanks after their last ill-fated foray outside their own solar system. It would take a few dozen Va'alen fighters to cause them concern now. They appeared in a new sector of the Centauri system within weapons range of each other and were ready to lay down supporting fire if things got hot.

"I've got… something…" the tactical officer said uncertainly.

"Do tell, Lieutenant," Halstead enquired with a hint of sarcasm lacing her tone.

"It's, er… it's debris, ma'am."

"Incoming hail from the *Hammer*," said the comm officer.

"On screen," Halstead told her, looking up to see the concerned face of Hayes staring back at her.

"You seeing what we're seeing?" he asked her with a frown.

"Not sure yet," she told him. "Just assessing now but from what I can tell, there appears to have been a scuffle out here."

A 'scuffle' was an understatement. At least one ship of a decent size had been destroyed, given the amount of electrically charged metal spinning around their immediate proximity. The only things in that sector, other than the scraps of evidence of a fight, was a large planet that resembled Earth with a little less water on the surface, and a forested moon. There was little chance of finding anything useful near either of the twin suns. They would burn up if they got close.

The two captains retired to their private offices and conferred. They ultimately decided to bring the admiral in to their discussions. The subspace link was activated and after a long wait the third portion of their screens blinked into existence with the harassed visage of Dassiova staring back at them.

Halstead filled him in on their findings with Hayes interjecting with facts and opinions at times. This clearly annoyed Halstead but she kept her lips pursed tightly together when the interruptions broke her flow.

"Conduct a search in grid pattern," Dassiova told them. "Start with the planet; that's where I'd ditch if I had to, because we know the atmosphere is good down there. No beacons detected at all? You're sure?"

"Sir, the *Tanto* isn't pinging on any frequency. If she's out there, she's gone dark."

"Understood," Dassiova growled. He didn't add that he was upset and concerned at the loss—the *potential* loss—of a rather valuable ship and a few irreplaceable members of the fleet. If it came to a fight on the surface of any planet, he would need those people to go in first and reduce the risks to his fleet and the other ground-pounders so that they weren't cannon fodder. He didn't tell the captains his concerns that not one, but two encoded messages had been transmitted back to Earth and that he had no way of knowing what those messages contained.

Understood was all they got and all they would get. The pressures and decisions of command were his to bear. The captains of his frigates, of his war hogs, had their own concerns without his burdens falling on them too.

On the surface of the exoplanet orbiting the larger Earth-like orb, a low-ranking pair of Va'alen warriors received an incoming message via the hardlines wired to their reinforced outpost. Their small bunker was uncomfortably short for their height and forced them to spend much of their time sitting down. It was linked to a mountain peak over a thousand feet above them. That mountain top, leveled and flattened by pulse cannon fire and an engineering team dropped off by ships, housed a single surface-to-space rail cannon, which was actuated and fired by the commands of the bunker built far below. That same cannon had sent a single shot at a falling object. The garbled message they had received told them the object might be human and, having scored a direct hit, they reported their success.

Once their report was made, the Va'alen went back to playing their repetitive game using datachips containing simple statistical values for fictional characters. They then bet those stats against the unknown card of the other. The winner kept the cards, and their game had gone on so long that both knew the deck inside and out.

When the comm link, another hardline from their main base fifteen kilometers away, buzzed unexpectedly they dropped their chips and rushed to respond.

"Rail gun bunker," the smaller one of them said.

"I know it's the rail gun bunker, you cracked-shelled fool," snarled the more senior Va'alen on the other end of the line. "Calling the bunker you are in was literally the last thing I did in my wasted life. Did you think it might be a wrong number?"

"I apologize, Aq D'marath," the Va'alen said respectfully.

"Stick your apologies in your—" The officer commanding the surface base growled and forced himself to give orders and not take out his frustrations on idiots. "There are two new enemy signatures in the sector. Keep the rail cannon charged to ninety percent ready to fire if they come into range."

"But, Aq, if we keep the cannon at ni—"

"I know!" D'marath snapped. "Don't let the capacitors overload and I won't have to inform your clan that you were killed for incompetence."

The line went dead, and the two rail cannon operators shrugged at one another. One leaned over and dialed up the charge to maintain a steady fifty percent until the coils would threaten to overheat; only then would they turn them down enough to remove the heat buildup. Until then, they went back to their game.

"It's clear," Brandt said over the team channel. "Zero, Payne, stay on station. Turner, bring your group in."

The round of acknowledgements rang out as she maintained a scanning watch on the lower ground all around them. Specter did the same, but his head moved faster, and his artificial eyes saw more details at further range than even her HUD could compute.

The advancing people came into view as the taller mech driven by Horne took point. He had the body of McMarrow mag-locked to the chassis. Behind him came the medic, who was half carrying Perez with one armored arm over his shoulder. Beside them came Paterson, now conscious but still evidently unsteady, helped along by Rogers.

It took them an agonizingly long time to negotiate the terrain with their burdens and Brandt could almost feel Horne's annoyance at not being able to unleash the power and speed of the battle mech. She focused on the mercenary and activated the HUD outline of his mech with her eyes to bring up the stats. Already the battery power had fallen lower and the figures she saw made her grit her teeth. If the mech was going to be needed in a fight, then they would need to conserve the remaining power it had or find some way of recharging it. Her absent-minded thoughts killed the time it took for them to make their final approach up the incline toward their position. The warning Zero called out burst that reverie.

"Movement, in the air," he said sharply.

"Where?" Brandt shot back as her head spun to find the source of the potential danger.

"Your six, high and far," the marksman said. "It's an animal. Flying."

"Everyone down," Brandt ordered. "Find cover. Zero, you keep whatever it is in your sights."

"Understood, Commander," Zero drawled back at her, every word exuding competent confidence and deadly efficiency.

She watched as Turner and Rogers deposited their buddies behind rocks and sank to cover them, with weapons raised. Specter stood tall. Her mind conjured the faint sound of his eyes whirring as he zoomed in on it. Horne's mech powered up as the canopy locked down and the arm cannons whined in readiness to fire the heavy bolts of directed pulse energy.

"Everybody hold your fire," Brandt warned. "Conserve ammo and don't attract attention unless we have to." She didn't wait for an acknowledgement but turned to address Specter alone by muting the team channel. "What do you see?"

"It's big," he said. "Like, the size of our mech big. Wide wingspan. It's just gliding this way, watching the ground like it's scanning."

"Predator?" Brandt asked again in utter betrayal of her fears. Va'alen warriors were one thing, but alien creepy crawlies and wolves scared her more than she wanted to admit.

"Large eyes, elongated beak, possible talons… I think, yes." The robotic twang of his words didn't soften the blow of the information one little bit. She reactivated her mic to the team channel.

"Zero?"

"Here."

"This thing looks predatory," she warned. "If it makes a move on us, I want you to take the shot."

"Understood," he said, again without emotion. It was a task. A mission. He was merely in the universe to be the matchmaker; to introduce bullet to target.

Seconds ticked by as slowly as if they were swimming through syrup. Every breath, every heartbeat made the distant shadow grow ever so slightly larger until it formed a distinct shape without magnification. Without warning, the direct approach vector switched to a lazy, looping arc as it lost altitude effortlessly.

"Hold your fire," Brandt reminded them, as much to calm her own nerves as theirs.

With a piercing cry the flying creature loomed into view overhead and flapped wide, leathery wings with percussive cracks. It slowed itself before the elongated talons of its hind legs gripped an outcrop of rock and scraped with a sound like a knife dragging over armor.

The creature settled with more flaps of its wide wings and slowly turned a long head to face them. It craned its head slightly and looked directly at Brandt, *through* her. She fought down the urge to open up on it just because the look of it terrified her.

"Hold your fire," Specter said slowly.

It was as though he had read her mind. He took over; the sight of the thing perched twenty meters from their position temporarily paralyzed Brandt. It looked at them intently, cocking its head to focus a bloodshot, yellow eyeball at them. It issued a chirping sound as it bobbed its head at them, somewhere between a questioning noise and a challenge, and stepped down from the rock to walk toward them awkwardly on all four legs. It raised the extended tips of its wings straight above its head and moved in the curious way that all graceful flying creatures had when relegated to the ground. The chattering noise came again, followed by the snapping of the large beak, exposing rows of sharp-looking teeth like neatly arranged drill bits.

"It probably hasn't seen humanoids before," Specter said over the channel. "It might not have a reason to be scared of us yet."

As if in answer to his words the creature made a series of darting movements in their direction as it chirped and snapped, as if trying to scare them into running away.

Brandt swallowed and got a grip of herself. "Hold your f—"

The creature exploded in a flash of bright orange light and dark red mist. The atomized cloud of blood and matter exploded out, cannoning a handful of smeared spots onto the front of her visor.

Her mouth opened to yell at Zero, to curse him for taking the shot when he didn't have to, but before she could start to speak, the facts replayed in her mind and she saw the slow-motion replay of the shot connecting.

It hadn't been a charged bullet from the high-powered rifle, not unless it struck something inside the creature that detonated. Instead, it must have come from the mech with its new alien-technology cannons on each arm.

"God*dammit*, Horne," she roared in unprofessional rage. "Stand down. *Now!*"

"Negative," he snarled back in fear. "There's more of the things incoming."

The words stopped her next curse in her mouth as she scanned the skies. Horne was right; a dozen more readings flashed up on her HUD from the same direction the first one had come from. She made an instant decision.

"Everyone inside the cave, *move!*"

They moved. Brandt and Specter held their ground together as though some unspoken order had been given. Both turned to face the visible wave of incoming beasts. The thin, dark line of their approach grew darker and thicker; it seemed to correlate directly with Brandt's own heart rate and blood pressure. As the team commander, she could access the details of every one of them, but she worried about her own icon on their HUD's flashing red to warn of medical problems. That kind of leadership crisis could be catastrophic for them all.

She glanced back, seeing the injured and impaired with their escorts moving as fast as was possible. Rogers and Turner had sacrificed the dignity of their burdens and thrown them over their shoulders to speed up their flight. Behind them Zero and Payne, weighed down slightly by the addition of McMarrow's big support gun, ran hard to make up the distance. She glanced back again; the dark line was now made up of individually distinct shapes, which, to her imagination at least, were larger than the one that was still partly smeared down the front of her armor.

"Come on, Zero," she said breathlessly. "Pick up your feet."

Zero didn't answer. She hoped he didn't answer because all of his energy and concentration was going into running.

Shrieks filled the air, sounding like the bird calls mixed with the yowling of an angry cat. The cries echoed all around them across the barren, rocky wasteland. Brandt turned her head back again and nearly let out a sigh of relief to see the others almost on top of them.

"Go, go, go!" she told them as they filed past.

Horne's mech stopped just ahead of her and he stepped aside to ready his weapons toward the approaching animals. Specter ordered him onward before Brandt could speak.

"Horne, push ahead and clear the cave," he ordered with a bladed gauntlet signal ahead into the darkness.

To Brandt's surprise, the PMC turned and did as he was told without argument. She looked back to see Zero and Payne had closed the gap and were bounding up the slope in long strides that wouldn't have been humanly possible without their armor. She glanced back at the flying threat to see that the line had split into three, with both flanks soaring in wide loops to surround them. She held her tongue, knowing that saying anything to hurry them up would only serve to fry their nerves instead. She dialed up the power on her modified weapon and settled it back into her shoulder, ready to fight if she had to.

"Why aren't they attacking?" Payne asked in between gulps of air.

It was Specter who answered. "They seem to be wary."

"You wonder *why*?" Brandt shot back. "They probably saw what happened to the last one."

They spoke too soon. The cries reached a crescendo until they seemed to fill the air with a continuous wailing noise that sounded ominous to all listening. Visors met as the soldiers imagined locking eyes with one another. The menacing sound spurred them on to run for the gaping, dark entrance to the world below the one with the flying beasts.

CHAPTER 10

Proxima B Orbit

The construction of the space station was a slow-burner. When Dassiova had first watched the graphic simulation of how it would go together, he had watched it on fast-forward. Too sluggish and boring otherwise. Having that quick imagery in his mind didn't help his mood as the sections unfolding from the retrofitted *Venture* moved so slowly that he had to fight the urge to find someone to yell at.

He called it encouragement. It was everyone else who thought he was yelling.

The painfully slow progress was unavoidable, but that wasn't to say that he couldn't make any other parts of their mission move a bit faster. The small station, rapidly prefabricated as much as it could have been in Mars orbit, required a well-coordinated team of a few hundred technicians and engineers, all trained for EVA—spacewalking. The process involved connecting everything together both inside and out. The central hub of the station, which was effectively a vertical and a horizontal ring around a nucleus containing the power supply, was just the starting point. After half a day they had succeeded in constructing the main support arms for three of the rings to be towed out in sections the equivalent size of a couple of dropships. The next step was to inch the sections of the support arms into place and lock them in. Lost in thought as he watched out the window, Dassiova almost jumped in fright when someone spoke to him.

"Admiral?" a female voice asked tentatively from a small knot of seamen passing by the corridor he had stopped in.

"Petty Officer Judge," he grumbled at the young engineer. She had been reassigned from his last flagship to the bigger carrier he now commanded. Reassigned and advanced on his direct say so, as if strings that couldn't be pulled by a fleet commanding admiral weren't even strings at all. "How are you?"

"Fine, sir," she said as she waved on the others, who were hovering uncertainly. "Good actually. I just wanted to thank you again." She brushed an imaginary speck of dust from the new rank insignia on the right side of her chest as she spoke.

"Thank me?" Dassiova said with a ghost of a chuckle at the proud attention she drew to her promotion. "You want to thank me for forcing more responsibility on you and assigning you to a dangerous mission?"

"Yes, sir, I do," she replied. The corners of her mouth twitched and made dimples appear in her cheeks as though they had been camouflaged until she smiled. "The team I have is good, and getting better every day. They'll keep your shields up and running, sir, don't you worry."

"I'm not worried, Judge," he said. "That's why I put you in charge of them. Carry on."

She seemed almost disappointed, deflated by the conversation ending, but she drew herself up and nodded; a gesture that passed for a salute to the senior rank when at sea.

She walked off, tools jangling in her utility belt as she hurried to catch up with her engineers. Dassiova sucked in a breath through his nose, held it for a moment, then let it out.

If I'd stayed on Earth, done something different with my life, she could be my daughter, he thought to himself wistfully. As his eyes caught the shape of her flight suit below the tool belt, he pushed that thought away quickly. He shook his head to clear his mind before resuming his brisk walk back to the bridge.

As he had done on Earth and while held at Mars, the admiral liked to take his meals whenever possible on the main mess deck among the crew. He felt it was important for them to see him, and for him to see them. They had to know that he was human, that he had to do mortal things like eat. Somehow that both perpetuated and undermined the myth that he was infallible. He needed his crew to know that he was mortal, that he could be wrong and could make mistakes. That way when he pulled them out of the fire as he had done time and time again during his career, they would idolize him all the more for it.

The bridge doors, activated by the chip in his left forearm, hissed aside to allow him access. Unlike the bridges of the frigates, which were dark and tightly confined, the bridge of the *Indomitable* was like a busy office with lots of different departments crammed into one room. The big boss sat in the center on a raised dais like a throne, looking down on them all. The admiral didn't like the grandiose feel of the command chair. Although it was extremely comfortable, with a heated massage function for when he had been sitting for too long, it gave off the impression that he felt superior to everyone else in the room.

The only thing that set him apart was his rank and position, but for the admiral of the fleet to walk around saying, 'Hey, I'm just one of you guys,' would be toxic. They had to see him as being the *man*. The one in charge, the big cheese, especially on the bridge, and the raised chair was just part of that necessary illusion.

"Good morning, everyone. Report?" he enquired politely to Massey, his flight officer. She ran most of the administrative issues onboard their ship without Dassiova having to dilute his concentration with the little things. She stood and smiled a corporate smile at the admiral, her eyes didn't match her facial expression, and rattled off the facts.

"Admiral," she bobbed her head in greeting, "*Hammer* and *Vengeance* are still searching the nearest planet and surrounding space for sign of the *Tanto*."

Dassiova nodded his acknowledgement, trusting the two tenacious frigate captains to do their best. He accepted a cup of coffee from a young enlisted rank who had clearly been delegated the task based on her utter lack of seniority. He took it and sipped, feeling the hot liquid connect to his senses like a weak stim shot.

"Our gun-buckets are holding position fifty thousand kilometers ahead in a defensive screen and the *Ichi* is still out in front, shrouded and scanning. Skies are clear, sir."

"Good," Dassiova said as he paused to take another sip of coffee. He tried to ignore his irrational flicker of anger at her derogatory description of the undocked gun barges. "Give Captain Torres my compliments and remind him that we have the best ships looking for his people. Scratch that; for *our* people. Tell the *Ichi* that their job is to be our eyes and ears and our first line of defense."

The comm officer, a woman with shoulder-length hair braided tightly back against her skull to show stripes of her olive skin between the lines, nodded and turned back to her terminal. She tapped out the message that she guessed was intended to keep Captain Torres and his crew from getting anxious that they'd been sidelined when their own people were missing. She knew she'd be feeling pretty bad if it was her ship, her crew, and because it was a small vessel, it occurred to her that those onboard the *Ichi* would be feeling it pretty sharply. With that in mind, she softened the tone of the message and added some more reassuring words on behalf of their fleet commander.

Dassiova sipped the coffee again and sat in the big chair, hitting the console beside him for the pre-programmed comfort settings to return to his preferred arrangement. He used two fingers to zoom in on the display of their sector of space, pausing as he noticed how skeletal their vessel appeared when the eight destroyers that formed the bulk of the midsection of the *Indomitable* were deployed. To his mind, their ship now looked like a mostly-eaten pear, leaving just a spine with a fore and aft section untouched.

He scanned further out, seeing how the line of gun barges rippled as comm traffic fed between them like they were a small organic network controlled by a central mind. Further out still and he saw the planned flightpath of the *Ichi*, but as they were shrouded, their precise location couldn't be pinpointed. Further back toward the red sun, the three large support ships were in close proximity to them, and all four ships encircled the space where the station was slowly forming.

"Okay, Massey," Dassiova said to his flight officer. "What else you got for me?" He sipped his coffee as the regular daily problems were laid at his feet for judgment like some medieval lord.

One light year away and closer to the rocky, forested moon where the *Tanto* had gone down, the crew of the *Ichi* went through a similar morning routine.

"Slight power surges detected in the number two propulsion engine," Sarvanto informed Torres. As always, he was careful to provide problem and solution in one sentence, "and I have Harris ready to shut it down and run a diagnostic if you require it."

"Do that," Torres said. He knew that if Sarvanto had suggested it, then it was highly irregular for there to be a better way of doing it. As usual though, the flight officer always left off some key detail which would either be picked up by the captain, reminding him why he was in charge, or else would serve as a last minute suggestion to make the tall Finn seem even less expendable than he was.

"Make sure he's ready to kick it back up to full power if we need to make a move," Torres instructed. "Other than that, give him what and who he needs to get it checked out."

"Already done, Captain." Sarvanto allowed himself a small smile. "Other than that, all ship's systems are running at optimal."

Torres thanked him, hearing from the comm and tactical officers in turn and swallowing a lump in his throat when the admiral's message was relayed. His inability to sit still or sleep was an obvious side effect of all those he cared about, his people, his friends, being out in the cold who-knew-where. If they were even still alive. Practicality kicked in and Torres temporarily filled Brandt's position with the woman now sitting beside him for the morning bridge briefing.

Her dark skin shone with an impossible smoothness and just sitting so close to her gave him the same adrenaline-fueled feeling he got when he was about to do a tactical insertion and jump from the open tail ramp of a dropship. He cleared his throat to clear his thoughts and asked for the projected flight path to be sent to his console. He took his time studying it and pretended he wasn't daydreaming.

Daydreaming about what others were doing when they should be on his ship.

CHAPTER 11

Unnamed Moon. Underground

"Rogers? You still with me?" Brandt asked softly as she shook his shoulder.

"Huh?" the pilot managed back. "Where…?"

"Still in the caves," Brandt said. "Still goddamned freezing, and still lost."

"Temporarily geographically misplaced, Commander," Zero corrected her. "You always said we're always where we're supposed to be; just not always relative to where others *want* us to be."

"Life is nothing without context," Paterson said weakly.

Brandt turned to look at him. He was sitting with his legs out straight and his back against the rough rock wall of the cave in what had been McMarrow's armor. Hours before, after the last time they saw daylight, the team had paused in the cavern to take stock of themselves. Paterson had been told to use the armor and to his credit had done so without question. He treated the body of the dead trooper with reverence as Turner had helped him lay the man down on the smooth rock floor of the natural cavern. The long, eerie shadows cast by their powerful LED beams made the darkness somehow more complete when not directly illuminated. Those deeper, darker patches of black held more promise of things from nightmares than they had before.

"It ain't natural, being underground this long," Horne complained.

He was back on his own two armored feet, having been ordered from the cockpit of the mech the second they stopped. Brandt stared hard at him for the three seconds he took deciding whether to obey her or not, then hit the canopy release and stepped down, abandoning the mech where he left it. She expected another confrontation with the company man then, steeled herself for it, but another voice removed Horne as one of her problems.

"With me," Specter told him as he stepped close to look down at the much shorter man. "Help guard the tunnel."

Specter glanced up at Zero, who nodded and turned to Payne. The slimmer armored figure said nothing, simply hefted the big gun that had belonged to McMarrow and walked to secure the opposite end.

"Flare out," Specter warned as he tossed one of the tiny tubes far ahead in the pitch-black direction they had come from.

"Flare out," Payne echoed as she did the same in the direction they had yet to travel in.

"Turner?" Brandt asked over the channel, looking around until her HUD flashed on the outline of the man kneeling down over the supine form of Perez.

"He'll be alright," the medic said in anticipation of her question. "I need to give him more oxygen and some steroid injections, but he'll make it."

Brandt paused a beat before asking the next question that made her feel like a grade-A shit.

"Can he be effective?" she asked simply. In order to best marshal their resources, she needed to find out if the man was an asset or a burden.

Turner's helmeted head dropped slightly before he responded. "He can man a position but with reduced lung function he won't be runnin' and gunnin' any time soon."

The visor of the medic turned to face her, and a private channel request popped up on the bottom of her HUD. She activated it.

"He's still probably going to develop pneumonia, which could kill him if I don't get him back to a ship with proper medical facilities," he said in a flat tone.

"Understood," Brandt replied. "Just patch him up as best you can." She cut the channel to minimize the time spent in obviously private discussion.

"You hear that, Perez?" she said in a lighter tone. "Restricted duties for you."

"Yes, Com—" He broke off into a racking cough that sounded like it had wet rocks in it. His mic muted for a few seconds until he had finished coughing and composed himself. "Yes, Commander."

She patted a gauntlet on his shoulder before walking away and addressing her entire team.

"Everyone stay closed down," she told them, using the ancient tank terminology. "We know the air is breathable up top, but I don't much like it down here. Plus, the temperature is too low so stay inside and stay warm."

"Temperature is dropping, actually," Paterson's voice drifted to her ears. "I'm guessing it's sundown outside."

"Yeah," Horne added, "and let's hope no creepy crawlies come out at night down here."

"Keep your eyes open and your mouth shut," came the unexpected reproof from Zero, who usually kept his thoughts inside his head. "And Commander? Are we gonna talk about what we saw out there?"

"You mean the huge flying dinosaur thing?" Brandt answered lightly, trying to hide the concern she felt for what had driven them underground like rats in the first place.

"It's not so hard to comprehend, is it?" Paterson asked in a voice marred by grogginess. "I mean, the environment exists here and on the main planet for life like ours to grow and evolve, right? So why aren't they dinosaurs?"

Nobody answered him, which he seemed to take as permission to carry on with his explanation.

"If there hadn't been an asteroid impact on Earth way back when, then who's to know that the dominant species on our planet would be us hairless monkeys? Why wouldn't huge reptiles still be rocking the top of the food chain?" Again, nobody answered him, so he carried on. "What I'm saying is, those things that we think looked like dinosaurs? Like flying dinosaurs? They were. They must be a kind of pterosaur that is unique to the environment it exists in."

"Wait a minute," Rogers cut in. Brandt looked over to him to see both gauntleted hands help up like he was trying to calm the situation. "You're saying we just got chased off the rocks by a bunch of pissed pterodactyls?"

"Yes," Paterson said.

Other noises filled the team channel at the answer. Noises of disbelief and at least one scoff.

"So, we've crash-landed on the surface of a moon that's what? Seventy or eighty million years behind Earth's evolutionary cycle?" the pilot asked incredulously.

Paterson made a high-pitched noise of pensiveness. "I'd say more *crashed* than crash-landed—"

"Whatever," Rogers snapped. "You're following the logic, right? So, we're expecting a T-Rex or something next?"

"No idea," Paterson told him. "It isn't like this place would necessarily have the same kind of species as we had on Earth. But, otherwise, yes; logic dictates that there would be large apex predators around."

"Well," Horne huffed to silence everyone. "That's just great. That's just... *peachy*!"

"Anyway," Brandt said to her friend who had once fought beside her before he became more academic than soldier. "I thought you did space science and shields and wormholes and stuff? Not this."

"I'm no paleontologist," he responded drily, "but if you can't accept what we've already seen, then it falls to me to point out the obvious. Plus," he smirked, "I'm not a dumb grunt and I actually read books. I don't eat them."

"One problem at a time," Brandt said a little too harshly as she tried to mask her fear and head off a quippy comeback from anyone. "Rogers, Paterson; help me bury McMarrow."

They settled on piling rocks over his body; there wasn't a single bit of dirt in the cave's ground to dig into. The temperature there would preserve his body and they marked their location to return for it when they were picked up. Though outwardly the team took these steps, privately they all knew his body wouldn't be there when—*if* —they did. They didn't discuss that possibility. The troopers held the cavern for a few hours so that Paterson and Perez could rest. The guards at either end of the winding tunnel were rotated and everyone took a turn at resting their eyes for a time. Brandt tried to decline, tried to stay awake and in charge the entire time but her stoically calm second-in-command quietly insisted.

The only one of them not to need rest was Specter, who maintained a ceaseless watch on the direction they had come from without faltering. Though she had given in to Zero's insistence, when Brandt tried to close her eyes, tried to find just a little sleep to recharge her own batteries, sleep stubbornly refused to come to her. She kept very still, as if she was sleeping, and used the visual interface to access the stats on the armor of her team. All of them were running at around sixty percent power, as was the mech, with the exception of Specter, who never dipped below ninety-eight percent. She knew what was contained inside his abdomen where his intestines used to be. Seeing as how he no longer needed them, the space was put to better use with the inclusion of a small singularity power source and a shield unit.

Shields, she thought. *We need to get top-side and retrieve the kit pack.*

She opened her mouth to call Rogers's name over the channel but recalled that she was supposed to be sleeping. Staying still, she used her eyes to link to his suit on a private channel.

"What's up, Grip?" he answered eagerly.

Brandt sighed. "First up," she said, not unkindly, "only us weird CP types call each other by the callsigns we were given. Unless you're Zero. Nobody knows his real name and I think he likes it that way. Secondly, any hit on the emergency kit you ejected?"

"Not under this much rock," he answered, sounding crestfallen. Brandt didn't know if it was by the gentle admonishment or the depressing fact that they had no idea where their emergency bug-out kit had landed. With the fact that it had ejected high up into a storm, chances were that it was miles away if they could even find it, and even then he would need to link to it and guide it toward them.

"So we get up top and we find it," Brandt said confidently.

"Yes, ma'am," Rogers answered, leaving out the attempt to sound like a special operator. He climbed to his feet and Brandt realized he must have assumed she meant immediately.

"Hold up," she told him. "Wait a while."

"For what?" he asked.

Brandt thought about it. "Good point." She climbed to her feet. "Let's move out. Keep on in the direction we're headed and look for a way back to the surface." Mumbles of acknowledgement rippled back to her as the others climbed to their feet.

"I've got point," Specter said flatly.

"I'm on you," Zero responded as he mag-locked his DMR, his precious dedicated marksman rifle, to his back and silently gestured for the heavy support gun still carried by Payne. "Payne takes the mech rig at the tail, injured and precious cargo in the center," he ordered.

And I thought you didn't want your own team, Brandt mused to herself with a private smile bordering on the kind of pride shown by a big sister.

They advanced maybe half a mile before Specter froze and threw up the fist of his right hand. The movement rippled back along the strung-out line until Payne at the back turned and watched in that direction.

Brandt took three careful steps forward, gun raised and HUD scanning the darkness ahead intently for any indication of the threat.

"I have movement ahead," the cyborg said softly, somehow more robotic than normal in the dark, echoing confines of their subterranean situation.

"What ki—" Brandt began, just as her own HUD came alive.

Outlines of things she didn't recognize lit up the cramped horizon as dozens of them crawled over each other in their bid to advance. The outlines flashed, confusing her suit's software as it tried to trace each reading to a correlating entry in a database. She had seen this before when they first set foot on the surface of Proxima b and nothing they saw made sense to their human technology. It slowed her suit almost imperceptibly then, just as it did now as the available memory lagged in the vain effort to understand what the things were.

"What the hell is that noise?" Horne yelled from behind as the dank air filled with a chittering cacophony like pebbles tapping against one another.

Before Brandt could answer, her suit registered two partial matches in the database. The legend on the lower left of her screen read:

SCORPION – 66.77% MATCH
COCONUT CRAB – 18% MATCH

"Oh, *hell*, no," she cursed as she turned away. "Fall back!"

They went. No ill-advised heroics from any of the team jeopardized their retreat but that made no difference. The clattering, chattering noise of hard, chitinous armor knocking together echoed behind them and sounded the advance of the unquestionably dangerous beasts behind them.

"Flares?" Zero shouted over the channel.

"Worth a try," Brandt yelled back. "Dump 'em."

Just ahead of her, lit sporadically by the moving beams of their suit LEDs like strobe lighting, she watched Zero in what seemed like motion-capture as he pulled a handful of the tiny flares and hit the activation patch on one end until his hands glowed like he held burning embers.

He scattered them with both hands over his head as he ran, raining down the lit flares to form a hopeful barrier against the onslaught.

They ran another fifty meters before Specter shot a glance behind them and called out a report.

"It's stalling them," he said, raising their hopes before dashing them in the same breath. "Cancel that, the ones behind have pushed over and through. Keep running."

It was a good idea, Brandt thought. Anything existing in the pitch-black underground would surely be concerned by the hot, bright light of flares but the sheer weight of the armored biomass behind them proved to be too much.

They ran through the wider cavern they had stopped in before, where McMarrow's body was so tenuously covered by piled rocks. As the tunnel widened to become the enclosed cave the speed of the advance slowed as more from behind that first wave flooded outward and caused a constriction as they tried to force their swarming way back through to narrower exit leading back to the surface. A glance behind her told Brandt that the scorpion-crab things, each one the mass of a medium-sized dog, filled the near circular tunnel behind her. She made a call to degrade the enemy's number.

"Payne, Specter, Zero—suppressing fire!"

She turned and dropped to one knee to bring the submachine gun into her right shoulder. Beside her, Specter turned and whipped both of the large pistols from his thighs and opened up indiscriminately on their pursuers just as she fully depressed her trigger without aiming. Their bullets, charged by the ethereal blue glow of the singularity power in their weapons, drilled a firework display of damage on the packed bodies of the creatures. The advance slowed as the living behind had to force their way through the suddenly dead. It wasn't enough to stop the assault.

Only when the huge bolts of orange energy rained laterally into them and blew great holes through to leave scorched and burning wreckage of dismembered bodies did the tide turn. When Zero added the insanely rapid-firing squad support gun with its heavier 12mm ammunition, the four of them shifted the balance and gained dominance over the wave of biological mass. The advance slowed, then stopped. Brandt wasted no time.

"Go!" she ordered.

All four of them turned to sprint for the exit where the dull smear of a gray and red dawn beckoned them. The rhythmic thud and robotic whine of the mech pounding ahead of them served like a heartbeat in her head as she almost held her breath to make it outside. The others were there, waiting, waving them on and readying weapons until she bawled at them to get clear and climb to higher ground. They emerged into the wan light of the dawn, turned in a switchback and began to climb away from the tunnel entrance, where they waited with ready weapons until the flood of dog-sized scorpion-crabs burst out into the open.

Instead of turning and climbing to get to them, the creatures spread out over the rocks to fan out and search for food.

They seemed to be acting on instinct alone and had no cognitive function to hold a grudge for the sheer number of them the humans had killed.

No sooner had the scorpions emerged into the open than the flying creatures returned to swoop down and pick off the smaller ones. The team stared for a while, watching alien nature take its course and reminding them that not everything, despite the in-built feeling of the human race as a whole, was about them.

"Commander?" Rogers asked in a shaky voice from behind.

She turned to regard him, expecting an attempt at humor when she was far from in the mood.

"I've got a read on the emergency ejection kit," he told her as he looked at the comm device on his arm. "It's down, and is about twenty-three clicks…" he moved round on the spot, spinning like the second hand of an analogue clock until he found the right bearing, "… *that* way."

Brandt turned back to watch the last of the scorpion-crabs emerging into the rocky plain as the pterosaurs, or whatever they were, flew off with their kills. She saw a flash of navy blue among the dark brown of their shells, and for a second, she thought she saw McMarrow's severed arm held aloft in a giant claw. She shuddered and turned back to Rogers's bearing.

"Let's move," she said.

CHAPTER 12

Bōken Sha Ichi

"You *cannot* be considering this?" Eze asked Torres as he paced up and down in her quarters. "You'd truly abandon our post and disobey orders? *Dassiova's* orders?"

Torres stopped, hands balled into fists and a look of impotent rage on his face before he breathed out and deflated.

"No," he admitted. "That would be the end of my career, despite the UNID intervening *or* my mother getting involved. Not that she would," he added bitterly.

Eze stood and took hold of both of his arms, running her hands down them until their fingers interlock and their eyes met.

"You need to stay strong," she told him. "Do your job and have some trust. Don't you think Hayes is capable? Or Halstead?"

He broke away from her and resumed his pacing.

"No, both of them are better captains than I am," he complained petulantly, "but they aren't looking for their own people, are they?"

"No, not unless you count *their people* as other members of this fleet. As other members of their species. Out here there is no crew rivalry or prejudice over the territory you were born in; out here it is as simple as us and them. And *they* are out there, which is why *we* are here to keep watch for them and protect the fleet."

He stopped pacing, screwed up his features and made a noise of frustrated anger, then rubbed his face with both hands, before returning to his agitated movements.

"As your troop commander, Captain, I'm giving you my best counsel. Take it or leave it."

"I'm sorry," Torres said as he stopped pacing again. "You're right. Let's get back to the bridge."

Neither of them felt much like conducting their usual routine when they managed to steal more than five minutes alone with each other, but Eze stood and pressed the side of her head into his broad chest with her arms around his waist until he relented and held on to her tightly. They stayed like that for a while, locked in an embrace of comfort as both ran through their private thoughts. Without speaking, they broke apart and Torres made for the doorway to slip out into the corridor and make his way to the mess hall for the sandwich that had been his excuse for leaving the bridge. Eze waited a moment, then left to head directly to the bridge where she sat working out the revised troop rotations on both the gun teams and the standby deployment crew, the revision necessary because of the loss of key personnel from their numbers. She was still doing that, tapping away at the datapad rested on her crossed knee to provide a makeshift workstation, when Torres walked back in. Sarvanto, sitting beside her, said nothing but stood from the command chair and straightened his uniform.

"Nothing to report, Captain," he said quietly as he stepped aside and allowed Torres to take his place again.

"Nice sandwich?" Eze asked innocently as she worked beside him.

"Fine, thank you," he replied, stifling a burp and wincing at the discomfort of indigestion as he had swallowed the sandwich necessary for his cover story in only three bites.

Three rotations, or watches, of four hours passed by with no sign on the long-range sensors and no communications traffic being sent or received. Torres was about to end the rotation and get some sleep when the tactical officer, the same young ensign who grated on his nerves almost constantly, made a hesitant noise.

"Er, sir?" the officer squeaked.

"What is it, tactical?" Torres answered, not bothering to hide his annoyance.

"I'm er... I'm picking something up on the sensors..."

"Well, do I have to guess?" Torres asked after no more information was offered.

"No, sir, it's just... it's just that I haven't seen this before, not in real life, only on the replays of the first time the Va'alen attacked the fleet."

Torres sat up, his attention suddenly electrified after so many hours spent doing nothing. He stalked to the tactical station in a few fast strides and pushed his way in beside the ensign who seemed to shrink away from his captain. Torres peered at the sensor data, recorded at the very edge of their range, and froze with wide eyes.

"All stop, shields to maximum," he barked confidently. "Sound battle stations. Helm, bring us about to bearing one-oh-eight and proceed at two-thirds power. Comm, lock everything down; no calls in or out in case they are detected. Shut down our sub-space receiver array." He turned to face a concerned Eze and addressed her by her brevet rank awarded in Brandt's absence. "Lieutenant Commander, ready the guns."

Sarvanto, in his polite and unobtrusive manner, pushed his way in to look at the console. "My God…" he whispered.

"Yeah," Torres said back. "We might need His help too."

He walked back to his chair and sat heavily, a frown of concentration and resolve on his face, which suddenly seemed older than it had a moment before. He hit the ship-wide comm channel and spoke clearly and confidently.

"Crew of the *Ichi*, this is Captain Torres. We have detected what appears to be a massive concentration of enemy ships moving at speed and under Shroud. Communication blackout is in effect and all crew are to remain at battle stations until I stand you down."

He killed that channel and called out to the helmsman. "Time to intercept?"

"Forty minutes, give or take, sir," came the response. "Passive sensors only," he ordered. "I don't want a combined reading that size knowing we're in the same sector if we can help it."

Beside him Eze brought up the sensor readings on her datapad and let out a gasp.

"I know," Torres said. "Each reading the last time was at least two if not four ships. Four readings merged together to make one about a tenth of the size of that, so we're looking at somewhere between eighty and a hundred and eighty Va'alen fighters?"

"That could destroy the entire fleet…" Eze said, trailing off. The obvious did not require stating right then.

Despite the aliens' obvious superiority in weaponry and shields the first time they had met, the Va'alen were still underequipped when it came to the delicate art of covert movement and subterfuge. Torres imagined their sleek ship, not for the first time, to be like the under-water submarines back on Earth as they slipped silently through the darkness stalking the fleet of surface ships above. One wrong move, one noise or a push of an engine too far and they risked detection and annihilation. Rising to the metaphorical surface to send a warning back to the rest of the fleet would, from what they had learned recently to their detriment, almost certainly spell discovery.

They slowed as they approached the single sensor reading, which they took to be a mass of enemy ships. Torres's theory, backed up by every scientist and engineer he spoke to about it, was that the Va'alen pushed their ship's engines too hard, which made their energy signatures detectable. For that precise reason they never moved at anything more than sixty-six percent of maximum when shrouded, and as they approached, they reduced velocity to a little over half. Their ship was faster than the enemy fighters, but even when mixing it up with just a few of the pairs, they were outgunned by the quick and irregular maneuvers of their newest foe. While their guns and shields had been upgraded far beyond any firepower conceivably required in their own system, the sheer number of shrouded Va'alen fighters made discovery within the range of their weapons a death sentence.

"Match course and hold us steady at their parallel," Torres said softly to the lieutenant at the helm of the *Ichi*.

That lieutenant, nervous to say the least to be promoted to the ship's primary pilot since Rogers went missing with the *Tanto*, acknowledged the captain and made fine adjustments to their course. They sailed alongside the mass of enemy ships which, even at that distance, made the stars visible behind them ripple in distortion.

"Holding steady at forty-thousand kilometers distance," he said.

"Good," Torres answered, placing a reassuring hand on the young man's shoulder to calm the tension that pulsated off him in waves. "Comm, are we picking up anything from them?"

"Bits and pieces, sir," the comm officer responded as she worked her console. "Nothing I can make out clearly and none of it voice. It's like there are... *data links* between the ships or something. I'm guessing, sir, obviously, but it's like they're all connected constantly, somehow."

"Keep on it," Torres told her. "Record anything you can for analysis." He turned away to his favorite ensign as she acknowledged her instructions. "Tactical, tell me what you know," he said with a hint of sarcasm.

"W... well, sir..." the ensign stammered. "Given the previous data recorded from Va'alen engagements, and going by the size of the distortion in space and the power resonation, I've developed a simple algorithm and calculated that the number of enemy ships inside the Shroud field, based on the estimate of how much space each ship occupied when we saw them before, that there are between one-hundred-fifty-six and one-hundred-seventy-one ships. I doubt the upper number because it's an odd number."

Torres stared at him, dumfounded by the sudden location of his wits, and remembered not to keep his mouth open. The ensign mistook his look of shock for misunderstanding.

"You see, sir," he continued, "they've always operated in pairs from every engagement we've seen, and if one loses the other half, they go berserk and turn kinda kamikaze, so it stands to reas—"

"Thank you, Ensign," Torres interrupted. "I'm capable of figuring that out all by myself." The young man, a boy really, turned crimson and seemed suddenly out of breath. Torres acted quickly before he had an aneurysm. "Good work. Stay on them and alert me if anything changes. Mister Sarvanto?" he asked as he turned away before the kid shed a tear in gratitude for the unexpected compliment.

"Sir?" the tall, gangly Finn answered.

"Would you man the weapons station, please?"

"My pleasure, Captain," Sarvanto answered. His usually straight face cracked into an evil smile more unexpected than Torres complimenting the ensign on tactical. The weapons station, a new addition during their minor refit, controlled the singularity warheads, what they still called their 'nukes'. Torres guessed it stirred something in their species memory and created a sensation of sheer destructiveness. The weapons pods, still only four of them but packing something much heavier than the charged slugs they used to fire, were ineffective over that kind of range and against so many targets. They were reserved for close encounters, which were supposed to be avoided by a stealth reconnaissance ship.

"Sir," the ensign on tactical piped up with concern in his voice.

"What is it?"

"The enemy trajectory, Captain," he replied. "It's a direct course for Proxima b."

"The fleet," Torres said out loud, putting his forefinger to his lips and holding his breath in thought. "Calculate their ETA."

Choices, he said to himself, thinking faster than he could explain in words. *Attack now and take out some of them? Jump back and warn the fleet? Contact the frigates on subspace and get them to jump in to help ambush the enemy?*

No, he realized, *a jump or a subspace comm would alert them and we'd have to jump away to save our own skin anyway.*

"Anyone care to take a guess at how far away they can detect our subspace communications?" he asked the bridge in general.

No answer.

"Don't be shy, people. The time and place for modesty is not here and not now."

"Going on the theory that they detected our jump signature almost a quarter of a light year away," the comm officer started but paused to try and work out the relativity of her train of thought.

"Jump signature and subspace communications differ by a magnitude of almost a thousand percent," the ensign on the tactical station offered. "Nine point four six trillion roughly divided by four is two trillion-three-sixty-billion. Our jump signature radiates that far...*ish*, which means that at best guess we'd need to be a little over two billion clicks away to be safe?"

Torres stared at him again, totally blown away by the young man who had clearly been hiding an incredible intelligence behind a nervous inability to make words when he was asked to.

"Too far," the captain said eventually. "We either give away our position and run away, or we give away our position, cripple them as much as we can, *then* run away."

"What are you suggesting?" Eze asked carefully, speaking for the first time since giving her orders to the standby gun teams to get to work.

In response, Torres smiled and spoke out one corner of his mouth as he kept his eyes on hers.

"Mister Sarvanto? How quickly can we unload all of our nukes?"

Sarvanto almost did a double-take but answered the question.

"We have thirty-six warheads on board and twelve launchers. That's three full launches and reloads. I'd say thirty to thirty-five seconds?"

"Helm, bring us toward the head of the distortion and prepare a jump course back to the fleet. Comm, prepare a subspace communication to both the fleet and the search teams, advising them of what we've discovered.

"Tell them that we've laid down as much firepower as we are carrying and if we don't make it back, to prepare for an assault. Send it the second we start firing warheads. Are you ready, Flight Officer?"

"Target coordinates laid in, Captain," Sarvanto called out. "Targeting the head of the distortion with a maximum spread. The second and third waves of missiles have a wider spread to hopefully catch any ships taking evasive maneuvers."

"Excellent work," Torres said as he took his chair again. "Fire when ready."

CHAPTER 13

Unnamed Moon Surface

"Everyone take five," Brandt said tiredly. The team approached the cluster of trees that offered a reprieve from the harsh sunlight. They had marched for almost four hours in the direction of their emergency kit crate, which had got lost up in the storm clouds and pushed far away from where the shuttle actually went down. The theory behind the kit crate being ejected in the case of a crash landing was for the precise reason they had encountered; emergency equipment was no good to anyone when it got vaporized or crushed by an explosion or a collapsing singularity drive that lost containment.

The theory was that the surviving crew could scout and secure a safe location, then the slowly descending crate would come to them and remove any need to haul the heavy lifesaving gear with them. The crate itself was designed to fold out into a small, rudimentary shelter, but having seen the schematics, Brandt doubted they could get even half of them under cover using it. What they needed, desperately, was the power source to recharge their suit batteries and the ammunition resupply along with the emergency subspace beacon, which she had thought long and hard about using; run the risk of discovery by the enemy or never be found.

"It's like it was back in Turkey outside," Zero said quietly.

He had that manner of speaking softly so much of the time that you were never quite sure if he was thinking out loud or talking to you. Brandt, the only other person to have been with him in Turkey not that long ago, made a noise of agreement.

Outside their suits the external temperature read close to a hundred and five degrees, which meant that the battery life of their armor was being greatly reduced as its internal air conditioning worked hard to keep them from becoming boil-in-the-can meals like the military field rations before their time.

"Same at night," Brandt agreed with the marksman. "Cold when the sun goes down…"

"Hot as *balls* in the day," Paterson finished loudly and crassly, "like our training exercise in the Sonoran Desert back in the day."

At his casual mention of the training exercise, their soldier on point stopped hesitantly and turned to look back at Paterson. The scientist noticed Horne tap at his forearm device and saw Specter waver before returning to his task.

"Out of interest," Rogers asked over the comm channel, "how hot *are* balls?"

Nobody answered him, and Brandt didn't have the energy, mental or physical, to save him from himself.

"Anyway," Zero said to change the subject, "everyone take on water and sound off a battery percentage."

"Fifty-nine," Brandt said flatly.

"Sixty-three," Payne responded. "The rig is at twenty-nine."

"Fifty-five," Turner mumbled, only half concentrating as he was checking Perez's vital signs. "Perez is at sixty-four."

Paterson chimed in next with, "Seventy-four. My err… my armor wasn't used for the first couple hours."

Nobody answered that. The memory of McMarrow's body was fresh in their minds.

"Fifty-six," Horne grumbled.

"Fifty-eight," Rogers added in a serious tone.

"And I'm at sixty flat," Zero finished. Specter didn't involve himself in the roll-call as his battery wasn't an issue. Nobody could miss the tall man in the unique matte-black armor who stayed unnervingly, *inhumanly* still when he didn't need to move, so it wasn't as though they were worried he hadn't kept up.

"Okay, like Zero said," Brandt told them, "get some fluids and take a ration pill; we could all do with the calories and the stim boost."

A couple of groans rippled over the channel at her last instruction, and she knew it was because the ration pills affected everyone differently.

The pills, the emergency rations developed to replace the bulky, ultra-high-calorie packs issued to all field active UN personnel, were a masterpiece in science and research. That was how they were described to the recruits. In reality they were dry, gray lumps, which were almost too large to swallow in one go. The alternative, snapping them in half, meant letting out the taste from inside that stayed on a person's tongue for about a month. They were packed with tiny particles that expanded to fill the stomach and release all the nutrients the body required, along with a sizeable dose of stimulant that was proven to increase a soldier's productivity. Unfortunately, the soldier's odds of committing suicide or suffering from psychosis if used regularly for extended periods also increased. That last part wasn't in the educational video given to new recruits.

One by one, visors on suits hissed open and faces were pulled as the pills went down. Brandt took hers first, knowing that the size of her stomach was marginally less than the amount the pill would expand to, so she suffered the taste by biting the end off a capsule and restoring it to the tiny pouch hidden in her armor.

She restored her helmet and took long pulls on the drinking tube to wash it down with the cool water and gave no thought to where the filtered, purified and chilled fluids had come from.

"Keep your lids on," she reminded them. "You'll lose too much battery power cooling you back down otherwise."

They complied, unhappily, but they did as they were told. In truth, even Brandt, who was well-accustomed to spending long periods of time closed down in her armor, was starting to feel the rub of claustrophobia. "How far to the crate, Rogers?"

"A little under six clicks," he said without checking, "but with the terrain change I don't know how long that will take us."

"Hmmm," the commander let out involuntarily.

The pilot raised a good point; their endless trek over rock-strewn wastelands had come to an abrupt end at a watercourse with trees and low bushes dotted all around. The foliage grew thickly around the banks of the stream and the air suddenly possessed a significant amount more humidity than the arid plain they had crossed. Luckily, they had seen no more flying reptiles or dog-sized scorpions, and amazingly, nobody had lost their mind over it either. Paterson had been right in saying that they had landed on a planetoid that possessed most of the same qualities as Earth for life to thrive and evolve, but also that it was younger in evolutionary terms. Their suit HUDs worked overtime to capture and log every new detail on the strange surface they found themselves on. Now as they moved into a world that was green instead of the reddish-brown plain, they faced a whole new ecosystem.

And nobody needed to point out that that meant a whole new set of potential predators with no clue what the little metal mammals were, or whether they were food.

They moved out slowly after a short break. Staying still too long was never a good idea. Their bodies would automatically want to shut down, especially after ingesting the ration pills. But the risk was weighed against giving the injured sufficient time to recover before moving again.

They went slowly, Paterson now fully in possession of his faculties after the side effects of too much adrenaline substitute had worn off. Perez was still weak and breathless. In the tight confines of what was evolving from a wooded area to something resembling a jungle, the clamoring movements of the mech rig made them all feel like they were advancing ahead of a marching band. Brandt's nerves couldn't take much more of it; she expected an attack by something at any point. She called a halt in a clearing.

"Rogers, distance and bearing to target?"

"Twelve hundred meters, dead ahead."

"Zero, set up three-sixty defense here. Specter, Paterson, Rogers—on me." The start of a protest began from the pilot but was rapidly abandoned as Brandt's visor swung to face him. "March order: Specter, Rogers, me, Paterson."

They formed up, spreading out so that they weren't packed tightly together and able to fit into the targeting scope of any weapon pointed in their direction, but still close enough to maintain visual contact at all times. Weapons drawn and advancing tactically, they moved through the forest with as little disruption as possible. Their HUDs flickered with half-seen movements as the software tried to recognize and catalogue the tiny creatures stirred up by their presence. Luckily, they all seemed too small and solitary to pose any kind of threat to them inside their armor.

"Fifty meters," Rogers said. "Must be just beyond those trees."

"Hold here," Brandt ordered.

She stepped up beside Specter and met his mirrored gaze. She nodded to him and both set off cautiously forward until the audible sound of the crate reached their suits. They were standing directly on the target coordinates and could hear the muted ping sounds of the supplies, but it was nowhere to be seen. As one, they both craned their necks to look upward.

"Shit," Brandt said.

"*Hijo de puta*," Specter added, startling his commander. She hadn't heard him utter a curse in Spanish since he had been Jake Santana.

"Come again?" she said.

"Someone needs to climb up," he said, stating the obvious and returning to his normal Specter self as though he hadn't just spoken in a second language.

"Are you volunteering?" she asked him

She received no immediate reply, so she called the others forward. They joined them in a little over a minute, and both looked up to offer their own opinions on the situation. The supply crate was hung up in the trees by the deployed canopy that slowed its descent back to the surface. The crate, too big for any two people to carry alone, swung ponderously in a gentle breeze that didn't exist on the leaf-strewn ground.

"Any takers?" Paterson asked before slapping the back of an armored hand against Specter's arm for his attention. "Want me to hold your beer?"

Specter stared at him for a few seconds before turning to look at Brandt. She didn't know why he did that, because if he was looking for help in understanding Paterson's humor her reflective face shield would offer nothing.

Unless those artificial eyes can see through my visor, she contemplated fleetingly before shaking her head to dismiss the frivolous thought. Specter mistook the slight shake for a negative from her and turned back to the scientist.

"You used to say that to me... to *Jake*... before you did something stupid," he said quietly.

"What the hell's going on there?" Horne's angry voice filled the channel. "You stop messing with our asset's head, you hear me? I swear, you godda—"

Brandt didn't respond, merely muted his mic from the channel, as was her privilege as commander.

"I did, buddy," Paterson said kindly. "Now which one of us dumbasses is climbing up? I'll be honest, I think you're in better shape than I am and there's no way we can let the girly go instead of us."

"Hey!" Brandt started, stopping when she realized both men were laughing lightly at her sudden anger as she primed the gender equality cannons to fire. She smiled, stepping back and giving a lavish gesture for them to proceed to the base of the tree. "After you, dumbasses."

The two men exchanged a look before Specter mag-locked both guns to his thighs and stepped forward. He looked around for a low handhold but found nothing under about thirty feet, which was beyond the limit of his augmented vertical leap.

"Need a boost?" Paterson asked him. "No, I need to be lighter." With that Specter stepped back and exited his armor after it unfolded to his silent command. He stepped forward out of it to expose his black-suited body. Brandt knew that the suit was actually part of his augmentation, one that made his artificial limbs seem more human than robot.

He walked forward, building up speed as he went until he reached the base of the wide tree trunk at a sudden sprint. He leapt into the air and planted a foot hard against the moist bark. His leg tensed as his body still moved in the air. He straightened the leveraged leg explosively to launch his body up and away from the trunk. In his launch, he gained the same amount of height again to reach out and grasp the lowest branch thirty feet up and fifteen feet out. He swung for a while until the pendulum action of his body wore off, then did a two-handed straight arm pull-up which he effortlessly turned into what the sadistic PT instructors called a muscle-up. He balanced his feet on the wood of the branch as it wobbled and flexed under his weight walking back toward the trunk. He performed a further series of jumps and muscle-ups until he was nearly a hundred feet in the air nearing the top of the canopy.

"You know," Paterson said quietly to Brandt on a channel he opened just to her, "I think little Mister Horne is hitting our boy with dopamine every time he has a Jake memory glitch."

Brandt turned to stare at Paterson, visor to visor, before she spoke.

"That little son of a bi—"

"Stand clear," Specter said over the team channel, interrupting them.

His voice surprised Paterson, who had never experienced him using the radio transmitter embedded in his brain. The sound of cracking wood and falling leaves echoed down to them as both retreated a few steps. A direct hit from the crate might not kill them, but their armor might not operate as well afterwards.

The crate hit the leafy ground and embedded one corner in the dirt so that there wasn't a single inch of bounce.

Specter followed, taking the quicker route down in three leaps between big branches before hitting the soft earth with both feet and cushioning the fall by sinking to one knee and arresting his forward momentum with an outstretched hand.

He stood straight, cracked a toothy smile at them and said in a deadpan voice, "Superhero landing."

Brandt and Paterson looked at one another in disbelief.

"Dude," Paterson said, conveying so much thought and emotion into the single syllable that mere words could not do justice. "You okay? Are you... *you*?"

Specter walked to his armor and turned to back into it now that agility was no longer required. He ignored the question and spoke.

"I saw something when I was up there. Looked like an artificial compound with at least one building."

"Man-made?" Paterson asked before correcting himself. "You know what I mean..."

"There was a faint energy signature coming from it. We should check it out."

CHAPTER 14

Unnamed Moon Surface

"Hold there," Zero's whispered voice sounded softly in their earpieces.

Why he whispered when the suit contained his voice was a mystery, but something in the way he spoke radiated caution to all of them. Brandt had gone ahead with just the cyborg and the scientist, who she had remind herself hadn't been a soldier in a long time and wasn't at the sharp edge of tactical movement and combat skills. He had been once, years before, but those years spent in classrooms and laboratories had softened their former squadmate.

"What do you see?" Brandt murmured back.

Her HUD flickered ahead at the plethora of new shapes and movements it was trying to catalogue. She had turned it off before; the constant working of the software annoyed and distracted her, not to mention removed vital memory capacity should she need to fight. But when the energy reading matched the signature of the Va'alen ships, she turned it back on in a hurry. Seeing the hulking, looming, four-armed outline of one of the huge warriors, one of the 'cockroaches', occupied a significant amount of her brain's concentration. She feared them, as any sensible person would, but her fear was not to be mistaken for cowardice.

"Nothin' much," Zero answered. "Just hold there for a while in case somethin' takes a peek out, alright?"

139

Brandt understood.

If a marksman could ever be rushed, were they even a marksman at all?

Patience, which she felt that she had, meant a whole different thing to Zero; the parameters were so vastly opposite that there should be another word for what he called patience.

She could bide her time better than most, but she doubted she had the mental and physical discipline to remain awake and in position, looking down the scope of a rifle for three days, just for a fifteen-second window of opportunity to take a shot and make it count.

They waited. Brandt expected Paterson, the civilian of their downed crew in most ways, to show impatience or annoyance at wasting the daylight. He surprised her by remaining still and focused; he still had the heart of a soldier. Something about her train of thought bothered her and made her go back over the word in her head until she found what was wrong.

Wasting the daylight.

"Anyone else notice," she asked softly and quietly over the team channel, "that the sun seems to be setting again already?" Silence reigned until the aggressive sulk of Horne's voice came back to her.

"So? It's a faster day rotation on this rock than you're used to. Scared of the dark, *Commander?*" Brandt sighed.

"Ordinarily, Mister Horne, I am not. But if a massive pack of giant carnivorous scorpion-crab-whatevers wanted to be underground and off the surface during the dark, does that give you any indication of where *we* should be?"

Horne didn't answer, but the conversation sank deeply into their minds.

"Okay," Zero said in the same controlled, implacable voice he always used when the customized rifle was in his hands. "Nothin' doin'. I'll cover your approach from this angle, but be advised that I do not have eyeball on the right side perimeter of the compound from my position. Acknowledge."

"Understood," Brandt said back just as softly. "Moving now."

She turned to look at Specter and Paterson, each about three meters apart and the same distance away from her. With her left hand moving in small, slow gestures, she ordered Specter to take point and Paterson to get on his ass and stay there. She finished by explaining that she would cover the rear of their approach. Specter nodded, drawing just the left pistol from that thigh and keeping his right hand free for any number of eventualities nobody wanted to think of in too much detail. Paterson, unencumbered of the heavy support gun which was back in the hands of Payne at the fallback position far behind them, tucked the submachine gun similar to Brandt's into his shoulder and adopted a tactical look as he followed. The compact weapon looked tiny in his hands, even compared to Brandt, who seemed just the right size to carry such a gun, but she knew the devastating firepower contained in that small package. The thought of his weapon made her glance down at her own for the hundredth time and check it; a nervous habit she had often been pulled up on. She had hoped for an alien energy weapon when they came back to the new and hostile system, but their technological advances in such a short time had limited them to ship and mech-borne energy weapons; they simply couldn't make the tech small enough in the time they had.

Her submachine gun, initially a Hyper prototype and much like Zero's 12mm marksman rifle and Specter's custom heavy pistols, was unique to her. It had taken her a while to grow fully accustomed to carrying such a small gun, missing the reassurance of the heavier Universal Service Rifle she had eaten and slept with during her basic training. But when she came to trust that the punch delivered by the lightweight gun was far superior to even the old squad support weapons, she had embraced it.

Now it was modified, overpowered, and tweaked to be perfect for her. She flicked the safety on and off to reassure herself that it was as ready to rock and roll as she was.

She glanced down at the action when she did it, seeing the custom etchings created by the old Teutonic armorer onboard the *Ichi*.

He had adjusted the weapon housing switch from "NO BANG" to "BIG BANG" on a sliding scale of how much singularity power was added to the charged projectile. She smirked, reassured by the joke covering the very serious nature of the controls.

"Perimeter fence," Specter's voice said, "damaged."

Brandt didn't respond verbally. Instead she had the patience to wait until her own controlled advance met the obstacle. She found a heavy mesh fence, three times her height, that was thick and tough but had a degree of flex to it. She knew that would make it harder to break though, as any attack on it would have the force distributed and dissipated by the give in the metal. She followed the obstruction to where Specter waited. There was a ragged hole about the height of him, where the edges of the metal were roughly mangled. Her HUD registered a chunk of something hanging from a jagged edge.

"Biological material," Paterson said helpfully. "Been there a while by the looks of it."

"Take a sample," she told him.

She expected a complaint about his field of science having nothing to do with taking biological samples. To her surprise he just took out a pack from a utility pouch on his armor and bagged the chunk of leathery flesh with only a single, mild protest.

"Ew," he whispered to himself, transmitting to the entire squad.

"Move inside," she instructed after he was ready again.

Specter moved through the gap with exquisite body control and without touching the edges.

They filed in after the cyborg, who had advanced and gone static to survey and support, should the need arise. Their progress brought the low building that had been covered by the small tree canopy fully into view.

"*Pheeeeeew,*" Paterson whistled softly in awe.

Few of them had ever seen an alien construction up close and his excitement was obvious. Brandt's was less so. Having fought their enemy under the shadow of two Va'alen ships, she recognized the style as being the same.

"Everybody stay sharp," she said softly with the tone of a knife blade being drawn slowly across a sharpening tool. "This had to have been built by the Va'alen."

She could almost feel the air over the channel grow cold and still as they realized the potential danger. Brandt caught Specter's attention and she nodded him toward the entrance to the building.

"Keep your eyes on us, Zero," she added, hearing a whispered acknowledgment from behind and above them.

"The energy signature is inside," Specter said, as though he could see the power source. "Room clearance?"

"Room clearance," Brandt agreed, before turning to Paterson. "You remember how to do a r—"

"Oh, *puh-LEASE,*" he complained quietly and sarcastically. He hefted the pistol and gripped it tightly. "It hasn't been *that* long, and I'm not so old as to start losing my memory just yet."

Brandt smiled behind her visor but nodded, then gave Specter the go-ahead.

Instead of kicking the door down and loudly announcing their presence to anyone, any*thing*, in hearing range, Specter instead placed a small device from an armor pouch onto the panel that appeared to be a locking mechanism.

It chirped and chattered for a while until a short buzz of static sounded and the large doorway clicked open a fraction. He removed the device and nodded back that he was ready as the second pistol appeared in his free hand. Brandt glanced at both men and nodded back.

Specter moved fast, almost impossibly fast as his superior prototype armor reacted to the superhuman speed of his robotic limbs inside the suit. Paterson and Brandt followed, weapons up and moving fast, to find a wrecked room with leafy detritus and crates littering the ground. Over the sight of her weapon, which moved everywhere her eyes did, Brandt got the immediate impression that she was in a field laboratory. They swept through the room, fanning out into a loose lateral line as they went, until they reached a door halfway along the abandoned chamber. Specter, the closest to it, went static there to cover it as the other two kept advancing toward the second door at the far end. Reaching that, they too went static and a chorusing echo of 'clear' ran through the channel.

Brandt told Specter to hold his position, before reaching out to hit the rounded control, which suggested some kind of emergency release mechanism, like the old push-bar escape doors back on Earth. That door led outside to a separate section of fenced-off enclosure where the trees had encroached right up to the wire. They closed the door, returning to where the only other exit from the room was covered by the unmoving form of Specter. He had one gun on that unopened door and another pointing back toward their entry point. That door was opened much the same way as the external yard one had been, and it showed a room of a similar size running off the one they were in, like the floorplan ran in a large T shape. They poured through the door and moved like water seeking the quickest way to return to a resting state. A warning came from outside.

"Movement," Zero said intensely but without a hint of panic. Panic only bred more panic when it was transmitted over a channel. "Three creatures, can't make 'em out fully, approaching the compound from the west."

"Va'alen?" Brandt asked, consciously trying to keep her own voice as level and cool as Zero's.

"Negative. Bi-pedal, feathered, elongated tails, rough height of a human."

Brandt's visor met those of the others with her and asked the question they had found themselves pondering more often than was comfortable on the surface of the moon they had crash-landed on.

Predatory?

Without a doubt, they had to be bad news. Brandt decided she'd rather lose her chance at this year's humanitarian award and stay alive. If she was wrong, then she was wrong.

"Take them out," she ordered coldly, waiting the split-second before a metallic *twang* thumped the air outside the building.

"One down, the other two scattered. No shot, repeat *no shot.*"

The three of them moved in an instant to find cover from the doorway just as a clattering noise sounded above them.

It's on the roof, Brandt thought before a noise at the doorway made her look back and widen her eyes in primeval terror.

Silhouetted in the wide, tall doorway was a thing that looked like a seven-foot-tall chicken with a long, muscular-looking tail like a massive alligator. It had a wide head brimming with long, conical teeth and feathers, which lent it the appearance of wearing a shaggy brown coat. It ducked its head as she held her breath and watched the HUD try to make sense of the new outline it detected. The wide

145

head swung from side to side, mouth wide open and long tongue snaking out to taste the air like a reptile.

"What the fu—" Paterson began.

It froze and cocked its head to issue a shriek in his direction from a beak full of sharp, conical teeth. Two shots rang out, so close to one another that they couldn't have come from the same weapon. Brandt followed the direction of the noise to see Specter with both of his heavy pistols up and pointing at the falling creature. Before any of them could react to what they saw, the sound of tearing metal sheets erupted from behind their position near the doorway. An ominous thud of a large body hitting the deck reverberated around the abandoned structure as all three of them turned to face the newest threat.

Slowly, the wide head brimming with teeth rose up from where it had landed, taller and wider than the one Specter had just killed without mercy. In place of the shaggy brown pelt of dull, bristled feathers, this one boasted a vivid plumage of red and a blue so bright that it seemed electric. The creature cocked its head, swung it side to side to take in all of them, before scraping a thickly scaled leg back and dragging elongated claws over the detritus in readiness to attack.

As weapons turned to face it, impossibly slow in comparison to how fast the thing moved, a flash of bright metal swung downward with a sickening crack. It beat down on the outstretched neck of the beast. It faltered, shrieking in agony and rage as it turned to the source of the attack. Emerging unsteadily from the shadow of a wide support pillar and swinging what looked like an ornate billhook the length of a human leg downward, came the shape of something instantly outlined and recognized by their HUDs.

VA'ALEN – 98.76% MATCH

The billhook-type blade rose a third time, pausing at the height of its upswing as though the thing wielding it, as terrifying to the humans as the beasts hunting them, summoned yet more strength to deliver the killing blow. Before the blade could bludgeon down on the layers of spiny feathers, the thing turned as it coiled, striking out with sharp teeth and both hind legs. Talons broke through the hard carapace of the alien and the teeth ripped hard chunks of it away. The Va'alen, already missing the arms on one side of its body, which seemed dull and dusty compared to the ones they had seen before, toppled onto its back and dropped the blade before it could strike a blow.

The three of them stood mesmerized for a second, unable to contemplate which posed the greater danger to them. Brandt sucked in air sharply through her nose and raised her weapon to drill a dozen shots through the thick coat of the animal and drop it lifeless on top of their enemy. All of them converged, ignoring the increasingly frantic calls over the radio for their situation, and pointed weapons at the badly injured Va'alen. The arms on its left side, the only ones attached to the big body, flailed weakly for the billhook. Specter, standing closest to the weapon, pushed it away with an armored boot. He kept his pistols up, one pointed at the alien's center mass and the other sweeping the room. It lashed out with a powerful leg to knock Specter down hard onto his back; the remaining arms snatched up the body of the brightly plumed predator and flung it at both Paterson and Brandt, hitting them in the chest plates and knocking them back. It rose, defying the sorry state it appeared to be in and threatening death to all three of the humans.

Its featureless face split open to reveal rows of elongated and very sharp fangs, as it roared a challenge at them, its arms spread wide. That roar, that deafening challenge, was cut short as Specter performed a gymnastic flip back to his feet and, ignoring the dropped pistols, snapped a wide blade like an ancient Roman short sword from the forearm of his armor. In one quick movement, he drove it deep into the chest of the Va'alen, until his bunched fist connected to bounce the dying alien off the blade and into the nearest wall, where it rebounded and flopped to the deck.

It looked up at them, and croaked a hissed sequence through obvious pain. The software of the suit translated the words as it repeated them again, louder, and it convulsed horribly.

[FOR THE HIVE LORDS]

"What the hell are the Hive Lords?" Brandt snapped, jabbing a boot into the fallen alien.

It didn't respond. Instead it convulsed one more time, more violently than before, forcing them to take a step backward and raise their guns, before it went still. Brandt's HUD flashed its outline from orange to red, indicating that it was dead.

"What? *Hive Lords*?" Paterson asked.

"Hive Lords?" Zero's voice echoed over the channel as the sound of their mech advancing echoed outside the building. "What in God's name are you three doing in there?"

"Everyone converge on our position," Brandt ordered as she glanced up at the darkening skies through the fresh hole in the roof. "I'll explain when you get here."

CHAPTER 15

Admiral's Quarters, The Indomitable

"Leave us," Dassiova ordered the other senior officers in the meeting, his unwavering gaze locked onto Torres unnervingly.

The room emptied in hurried silence.

"Out of a sliver of respect for your tenuous rank and position in command of what is becoming an iconic ship in Earth's fleet," he said carefully, "I'm going to give you the opportunity to explain to me personally exactly what happened."

Torres swallowed, glancing at the chair in front of the desk where the admiral sat. Dassiova glanced at it too, not extending the junior officer an invitation to sit. Instead, Torres remained standing to attention, the best way to prevent further punishment, in his experience, and explained everything.

"Sir, we detected a sensor reading indicating shrouded enemy ship movement at the extremity of our visible range," he began stiffly. "Based on calculations and some informed assumptions, we believe the enemy force to be in excess of a number the entire fleet could expect to repel."

"Not your decision to make, Captain, but go on," Dassiova interrupted quietly.

"I gave orders for our entire arsenal to be unloaded at the enemy mass in order to degrade their forces before they arrived in this sector, which we anticipate will be in—"

"Will be in a little under three weeks, if my calculations and assumptions are correct," the admiral said, "which is more than enough time to deploy a minefield, plan an ambush of their approach trajectory and formulate a disciplined defense, wouldn't you agree, Captain? Which would have been entirely possible, had you fallen back out of range of detection and reported the enemy disposition instead of basically closing your goddamned eyes and pulling the trigger on full auto?"

Torres was trapped. The plan Dassiova had just suggested was a good one, despite a couple of stalling points he could envisage right away. To disagree was lunacy. To agree was to shoot himself in the foot. He chose to appear wrong, as opposed to appearing foolish and arrogant.

"Yes, sir."

"And what did you discover after you launched every last one of a finite supply of heavy munitions?"

Torres swallowed again and told the story.

~

"Fire when ready," the captain of the *Bōken sha Ichi* called out confidently, feeling the crumps of vibration as the rippling line of warheads erupted from their firing ports.

"First salvo away," Sarvanto said. His fingers danced over the console, ready to fire the next wave as soon as the tubes were loaded again. "Adjusting target coordinates... second salvo fired."

The familiar shakes translated up through the deck, into the chair and were interpreted by the captain's body.

"Comm bursts transmitted," the communications officer reported.

Before the report of the third round of nukes could reach Torres's satisfied ears, the yell of warning came from the ensign at the tactical station.

"Three enemy signatures on our six, they're firing on u—"

The ship shook unimaginably hard as impact after rapid-fired impact pounded their shielding. Torres was almost knocked out of his chair by the savagery of the unexpected onslaught.

"Where the hell did they come from?" Torres yelled.

"Sir," Sarvanto cried as the sudden movement of the ship forced him off balance, "shall we return fire?"

"Yes!" the captain replied as he regained his wits. "Gun teams lock on and fire at will. Helm, evade. Tactical, talk to me."

"Six ships, standard attack pattern; two coming directly at us and the others flanking each side," the ensign snapped back.

Another burst of heavy ship-to-ship fire slammed into them and rocked their vessel violently.

"Get us away from them, Lieutenant," Torres ordered the pilot.

"Trying. Can't shake them!"

"You're thinking two-dimensionally," the captain responded. "Drop us down and punch it."

The pilot did just that, evading their Va'alen ambushers for maybe half a minute before the hits started to batter their shields once more.

"We've lost the outer shield," tactical shouted. "Seventy-three percent." Another flurry of direct hits rocked them at their consoles and in their seats. "Fifty-eight percent!"

"Guns, give me something," Torres growled.

"Working on it, Captain," Sarvanto answered through gritted teeth.

"Direct hit on nearest pursuit ship," Eze called, gripping onto the arms of her unfamiliar chair as she monitored the progress of her people manning the turrets.

"Destroyed?" Torres asked with visible concern.

Eze paused, looking at the console for the sensors to refresh.

"Yes."

"Full rear shields," Torres cried desperately, "fire everything before that second ship ra—"

He didn't get to finish giving his orders before the solitary Va'alen accelerated impossibly hard into the belly of the *Ichi*, crushing its way through what remained of their shields. The lights on the bridge flickered and blinked into darkness before returning to illuminate the room. Shouts echoed all around the bridge as everyone tried to call out reports or give orders at once. The gravity failed for a few seconds, raising all of them up in sudden weightlessness, before the power was restored to the grav emitter and they dropped back down.

"Damage report," Torres breathed.

"Shields restored to twenty-five percent; we're down to our last emitter," the ensign at tactical said. "Hull breach on lower deck… we're venting atmo. All damaged compartments are sealed off."

Torres grimaced, shutting his eyes for a moment to compartmentalize the pain of the loss he knew would sting him for the rest of his life. He opened his eyes, cutting away from the momentary flash of self-pity, and gave his next orders.

"Tell me the Fold Drive is online."

"Affirmative, sir," replied the helmsman. "But we can't jump at these speeds; the sensor array is on the fritz after that last hit and I wouldn't be able to program it safely enough."

Torres thought for few seconds, not wasting time but investing it in a better plan than they currently worked to.

"Can we restore the Shroud?" Another pause.

"Yes, sir," came the response from tactical, "but I don't know how good it'll look."

"It doesn't have to pass muster for long, Ensign," Torres told him. "Helm, at your discretion, full stop and radical course change. Tac, as soon as he hits the brakes you get us under Shroud. If we can throw them off for long enough to calculate the jump, then do it." He didn't wait for a reply, instead hit the ship-wide intercom and called out a warning to his crew.

"All hands, brace for emergency jump. Damage crews stand by."

~

"Captain Torres," Dassiova said coldly. "I am all for tenacity in leadership, but let me be absolutely, one-hundred percent crystal goddamned clear on this; the next time you go off half-cocked and show a lack of planning and good judgment in your decision-making, the next time you put your and the lives of other ships' crews in danger I will personally remove you from command of that ship and put someone there who is more worthy of it. Hell, in fact I'll give it to Wright and make you serve under him as a Lieutenant. How does that sound?"

Torres didn't like the sound of it one bit and hoped that the question was rhetorical. Luckily, it was.

"You know where the term 'half-cocked' comes from?" the admiral asked.

"No sir," Torres lied. It wasn't wise to interrupt an admiral in the process of chewing his ass off with a smart-mouthed answer.

"It stems from an infantry term way back in the sixteen or seventeen hundreds, before the old United States fought for independence from Europe, back when the soldiers' personal weapons had to be loaded for every shot. You see, they had to prime the firing pan, pour the charge and the wadding and the bullet down the barrel from the business end, then use a bit of metal called a ramrod to tamp it down so the damn thing didn't fall out. Inexperienced troops, you know, young kids and battle virgins and the like," he said, watching Torres for a response to his goading, "well, they had this habit of panicking and firing their gun without remembering to take the ramrod out. That meant they fired it at the enemy and generally couldn't use their gun again because it was useless. *That* is what I mean by going off half-cocked." He paused, taking a few long breaths to recoup his oxygen loss during the rant.

"Now I've got enough problems with missing ground teams, enemy fleets, slow-moving space station builders, complaining friendly aliens, and the purse-holding puppeteers both here and back on Earth, without your incompetence causing me a fresh new stomach ulcer. You fire your goddamned ramrod at the enemy again and you'll be commanding the mess hall on a support ship, or else making Wright's goddamned Earl Grey onboard a ship that *used* to be yours. Dismissed."

Torres stood fractionally taller, and despite the standing orders not to salute the admiral while at sea, he cracked off a crisp one. He held it for three seconds before dropping it and walking out of the room with his face set in a stony mask.

Nothing the admiral could say could assuage the guilt and pain he felt for the loss of his people, something he felt even more keenly as the *Tanto* was still missing. It was like he was stacking failure upon failure, but the loss of his command would sting him forever. It would disgrace him, and effectively end his career. Even if they let him keep his relatively new rank, which he doubted, he would likely then find himself shut out in the cold from the warm and influential embrace of the UNID, the Intelligence Directorate, who had advanced his career so far in a short time. He would find himself commanding water resupply runs to Mars without a Fold Drive or access to television archives.

Torres stalked the corridors of the *Indomitable* as he headed for the nearest of the three shuttle bays onboard the enormous carrier. Out of one of the rare portholes he saw the progress of the space station, over halfway done, he guessed, the external construction, anyway. As he neared the shuttle bay, a dark blue figure in a flight suit pushed off lightly from one wall and dropped in behind him to match his pace among the busy decks where many others wearing similar uniforms were going about their tasks. Torres, no stranger to covert surveillance work in crowded areas, made his tail after a hundred paces and two turns. He stopped a junior rating, a kid who couldn't have been much older than Torres had been when he was first posted to the Lunar base, and asked him for directions he didn't need. The kid, seeing the commander's rank on Torres's flight suit, stammered and pointed as he babbled out the directions and managed to get them wrong. Torres thanked him anyway and carried on, having taken the opportunity to face back the way he had come from during the brief conversation, and seen nothing of any surveillance.

Pretty good, he told himself before resuming his journey.

He arrived at the nearest shuttle bay and cut the line waiting for transport, as he had a dropship waiting for his return. Anyone with the authority to have their own dropship on standby wasn't someone you wanted to have pissed at you for an attitude problem. Torres stopped at the foot of the ramp and watched the door behind him, expecting his shadow to appear at any moment. He was startled enough to jump slightly when her voice sounded close behind his ear.

"Boo," she muttered.

"Dammit, Amare!" He held a hand on his chest briefly. "Don't do that. How the hell did y—?"

"Would you ask a magician to reveal the truth behind her tricks?" Eze asked with a wolfishly playful smile.

Torres ignored her question; he wasn't in the mood to be drawn into the conversation. He didn't feel much like talking at all, not after having to check he still *had* an ass, in case the admiral had inadvertently chewed too hard and removed it for him. He hit the button to seal up the ramp, annoying the dropship's loadmaster, who had just had his only job done for him by a senior officer. Torres held the handrail above his head with both hands for lift off.

"Bad, huh?" Eze asked him.

Torres gave a slight nod and a grunt, which hinted at an affirmative. As the dropship phased through the single layer shields of the carrier and set off toward the *Anvil*, he remained in unhappy silence. His ground commander, his lover, remained in companionable silence beside him as they crossed the distance to the massive forge vessel where their much-loved *Ichi* was currently suspended in a dry dock, undergoing emergency repairs.

They had a ceremony for the eight crewmembers lost during the Va'alen ambush, though they only had two bodies to bury at sea. The other six had been sucked out violently into the void of space, where they instantaneously froze solid as they suffocated. As far as violent deaths go, it must have been pretty awful to know you were going to get vented. As for their attempt to degrade the enemy numbers, the sensor data had been pored over by, not only their own crew but by that of the dedicated intelligence cell on the *Indomitable*. Their hopes of destroying forty percent or more of the Va'alen strike fleet were dashed when the true estimation was closer to twelve percent.

Twelve percent of an armada still too big to defend against was pointless. It wasn't worth the near catastrophic damage to their recon ship, which was useless in defense of the rest of the fleet when it was in dry dock, and it wasn't worth the lives of eight crewmembers.

"That's nineteen now," Torres said with a dry throat. Eze said nothing. "Nineteen of my crew dead or lost. My ship battered to hell, my shuttle lost along with some of our best people, and my command heading for the crapper."

Eze, unsympathetic to any hint of self-pity, said nothing.

She knew she should have said something; Brandt would have told him to get a grip, to focus on things he could have a positive effect on and forget the rest, but the words escaped her. Not caring if the sulking loadmaster saw her or not, she took a step closer and snaked an arm around him to give comfort to both of them.

CHAPTER 16

Abandoned Va'alen Outpost

Zero's obsessive organization of their defenses was a fieldcraft masterclass in fast-forward. Within thirty minutes he had managed to get the supplies from the recovered crate brought down, he had secured the two gaps found in the perimeter fencing and he had cleared every inch of the T-shaped building that appeared to be a small alien outpost probably designed for research. Brandt had been working with Paterson on their biggest discovery, biggest since finding a half-dead but still lethal Va'alen warrior and a trio of carnivorous ostrich-type birds, that was. She focused on the energy reading Specter had first detected.

"Okay, smart guy," Brandt said hands on her hips and taking bigger breaths to suck as much oxygen from the nitrogen-rich air as possible. "Tell me what I'm looking at."

"Okay," Paterson said, his own helmet removed also. "The eddy current caused by the magnet generates a braking force against the copper."

"Dude," Brandt said with an eyebrow raised. "English."

Paterson thought for a moment, his face resetting before he began again affecting a voice like a dumb but excited cartoon character.

"Err, duh magnet inside duh copper ball goes, err, spinny-spinny and err—"

He stopped quickly as Brandt took a pace toward him and turned her body slightly sideways. He was smart enough and still recalled enough of his time in active service to know when he was about to get smacked.

"Alright, alright!" he said backing off with his hands up. "Way back when, like the nineteenth century, I think, a guy called Lenz figured out that overlapping magnetic fields did… *stuff*…"

"I assume by '*stuff*' you mean complicated physics shit I won't understand?" Brandt said in a dangerously measured tone.

"Exactly," Peterson answered, continuing before he fetched a lesson in cranial kinetics. "Basically, the two objects spinning against each other are generating electrical fields. This is a generator, and I think it's the same kind as they put in their ships."

Brandt had a whole dropship full of questions, but she limited them to what she needed to know right then and how it affected their mission. She looked up at the brassy-looking sphere, which seemed to hum imperceptibly as it spun lazily. Through the round holes in it she could see the darker, almost blue shade of the cube of metal suspended inside. The inner piece, the powerful magnet as she had been informed, also spun around but faster than the spherical housing it hung inside of. The pattern of the spin seemed almost random, but as she widened her eyes and allowed her sharp focus to fade, her vision melted a little to show the magnet more clearly. She had no idea how a spinning magnet inside a metal ball could generate power, let alone enough to power a space-faring ship, but she knew enough to know not to concern herself with too many 'hows' and focus more on 'whats' and 'whys'.

"So," she said, changing the subject back to something more pressing, "can you turn it into a battery bank for us?"

Paterson frowned, as though his friend had suggested pulling pages from a rare and treasured book to use as toilet paper.

"I need to study it a little," he said reluctantly, "figure out the controls so it doesn't go boom."

"It could do that?" Brandt asked, her eyes widening.

"Remember the sensor readings of the booby-trapped ship back on *b*?" he asked.

Shortening the name of Proxima b, the dark planet under the glow of the red dwarf, confused her for a moment. She did remember, and nodded to Paterson for him to go on.

"Well that was either a separate bomb rigged to blow on a kind of anti-tamper device or it was the energy source …*collapsing*."

"What are the odds?" she asked him, wanting things simplified to make her decisions quicker and easier; a born officer.

"Best case? This thing malfunctions and we're looking at an EMP the size of our ship. The *Ichi*, that is. Worst case?" He said nothing further but opened his eyes wide, puffed his cheeks out like a hamster and mimed an explosion with his hands growing outward until he stopped them and slammed them back together with a sudden clap.

Brandt understood.

"Try not to screw it up," she told him simply. She walked out of the chamber and cycled the menu options on her forearm device to find Zero's suit on the comm link. She ordered him to her and heard him realigning their temporary defenses to cover his position. Brandt waited for him outside the small structure, built on a single level in the shape of a T and raised from the ground on adjustable legs like landing gear. It annoyed her how much she relied on the HUD instead of on her senses as Zero approached and startled her slightly. She shook it off, annoyed with herself for becoming reliant on the technology, especially as she was running at less than forty percent battery charge.

She filled him in on what they had found, and added that hopefully it could be used to charge their suits and mech.

"It's going to be an issue if we can't," she told him, "because the temperature alone will seriously damage us if we have to walk around in our own skin."

Zero didn't need that explained to him but he kept his mouth shut. He had removed his helmet with the eye controls to talk to her, revealing scruffy hair that looked even worse than usual, but power was a serious concern of his, too. He had adjusted the temperature controls of the suit by a few degrees, which he knew he could cope with; too cold in the night and too hot in the day meant that the suit was working constantly to maintain a steady body temperature, draining vital power.

He wasn't concerned with his own comfort, as the sweat caused by the humidity under the tree canopy proved. Instead, Zero was more concerned with losing the HUD capability of his suit and the uplink it had to his rifle's scope. He needed that power to give him targeting arcs and calculate trajectories. He also needed the faint scrambling fields that minimized the chances of his prone form being detected by the enemy before he had the opportunity to offer group discounts on lobotomies and decapitations by fast-moving 12mm.

"Any sign that the Va'alen are coming back here?" he asked.

"None," Brandt told him confidently. "Whatever went down here, we definitely missed it. Looks like if there were others, they took off and abandoned this place."

"For good reason," Zero chimed in. "What about the one left behind? The dead one?"

Brandt didn't need reminding *which* of the deceased aliens she had ordered to be wrapped up in a body bag, to be recovered if possible. Specter had done it, along with Turner and Horne as the three of them manhandled the surprisingly top-heavy corpse into the tight-fitting bag.

Black gore had oozed from the deep wounds caused by the carnivore's long talons and Turner commented that they seemed incapable of having caused the alien's death.

"It's dead," Brandt told him simply, "and hopefully we can get it back to the fleet and autopsy it properly; look for a physiological weakness or something useful."

Zero chuckled briefly. "Like finding out its balls are actually under the armpits or something?"

Brandt, despite herself and the gravity of their situation, also laughed.

"Yeah, something like that. Still, would be good to know if the assholes have a sweet spot," she said as she tapped a finger on the soft flesh under her nose.

Zero knew exactly what she meant; a headshot on a human target face-on through that spot would obliterate the brainstem instantly before any signal could be sent from the brain to a trigger finger. Even in death, humans were dangerous creatures, but less so if they were suffering complete brain death in an instant. As a precision tool himself, Zero appreciated the thought of a magic target against an enemy that had been fairly bulletproof the only time he had met them.

"Turner said this one looked smaller than the others?" he asked, confirming.

Brandt had puzzled over the same fact and told him that it was indeed much smaller than the ones they had already gone up against.

"Like, a couple of feet shorter. Only just a little bigger than Specter," she said.

"Maybe they aren't all warrior caste or something?" Zero guessed. "Like the smaller ones do the science and stuff?"

"Makes sense," she agreed. "Anyhow, where are we on defenses?"

Zero filled her in, and it wasn't all good news. The area where the outstation, or whatever the Va'alen had intended the small enclosure to be, had been built was in a shallow depression with tree cover all around. From a marksman's point of view, which Zero considered to be his primary function in the universe, it was a bad move. He used a colorful expression to give his opinion on the site from a tactical defense point of view and saw his commander frown at his choice of words.

"A gang fu...? Anyway. What's the plan?" she asked, steering the conversation back above the belt. She was happy to delegate such matters to her second-in-command, but that was because she knew and trusted him to lead the team in her absence. She was by no means a hands-off kind of commander.

"During darkness we'll be forced to consolidate inside," Zero said. "I don't like it but there's no other way. There are no natural underground structures here, not that I'd recommend tunnels again after the dog-sized scorpions gave me nightmare material for about a hundred years. We can't stay outside in darkness, because there are clearly pack-hunting carnivores on this planet—which is another thing nobody's talked about— and the only other option is to get up high."

"How would we do that?" Brandt asked, genuinely curious about the suggestion. "Trees?"

"Yep. It's the only way, but it means leaving the mech and the supplies on the deck for anything to get at them. If it were me, if I was the Va'alen asshole given the job of putting an outpost here? Well, let's just say I wouldn't put it here, and I hope the dead 'roach down there is the asshole responsible. If he is, son of a bitch got what he deserved for being a dumb son of a bitch."

"Learn from your mistakes?" she asked him with another eyebrow raised.

"Yeah," the marksman said, "and death is a very strong motivator to not repeat someone else's screw up."

Brandt had followed Zero's advice and consolidated her entire team inside the smallest room of the outpost they could realistically fit into. The entrance door to the outpost was too small for the large mech to get inside, and rather than run the risk of losing it they hid it under foliage. All sat in silence as they tried to ignore the cacophony of animal calls outside during the darkness. Twice she swore she heard the sound of something getting caught and killed by something bigger, and her imagination ran riot.

The three carnivorous bird-things they had encountered played on her mind too. The one Zero had killed was similar to the one taken down by Specter—smaller and seemed to be wearing a shaggy brown fur coat of spiny feathers. The one she had killed, a larger and a far more dangerous specimen, was brightly plumed. Her knowledge and logic told her that this was the male of the pack. Hopefully the alpha male, as she didn't much like the thought of the rest of their little herd coming to look for their missing birds.

The small energy source sat humming lightly on the deck between them; it was essentially a large single-use battery pack which snaked out wires to their suits, except Specter's and the mech.

Paterson told her it would probably top them all up to ninety percent, but that charge would be lucky to last them another day like the first one they had experienced on the surface of the exoplanet.

Brandt sat between Paterson and Specter, their shoulders pressed close as though proximity could provide the warmth that their suits managed for them. She leaned forward, stealing a glance at Horne, who was asleep. She used her command override to access his suit, resting the tired muscles in her eyes by raising her hands to access the HUD menu, and checked his activity log. Three times since landing—since crashing—he had accessed Specter's suit and administered something not recorded in the log. It seemed that Hyper wanted their cyborg escorted at all times to keep his true mind from reemerging. The substance, which Paterson had guessed was dopamine or something similar, was being used to keep the emotions dead to him. She accessed Horne's suit's mic, opening it on her override authority, and caught the faint sound of a wheezing snore. Satisfied he was asleep, she isolated him from the comm net temporarily and sat back with another channel open to Paterson and Specter.

"Hey, who mentioned the Sonoran Desert earlier?" she asked, feeling both of them stir, even though she doubted either was asleep. "You guys remember that training ex?"

"How could I forget?" Paterson asked sourly. "A million degrees in the day and minus a million and four at night. Damn, those old tin can suits could never keep up with my body temperature. I'm warm-blooded, you know?"

Specter huffed. "You always got in trouble for messing with your suit's temperature controls."

"Yeah," Brandt said carefully so as not to break the spell of Jake's memories coming out, "and I was the one who had to chew him out for it, even though the ass never listened to me." She leaned to her left, lightly clanging her helmet against Specter's in an unintentional gesture from the depths of her memory.

CHAPTER 17

Sonoran Desert

Eleven Years Earlier

"Hunker down, shut up, don't move," Master Petty Officer Carter snarled at the newest recruits to pass out of basic. They had earned their combat rating and were now officially seamen instead of recruits, but the hopeful thought that the new designation meant that they had earned the right to be shown any respect was quickly extinguished.

The three new additions to the unit had graduated and been shipped in just in time to suffer one of the biggest career tests of all of the American UN's ground pounders, simply referred to as the 'desert exercise.' The sheer casual simplicity of the name did nothing to advertise how grueling the experience was. It was ten days and nights spent infantry maneuvering and digging-in defensive positions without aerial or vehicle support, that culminated in a mock assault on a defended position.

At the time, none of the three seamen referred to as 'fresh meat' realized that the exercise was pure market research by the UN and their private partners in tech R&D. The last iteration of the powered armor suits had been in service for close to a decade and questions were being raised as to their effectiveness.

What better lab rats to use than dumb grunts who bought the lie that the war games were a method of selecting candidates for promotion?

Santana, Paterson and Brandt all hunkered down, shut up, and didn't move. The smallest figure of the three tapped awkwardly at the comm device on the left forearm of the suit. The earpieces of the other two beside her in their tiny foxhole crackled as the telltale sign that a comm channel had opened.

"Hey," Brandt whispered, "do you think we'll get attacked tonight?"

"What does it matter?" Paterson groaned back at her.

"Attacked?" the Latino-accented voice of Jake Santana asked. "I'm... more likely to die of exposure than I am a bullet. *Carajo*, it's cold, man!"

"Stop complaining," Brandt told him. "Don't you have cold temperatures in Mexico?"

"I'm from California," Santana answered flatly. "Can't we like, I don't know, cuddle up to share body heat or something?"

"Through multiple interwoven layers of carbon ceramic polymer-alloy which has been ultra-heat treated and set? Sure, dude, bring it on in." Paterson lifted an armored arm to invite Santana in for a hug.

He almost accepted before he paused and slapped the arm down to mutter a curse at him.

"You're funny, asshole. I'm just saying, isn't anyone else freezing their ass off?"

Another telltale crackle of static hit their ears, indicating that their private chat was being interrupted.

"Is there something you little pukes want to share with the rest of the unit?" Carter snarled at them. He had seen their private channel courtesy of his command override authority.

"Sorry, boss," Brandt answered for them, eager to take the full blame. "I opened the channel an—"

"I *literally* do not care," Carter responded. Everyone knew he was angry because he was due for a promotion to command chief, but their unit's senior NCO seemed incapable of being killed or retiring from service. Carter was left with the choice of waiting patiently in line or leaving for any other unit in the territory that had an opening for a senior chief NCO.

He had decided to stay and he made up for it with sheer malevolence toward the fresh meat. "If you want to cuddle up and have some kinda twisted ménage à trois, then do it on your own damn time and not mine. Now. Hunker down, shut up, and don't move."

They did as they were told, keeping their mouths closed; anything they said would be transmitted over the squad channel and be picked up by NCOs and officers who would be just as willing as Carter was to tear them new waste chutes. Shivering throughout the night, the three of them alternated turning and half standing to put the very top of their helmets above the dusty level of the hole they had dug. This allowed their rudimentary HUDs to link up with the drones providing overwatch to their camp. Nights like those were long, exhausting and so uncomfortable that they left a memory strong enough to last a lifetime.

Some units were lucky and never caught the exercise, whereas members of others were unlucky enough to live through it twice in their careers. That was only likely if you served more than your mandatory minimum to earn the civilian privileges the UN used to lure recruits to them.

The unit commander, a hard man who had served twice in the vaunted CP special operations division, was in just as foul a mood as

Carter had been when he caught the new additions to the recon squad chatting like girls on a sleepover.

He had been on that same exercise as a lieutenant, and it didn't get any easier with rank advancement.

"All units," he said into the microphone built inside his uncomfortable helmet. The clothing he wore beneath the armor suit rubbed and itched and he pushed the discomfort away. "This is Dassiova. I want all sentries to have their heads on a swivel throughout the night. Make no mistake, there is every chance we will be attacked at this position during darkness. Do your jobs. Out."

Brandt glanced at her two friends either side of her, both of them turning to meet her slight sheen of visor reflection in the gathering dark. She imagined them both looking as frightened and cold as she did.

The watch chime, set to sound every four hours, jolted Jake even though he was expecting it. The sudden sound, no matter how soft it was, came through loud and harsh to him. He steadied his breathing, glancing at the rudimentary HUD display to see how much his heart rate had elevated, before reaching down to nudge Brandt awake. Jake had taken over from Jamie Paterson and both of them were tall enough to lay their service rifles over the lip of their foxhole and lean over it. Their only female comrade in their position had to stand upright and not lean to rest her body weight; she was fractionally too short.

"You're up," he whispered to her with a light tap on her shoulder.

She looked up, glanced at her forearm device and tapped it to speak to him alone, and stood stiffly.

"Anything?" she asked him in another whisper.

"Don't you think I would have woken you up if there was?"

170

"True," Brandt acknowledged.

"Link to the drones," Jake told her. "See you in four hours." He withdrew his rifle from the lip of the trench and nudged

her armored shoulder with his own in a gesture of muted solidarity. She hefted her own gun, used the comm device on her forearm to show the active sweep from the sentry drones on her HUD, and settled in to wait.

The chime of the watch bell woke her, making her take a gasp of still air from inside her suit as momentary panic filled her mind. *I fell asleep? Oh my God, I fell asleep!* She looked around her, expecting to find the commander or the chief or Boss Carter watching her as she nodded off on her feet like a farm animal, but nobody was there. She closed her eyes, breathed out to calm herself, and opened her eyes again.

To see a flashing red icon on the HUD.

She opened her mouth to say the words, but nothing came out. The breach of their virtual perimeter was there, right in the sector manned by the three new soldiers fresh out of training. She hadn't seen it. She hadn't called out the warning. There should have been a central overwatch, a command-level operative watching all the feeds, but still nobody had seen the breach. She tried to speak but a single, strangled noise came from her throat and made her cough.

"Contact," Santana's voice barked over the squad net with authority. "Perimeter breach in sector two, permission to engage?" He was suddenly beside her, the bulky service rifle next to her as he took aim with his left index finger on the trigger guard, ready for the orders he anticipated.

"Recon squad, open fire," came the order through their suit speakers.

Jake squeezed the trigger, rounds ejecting and pinging her in the visor as rapidly as if she was being shot. She heard grunts and noises of confusion as Paterson rose, watched where the bright blue tracer was going and added his own gun to the fray. Brandt, realizing that her first live exercise had resulted in a monumental choke, clicked off her own safety and let loose with the non-lethal training rounds toward where one of the other units was attacking their temporary camp.

Brandt was sheepish an hour later when the sun rose rapidly. Her squad had been sent to make the 'bodies' of the dead enemy safe and to provide emergency battlefield medical care to the ones designated as casualties. She was on body clearance with Paterson and Santana. The process involved scanning the supposed corpse for life signs and any evidence of active circuitry, which could be an explosive detonator. When they were satisfied there was nothing obvious, one of them activated a small damping field of electromagnetic energy to stop any remote line of sight triggers, and one unlucky trooper got to do what they called 'the roll'.

"You're up," Paterson said to Jake.

He activated the damping field on the heavy case they had to lug around on body duty. Santana sighed, handed his rifle to Brandt, who locked it to her free left leg. She covered him as he lay on top of the armored soldier playing dead and rolled onto his back, using the strength in the suit to roll the body with him and expose the front.

"Clear," Brandt said.

She watched as he pushed the body back off him and got to his feet before marking the position on his comm device as having been secured.

172

"Can't wait for our turn at this," he complained. "Knowing our luck they'll kill our suit's aircon as well as the movement actuators and let us cook to death out here."

Brandt didn't like the thought of that. She tried to push it from her mind as she handed Jake back his rifle. She hesitated, opened a channel between them and ran the risk of another unpleasant horoscope reading from Carter, and said what was on her mind.

"Thanks for this morning," she said briefly. "You saved my ass."

Jake didn't look at her, didn't give any physical indication that he had heard her words, but answered casually.

"It's what I'm here for."

Abandoned Va'alen Outpost, Unnamed Moon Surface

Brandt moved as quietly as possible to try and find a more comfortable position to sit in without success. She glanced at the readouts for the others. Payne and Specter were awake; Payne on duty watch and Specter... well, because he was Specter and probably didn't need to sleep.

They had argued about deploying the single reconnaissance drone from the emergency crate as it acted as a comm relay. Zero made the point that in the deep canopy where their shelter was the drone was fairly useless. It had too small of a field of view. They had settled on leaving it on the highest point of the building and set to activate on remote control if they needed it. As ever, Horne had supported whatever plan offered him the highest probability of personal survival, revealing once again that the world of private military contractors didn't exactly support the team mentality of the UN forces.

Brandt couldn't sit still any longer, and rose as quietly as she could to walk to the other side of the room. An expanded submenu on her HUD showed the outside temperature as being a little above freezing, with traces of a brutal wind snaking through the thick jungle. She closed that submenu with a blink of her eyes and glanced diagonally downward to minimize it before she brought up the analysis of the local wildlife. It didn't make for relaxing reading, especially not to someone who was already struggling to find sleep.

"Can't sleep either?" a familiar voice asked, startling her slightly.

Brandt looked at the comm icon and saw no open channel. Specter had literally transmitted his thoughts into her head. For some reason she couldn't comprehend, that voice still had the same robotic twang to it, like it was synthesized, even though he wasn't speaking.

"Jesus, Ja—" she gasped and stopped herself. "Jesus, Specter, don't do that."

He chuckled softly, the sound undulating over her eardrums and soothing her. She smiled and relaxed despite the fright she had just received.

"I knew you'd fallen asleep, by the way," he told her softly. "What? What are you tal—"

"Back in the desert, when we were first posted to Dassiova's command. He hasn't changed much, has he?" Specter asked.

"Hasn't changed... he's older, but then aren't we all. Hey." She stopped, shaking her head to get back to the first thing he said. "What do you mean you knew I'd fallen asleep? That was years ago before you were... *you*." He chuckled again.

"I couldn't sleep. I told Jamie I was too cold and begged him to show me how to trick the suit into letting him turn up the heating, but he was being an asshole and trying to make me buy the information from him. I tried to talk to you, but you were out on your feet, so I took over your watch and called the attack when I saw it. I tried to wake you first but… anyway, I don't know why but I just wanted you to know that."

Brandt stared at him, totally lost for words. "Jake?" she asked hesitantly. Specter sighed.

"I'm still in here but being around you two makes me come out more. Specter is more like… more like my callsign now, you know? He's like my front, just like James over there gets all pissy when people don't call him Zero. It's like a personality front. Anyway, this *cabron* keeps hitting me with dopamine shots or something every time he thinks I'm slipping back. Him or one of his other Hyper buddies. I've tried to override the command, but… I'm hardwired not to be able to mess with it. I hate it. It makes me go all… fuzzy. Reckon you could disable it for me?"

Brandt was still speechless at his words, like she had agreed to partake in a séance and found herself talking to her dead friend through another person's body. "I…" she stammered, "I might not be able to, but Paterson definitely could. I'll wake him up—"

"No," Jake interrupted. "Tomorrow. Let sleeping dogs lie and all that, eh?"

"Sure," Brandt agreed in a daze. "Tomorrow."

CHAPTER 18

Proxima Centauri, Deep Orbit

"Save me the excuses, Captain," Dassiova said from behind his hand rubbing his furrowed brow. "Just tell me the earliest time for completion."

"Sir," Massey interrupted from the doorway of his cabin. "You need to see this."

Dassiova nodded at his flight officer and turned back to the screen.

"Get it done, Captain," he told the officer commanding the *Venture*. He wanted the space station operational. "Unless you feel like repelling a few hundred Va'alen ships with love songs and messages of peace." He cut the transmission before his sarcastic comment could generate any response, then he stood and followed Massey onto the bridge.

"What am I looking at?" he asked, squinting at the large display screen showing the whole system.

"You're looking at the best estimation of the Va'alen fleet arriving in this sector," she told him, "and the route they will have to take to avoid an anticipated asteroid path. That will lead them through this part"—she pointed at a bit on the display— "of empty space. Captain Novak is confident that the shrouded mines you requested will be manufactured in nineteen days."

"Nineteen days gives us about thirty minutes to deploy them before that damned armada knocks down our front door. Tell him to speed it up or else lower my expectations. Either way, tell him to pull his Russian thumb out of his ass and not to waste time on excuses."

"Sir," Massey said reprovingly, "he also wanted it noted that the manufacturing time has been delayed because he has had to redirect key personnel to the repair of, er, *essential fleet assets*."

Dassiova growled to himself, turning the noise into a throat-clearing cough. The 'essential fleet assets' referred to was the battered and damaged *Ichi*, which Dassiova had ordered repaired as a priority. The fleet needed to get their recon ship back in play. He bit down another loud cursing of Torres, knowing that the impetuous call he had made wasn't necessarily the wrong one, though it had turned out to have been a catastrophe. He paused, staring at the display screen and thinking, which lent him the appearance of being about to explode in rage at any moment.

"We're confident they'll be forced to come that way?" he asked, looking at the three-dimensional map of space before him.

"Yes, Admiral," Massey said.

"Good," Dassiova answered, giving nothing else away and changing the subject. "Anything from the *Hammer* or the *Vengeance*?"

"Negative, Admiral," one of the comm officers answered. "No update scheduled and no emergency subspace bursts."

Dassiova pulled a face, weighing the risks and the odds that the two frigates were running on low power, while a superior Va'alen force searched for them. He decided that neither of those captains were the 'hold their breath and hide' type, which was precisely why they commanded the big space tanks the frigates had been turned into.

"Send a message on subspace to both ships," he ordered. "My compliments to both captains; they are to search for ten days, then jump back to prepare for a fleet defense operation. If there is no sign of the *Tanto* by then, we will have to declare them officially MIA. I know it's harsh, but the lives of everyone up here and everyone who'll follow are more important than the few we have out in the cold."

The comm officer acknowledged him, just as the door to the main bridge hissed open and in strode an alien on a mission.

Asha walked to Dassiova and stood tall, towering over him, though with a third of the body mass. A wave of deep concern spread over the bridge, despite the Kuldar's evident attempts to keep his emotions in check.

"*Ahhd-mee-rahl*," Asha said with a bow, still stumbling over many human words and unable to grasp the concept that a person in charge was not royalty, "I implore you that we may speak for a time that is short."

"You mean you want to talk to me for a minute?" he asked. He continued before the confused alien could respond. Asha's grasp of English was improving massively each day, but his translations were often literal as he learned the language from the translation software from a comm device. "Sure, come on." Dassiova walked past the concerned alien and entered his cabin, pausing at the door for Asha to follow. Massey made to accompany them, but the admiral shook his head to tell her to stay put on the bridge.

Dassiova sat on the uncomfortable couch built into the outer room in his private quarters, holding out a hand to invite the gangly alien to join him. Asha bowed again, sitting delicately and wringing his hands.

Another wave of worry escaped and threatened to take the admiral's breath away. Whatever was on Asha's mind must be bad.

"I can feel the concern, Asha," he said gently. "Tell me what's eating you?"

"What is… *consuming my body?*" he asked with incredulity and concern for his own safety. He tapped at the comm device offering the translation.

"I mean," Dassiova said as he tried to stifle a laugh. It would have escaped had he not experienced the confusion and fear through his telepathic alien advisor. "What's the matter? What is eating you up inside and causing you to worry? It's a human thing; a colloquialism."

"Oh," Asha said, embarrassed, "I, ah… I have seen the reporting of Captain Torres, and I think I know what the anomaly was which they witnessed."

Dassiova racked his brain.

"Oh, the… er, the *thing* the two Va'alen fighters were towing?"

"Exactly this," Asha said. He produced a datapad from inside his flight suit. Dassiova managed to stop his face from wrinkling up; he didn't like the thought of wiping alien sweat off a screen he was touching. He was grateful that the telepathy only worked one way. He leaned over and took the pad, seeing a screen grab of a recording from the *Ichi* depicting the unpowered vessel. It was zoomed in to show 'glyphs on the outer hull.

"You know what that thing is?" he asked.

"I have suspectings," Asha said awkwardly. "But for me to tell you what I have thinking, I must admit to a thing which you do not know."

Dassiova leaned forward and stared hard into the large eyes through the dark goggles, wishing that he would just allow the translator to work instead of mangling the grammar.

"A lie? You mean you decided *not* to share important intelligence about the enemy before we came back out here?"

A sensation of shame mingled with a little fear swept the room before Asha spoke.

"The lie is not about the Va'alen," he admitted, "but about our own species. We Kuldar are not how our whole race was before the Great Journey of my ancestors… we are… we *were* what the others called…" He hesitated, lifted the comm device and made a series of rattling, clicking noises until the translation showed on his screen and he said the word.

"*Uhn-der-lingss.*"

"Underlings?" Dassiova asked, taken aback. "Why?"

"You identify our ability to project our mindsets? Our *feelinghs*? It is something which only the matured ones of our species can be doing, and many of us that are not able. I, like only a few of my kind, are able to make a limit on our projections."

"So…" Dassiova prompted.

"So if we were the underlings of our kind, the higher caste of our peoples were the Overlords. Their minds can project not just feelings but controlling thinking. According to our legends, the few who were born with this power made the others of our kind do their bidding."

"Aaand…" Dassiova prompted again, not liking where the conversation was heading.

"And the markings on the device the Va'alen are towing are not Va'alen at all, but old, *very* old Kuldar. They have at least one of our higher kind, and I do not know how they could be a prisoner."

Dassiova stared blankly at him for ten long seconds before responding simply with, "Aaaah, shit."

~

The comm officer on the bridge of the *Vengeance* jumped in alarm as her console lit up. "Ma'am, incoming hail from the *Indomitable*. Requesting an all-clear before they continue transmission?"

Captain Nicola Halstead frowned at the breach of protocol, quickly finding that annoyance pushed aside by a tight knot of fear in her stomach. She glanced at the tactical officer, seeing no concern that the subspace link had awoken any shrouded enemy fighters nearby, and nodded her assent to the comm officer.

"On screen," she instructed, her voice level and in control. "The comm is marked for your eyes only, Captain." Halstead rose without speaking, nodded to the Lieutenant

Commander beside her to take the chair, and walked into her quarters, where she activated the viewscreen at her terminal.

"Admiral," she said in greeting, seeing Dassiova's drawn face nod back at her moments before Captain Craig Hayes's welcome and rugged mug blinked in to fill the right half of her screen. Her breath caught for an instant and she stifled the giggle that threatened to escape her mouth; Hayes had clearly been sleeping and looked groggy.

"I'll be brief," Dassiova said. "I apologize for breaking protocol, but this can't wait." He sighed heavily, like a parent with twin toddlers trying to keep them from killing each other in public.

"It appears that our new *allies*," he invested the word with some acidity, "have neglected to reveal certain aspects of their history to us until now. Long story short, there is a sub-species of Kuldar, or maybe the ones we know are the sub-species, I'm not sure," he shook his head, annoyed with his own wandering logic, "but anyway... the thing that Torres's ship saw the Va'alen towing is a kind of higher-level Kuldar with... I can't believe I'm saying these words, but hell... with *mind control* abilities. Odds are, these new sons of bitches are allied with the Va'alen and kinda hate the ones on our side. Just to make it more interesting. No idea of their combat or tactical capabilities yet, but it changes the game." He paused, watching for any response to his words and waiting for them to sink in to the minds of the two frigate captains.

"What do you need, Admiral?" Hayes asked in a half growl, half croak.

"I need you to jump your ships back to us," Dassiova answered. "There's an incoming enemy armada with an ETA of a little over two weeks, and I plan to use you two to harry and harass the sons of bitches all the way here before we crush them."

"And the missing crew, sir?" Halstead asked. She noticed a tightening of concern on the fleet commander's face.

"I can give you another twelve hours tops," he said grimly. "After that, I see no other option."

He left the rest unsaid. He had no other option but to declare them all missing in action, presumed lost. Presumed dead. In terms of personnel numbers it was nothing; a mere shadow of the crew lost by either Hayes or Halstead on their last foray into the system, but in terms of fleet morale and irreplaceable people, the cost was high.

"Understood, Admiral," Hayes said. "Anything else, sir?"

"No," Dassiova replied. "See you soon. Out." The left half of their screens went dead as the faces of the two remaining captains enlarged, each to fill the display of the other. They sat across from one another, face to face but separated by half a million miles, in a moment of introspective silence before Halstead spoke.

"No sense in stealth now?" she asked.

"Nope," Hayes replied. "Double up or spread out?"

"Double up," she answered. "Active sensors and weapons hot." Hayes nodded agreement.

"We'll jump to you," he told her. The *Hammer* had been scouting away from the planet. "Three full orbits with active sensors and check out that forest moon before we go back?"

"Fine by me," Halstead told him, nodding before she cut the comm to leave the other captain on his own.

"Weapons hot?" Hayes asked himself out loud, his voice still croaky after the full ninety minutes of sleep he had been blissfully enjoying. A smirk crept onto his face as his brain caught up with the conversation. He shook off the childish excitement her words gave him, put on his game face along with a fresh flight suit, splashed water on his face and short hair, and stepped back onto the bridge to give his orders.

CHAPTER 19

Va'alen Base, Unnamed moon Surface

The arrival of the Hive Lord had caused a massive volume of unnecessary work for the handful of bored Va'alen warriors deployed to the surface. They had even been ordered to clean up their barracks in case an inspection was carried out, as if their mythical overseers cared about such things. The sullen feeling running through the small ranks, as the young Aq in charge bossed them around to demonstrate his power and mask his fear, was unmistakable.

"Who does the small one think he is?" one warrior complained to another. "My mate is larger than he is, and he hasn't even fully grown his teeth in yet."

"He is our Aq," the other answered blandly.

"Only because his sire is an old Muq," the other complained in a quiet, hissing growl as though they could be overheard. "I'm sure if *my* sire was a warrior of renown, then *I* would be in command and not him."

The other warrior beside him turned and adopted a slightly lowered stance: body language for a challenge.

"But he was not, was he? He was just like you and just like me. Like my sire was and like our offspring will be. Stop running your mouth over nothing and do as we have been commanded."

The complaining Va'alen said nothing, ignoring the challenge in the words and stance, but he stopped talking nonetheless.

"Why is it here, anyway?" the braver of the two asked after a moment's silence. "What does a Hive Lord want with this bastard of a rock?"

"The minerals?" the other guessed.

"Why would a Hive Lord want minerals? I think it is here hiding. I think the humans have come in force."

His words got the other thinking. The pair walked back to their assigned perimeter defense position where their mates had been keeping watch at the high gate overlooking the plains and the distant mountains. The news of a human spacecraft crashing on the moon had caused great excitement, but that had been short-lived when the team sent to recover their bodies and equipment found only an impact crater the size of a transport ship. After that brief interlude of excitement, they had gone back to the monotony of keeping watch for any concerted effort by the indigenous wildlife to breach their walls, or the attention of the larger types of reptilian predator to come into range so they could kill another and recycle its biological matter to feast the whole base. Such demonstrations went a long way to raising the standing of a Va'alen warrior who had no family ties to call on. Killing more than one of the large beasts would create a reputation. Reputation, at least when it came to being noticed by a more senior and well-connected warrior, was everything.

Their contingent of twenty warriors, with triple that number of supporting engineers, had been degraded by the hostility of the alien world and the monsters that inhabited it; this resulted in the spineless Aq in command ordering them to fall back and reinforce the defenses of the main base that he had not left since the day they had arrived. The warriors had abandoned their outposts, with the loss of every

Va'alen posted there as well as the equipment and power generators installed at great cost to their expedition.

Flight inside the atmosphere was treacherous due to the ion storms that ravaged the skies higher up. Flying close to the terrain had downed a ship after it ran into a flock of flying creatures. The only exception to the rule that nobody left the mining base was the rotation of the pairs of warriors controlling the orbital railgun command bunker.

As the two bored and sullen Va'alen returned to their given position near to the main gates of the compound, they viewed their mates standing stock-still to watch their approach. Something was wrong, *off* somehow. Neither of their females bowed their heads in respect and deference to their mates when they saw them. Both males growled warnings as they neared but still no deference was shown. Before they could speak and berate them, a coldness swept over their minds and paralyzed their bodies.

The words somehow sounded simultaneously in their minds instead of travelling through the air and into the tiny holes that were their ears.

"*Weak fools,*" the voice boomed with a vibration that shook their bodies into terrified stillness. "*You complain about your commander? About MY presence? I should force you to recycle each other slowly and listen to your screams of agony.*"

Both dropped to their knees and put all four of their upper limbs onto the dusty, flattened surface beneath them. The movement was involuntary—it was *commanded*—and both let out a keening noise of a cornered predator with a grievous injury. Their thoughts poured from their mouths without their permission and both babbled incoherent apologies and pledges of fealty to obey everything. They were powerless to stop the Hive Lord from controlling their bodies and

186

minds. They had still not seen him, but knew he must be close to have heard their words and exerted such will over them.

As suddenly as they had been gripped by the powerful telepathy, they were released to drop to the dirt in agonized silence. Both rose to their feet hesitantly, glancing around for any other Va'alen who had seen their humiliation, and shooting vicious glances in the directions of their mates, who had not warned them of the presence of a Hive Lord. Wordlessly, both took up their positions and remained silent for an entire rotation of the moon, through the scorching heat and freezing night, without uttering another sound.

~

"Incoming target coordinates," announced the mate of the Va'alen warrior in charge of the railgun battery.

Her mate said nothing in response, still maintaining his hostility toward her as a way to cope with the boredom and isolation of the deployment that grated on all of them. What had been sold to them as a profitable expedition had instead become a dangerous detail defending a wall and mining operation from the horrors of the indigenous wildlife, which was somehow more savage even than they were. His complaint to his superior officer about their fate had resulted in the reward of command; albeit command of the sole anti-orbital gun battery that had never been fired since it had been first tested, and a team so small it was likely to result in the unsanctioned murder of a fellow warrior. Only he and his mate were deployed there with another warrior pair. The commander had spitefully chosen his subordinate with exquisite care. The two families within the same clan had a conflict spanning generations over a claim to clan seniority.

That feud had resulted in a bloodbath long before either of their sire's sire took their first steps, but their sense of clan memory was as fierce as it was illogical.

He inputted the coordinates, feeling the dull vibration of the huge gun on the distant mountaintop articulate, and he turned the barrel longer than a ship to point at the given location.

He stopped. He stared at the magnified screen in disbelief as the outline of an alien ship was joined by a second, appearing as an angular shape of lighter gray than the sky below it. His clawed hands caught up with his brain moments later, and a firing solution was inputted to the targeting computer.

"Charge levels?" he snapped at his mate.

"Sixty-two percent," she replied, "and falling… one of the power lines is failing."

"No!" the warrior in charge roared, flinging out his left hands to slam into the mate of his blood enemy and knock her to the ground. "Go and fix it. Now!" he snarled. He looked up at the hostile stance of her mate, who was on the verge of challenging him. Had they not been given a sudden mission to destroy the enemy in orbit, he would have raked the claws of all four upper limbs across his chest in an X and demanded that the other warrior fight him to the death.

That would have to wait until the humans were obliterated.

He leaned down, not taking his eyes off his enemy, and lifted his mate to her feet. Next, he grabbed up two of the bulbous rifles from the weapons rack and walked to the exit of the bunker. His mate, knowing as well as all of them that she would be forced to fight with the other female if their males made a challenge, shot the other a hateful stare on the way past.

"Ignore them," the warrior in charge said. The bunker door was slammed so hard it failed to engage the lock. "We will deal with them after we have destroyed the humans."

The two Va'alen sent from the bunker said nothing to one another. Both knew the inevitability of what would happen that day. At least they thought they did.

They followed the two thick, snaking power lines running along the dusty surface of the moon toward the distant peak as they checked for signs of damage or a disconnected junction. They found the source of the power failure after a mile. Sparks of blue power arced from the damaged cable beside the charred corpse of one of the large predatory birds. They had encountered these creatures enough times to know to shoot first when the birds were seen loitering around the edges of their peripheral vision. They never showed themselves fully unless they were attacking, and once they did it was often too late. They hunted in packs ranging from a trio to over two dozen. As the corpse was evidently alone—though the mist that reduced their visibility to twenty paces—both laid down their weapons and reached for tools on their utility belts to bypass the damaged section and restore power to the railgun.

Both Va'alen dropped to their knees, working as fast as possible while the cold wind howled around them and flickered the edges of the mist to play tricks on their minds. A chattering noise rang through the air, snatched away by a gust as soon as it was heard. Both kneeling Va'alen stopped and faced one another.

"Just the wind," he said, not entirely believing his own words. "Keep working. We will fix this, shoot the human invaders out of the sky and tear those two limb from limb."

"What of the blood price?" she asked him as she worked.

"What of it?" he snapped back. "The challenge is legitimate; no Va'alen has the right to strike you down but I. He overstepped, and he should know the consequences."

The same chattering rattle sounded again, this time answered by a second call that could not be ignored.

"Keep working," he ordered as he stood and raised his rifle.

He scanned the fringes of the mist in all directions, his nerves growing more taut with each passing second.

"Hurry," he growled at her.

He heard only an answering, guttural noise before a thud and the sound of sharp claws on hard carapace. He spun and looked down at his mate, her mouth wide in agony. Her outer layers of biological armor were punctured by the elongated hind talons of the creature latched onto her back, about to sink rows of sharp, conical teeth into her head. His rifle pulsed once, shredding the beast's head clean away from the ragged and bloody stump of its neck as the body fell away lifelessly. He opened his mouth to issue a bellowing roar of rage as his mate twitched and spasmed on the dusty ground before him. Scratches of claws on rock made him spin, firing the rifle as he did, and picking two more of the animals out of the air as they launched themselves at him. An involuntary squeal of pain sounded again, punctuated by growls and cracks of his mate's shattering hide as more erupted from the mist behind him to tear at her. Her scream of rage and pain was cut short as one long talon pierced her chest and punctured the soft core inside to kill her.

Instantly, the male, now devoid of a mate and robbed of the neurological link created when they bonded for life, turned berserk.

He switched his rifle into the lower of his left hands and drew the curved blade from behind his back. He swung it in a vicious arc to cut the top of a creature's head off through its open mouth as it shrieked at him. Kicking out with one powerful leg to push the dead beast off his mate's corpse, the momentum carrying her body to flip it over onto her front, he reached down for her own blade and rifle. Weapons in hand, he rose to his full height to fire both guns, and swung both cruel-edged blades at the beasts attacking inside the radius of the gun's effective fire. Bodies piled up around him, dying in droves. His rage at losing his mate pushed him through one of the largest and most effective ambushes laid by the hunters.

Sheer numbers were triumphant as one lucky creature, a young male with the start of the bright blue plumage growing around his neck and chest, made it through the twirling maelstrom of directed energy bolts and swinging curved swords. It struck a successful blow with both back feet as his talons cut into the arms of the Va'alen's left side. Both weapons dropped uselessly as the predator fell hard onto its back and flailed to get back to its feet inside the ring of dead pack members. The Va'alen rounded on it, stabbing down with the sword to pierce his attacker through the chest so hard he pinned it to the dusty ground, where the weapon stuck around its squealing, writhing form. Unable to free the weapon, he let it go and brought the single rifle back to bear. Three more creatures fell to his wrath before he was overwhelmed, forced onto his back on the dusty ground, and killed by the pack.

When both Va'alen had been torn and shredded into black, pulpy messes, the pack responded to a single sound like a whistling

birdcall, and, as one, they set off for the open door of the command
bunker.

~

"Power at sixty percent still," she said to her mate, who slammed a
pair of clawed hands into the console again.

"We have no choice," he muttered as he flipped up the safety
device to expose the firing command level.

He pulled it, sending the projectile up the long barrel under the
force of the magnetic fields charging it to impossible speeds. The slug
the size of a mature Va'alen left the barrel, spinning at an incompre-
hensible rate, to create a sonic boom and shockwave that cleared the
mist around the mountain for half a mile. The wait was only seconds,
but they never got the opportunity to charge a second shot and destroy the other ship in orbit. As the new targeting solution was being
typed into the controls, the door of the bunker creaked open and a
vicious, chattering snarl filled the chamber.

CHAPTER 20

Orbit of Unnamed Moon

"Sir! Massive energy reading from the surface," cried the tactical officer on the bridge of the *Hammer*. "I think it's a weapon discharge."

"Shields to maximum," Hayes barked as he took his chair to end his usual pacing.

"They are," came the terse reply. "Weapon discharge detected. Small reading heading our way, fast!"

"Helm, evasive maneuvers. Signal the *Vengeance* to get the hell out of here."

His orders were acknowledged as the slight, almost imperceptible lurch of the ship betrayed the incredible forces in play fighting against their grav emitter. A colossal boom and answering shudder rocked the *Hammer* as the lights on the bridge flickered in and out like eyelids fluttering.

"Damage report," Hayes called out, fearing the loss of more of his crew in this godforsaken solar system.

"Glancing blow to the forward shields," the tactical officer answered. "Down to fifty percent but rising, sir."

Small mercies, Hayes thought as he resisted the urge to genuflect to a God he didn't wholly believe in but who had been such a large part of his upbringing. He guessed that had the charged projectile hit them dead-on, even the full layer of all four shields would have been insufficient to save them from a follow-up shot.

"Keep your eyes on those sensors, Tac," the captain ordered. "Another reading and we jump; I don't care where to. You got that, helm?"

"Understood, sir," the pilot snapped back. "Emergency tenth of a second jump course laid in."

"Good," Hayes replied. "Hit that base with a return barrage—energy weapons only—and get me a full active sensor sweep. After that, get us the hell out of here."

Dawn came as fast as sunset on the surface of the moon. The night spent huddled in the cold of the abandoned outpost rapidly gave way to a morning of instant humidity and rising temperatures. Brandt ordered more ration pills to be taken and for everyone to drink from their tubes. She had Turner check everyone's vital stats for signs of dehydration. Zero had 'taken in the morning air' as he called it, climbing to the roof of the structure to assess the closed-in lie of the land. A distant, percussive *crump* sound drifted to her via her suit sensors.

"Grip," he called over the open channel. "Better get up here."

Brandt didn't wait for any further explanation, nor did she expect one from her marksman. She locked her submachine gun to the front of her left thigh and walked rapidly outside where she jumped to catch the lip of the roof and hauled herself up. Zero said nothing, simply pointed to the distant sky where a dead-straight vapor trail showed the trajectory of something tiny launching upward at an angle. Moments later an answering burst of bright blue temporarily lit up the unmistakable shape of one of their frigates.

"Oh, my God..." she said. "Is that..."

"Has to be one of ours," Zero answered. "Looking for us probably."

Both of them stared upward as the outline flickered away to become a dull, gray ghost once more. It didn't disintegrate or break up in sparking ruin, so whatever had fired on them hadn't scored a killing hit. They hoped. The answer came seconds later when a rolling barrage of bright orange flashes poured downward, following the reverse trajectory of the vapor trail. Hundreds of shots rained straight down without deviating, likely obliterating whatever had fired the initial shot, before both of them woke up to the prospect of rescue at the same time.

"Comms!" Brandt snapped, her voice mingling on the channel with Zero's call for the comm device to be set up.

"I've got it," Payne's voice came back. "What do you need?"

"Send out an emergency pulse, nothing specific, just aim it upward and send. Quickly."

A few seconds passed before she came back on the net. "Done, what now?"

"Now," Brandt said, "we wait." They waited. Ten seconds. Fifteen. Without any reply, the shape high above them blinked in a dull flash, and was gone. Brandt sank her head.

"Did it send?" she asked. "Did it get through the atmosphere?"

"Can't tell," Payne replied. "I sent a broad spectrum emergency beacon burst like you said—no direct link established."

"Goddammit," the commander muttered, cursing herself for betraying her dismay to the others under her command. "Okay, people—"

"Incoming message..." Payne interrupted. She paused as she read before speaking. "It's the *Vengeance*. They have our beacon, and they promise they'll be back."

"Did they say when?" Paterson asked hopefully.

"Negative… They're gone."

Brandt took five long, deep breaths before she spoke. She wanted her voice calm and measured, as though this was all expected and okay when inside she wanted to scream at the sky and beg their ships to come back for them now.

"Zero? Overwatch. Specter and Horne, conduct a perimeter check. I want this place locked down as best we can for now. Paterson, get back on that energy source and see if you can't speed up figuring out how to make it work for us. Everyone else, police up the camp and prepare to dig in. Payne on me, we need to find a water source to purify. Like it or not, this place could be home for another day at least."

The stranded team took the news in their stride, even if most of them were quiet and a little subdued. Brandt moved slowly through the thick foliage, which seemed to grow even thicker as they descended a slippery drop to the clearing of trees at the water's edge. It was murky, with an oily film resting on the top and the dark promise of things unseen lurking below the surface. The state of the water didn't matter too much. Whatever pathogens and chemicals lay inside it would be filtered and neutralized by their emergency water purification module.

Her mind went back to basic training, when the petty officer on the training staff took great delight in unfastening his uniform pants in front of their whole squad and loudly filling the container from his bladder as the horrified recruits looked on.

"It don't matter what you put in here," he told them with a smirk and evident pride in the weapon he held in both hands, "as long as it has good ol' H-two-oh at its heart, then you'll get the freshest mountain dew in return. That thing about not eating yellow snow? Well stick that snow in one of these bad boys and you're good for days."

He had zipped himself up and waited, still smiling as he wiped a sprinkled hand on his uniform pants. He took a canteen and filled it with the cool, crystal clear liquid already filtered through, and took a long, satisfied slurp, like it was his first beer after a hard day's work.

"It's sterile," he bragged before taking a sip and making a theatrical sigh of satisfaction, "and I *do* love the taste of my own brand… *ahhhh.*"

The recruits tried hard not to make faces or fall over laughing, at least those who weren't still stunned by the tool he'd used to fill the module—young Leslie Brandt being one of them. They lined up to take enforced turns to sip the recycled urine of their training master, much to his great delight. After a tentative sip of the end product, the squad was converted.

"What the hell is that?" Payne gasped as she fell back from the muddy bank and landed on her back.

"What?" Brandt asked, torn from her reverie by the panic in the other woman's voice.

"Something moved. Something… *big.*"

Brandt reached for her weapon as she spoke. "Get back, slowly…"

Before she could say anything else the water erupted as a muscled tail the length of a full-grown man whipped back and forth to propel something shaped like a crocodile fast up the bank out of the water. It shot directly at Payne, who was flailing about in the mud. Brandt's gun rose, her finger already on the trigger before she had fully aimed, and her thumb cranking the safety spectrum all the way to maximum. Rapid fire tore the heavy air, shredding holes through the open maw of the animal, which seemed as wide as the ramp of a dropship. It kept coming. Brandt walked her shots toward the back of the open mouth, seeing a glimpse of more teeth than a hundred crocs should possess, until her rounds found something in control of the body.

The mouth slammed shut with a percussive clap, the long jaws falling lifelessly into the mud and sinking between Payne's legs only a hand's breadth away from her armored crotch.

Only rapid breathing filled the channel before she erupted with shock at her lucky escape.

"What the *shit*!" she cried, scrabbling backward to her feet and snatching up the full water purification module. Forgetting herself, she threw her body into Brandt's arms and shook violently. "Did you see it?" she babbled. "It… it…" She stopped, lost for words as the adrenaline removed her vocabulary.

"I saw it," Brandt answered, their armor plates clanging against one another as she held on tightly to the younger woman.

"It nearly got me!" Payne said waveringly. She fought back the flood of adrenaline-induced tears and the shock of having survived a primeval threat to her life.

A rumbling growl, like the rolling thunder of a sudden storm, filled the air ominously. Both women turned to look at the animal they had thought to be dead. Its one yellow eye locked its focus directly on them, coiled its massive tail again, and launched itself forward off the muddy bank.

Brandt, watching in slow-motion as she tried to turn and fling Payne out of the way of the opening jaws, saw a blossom of purple against the forehead of the monster. Daylight showed behind it in a blink of an eye. It slammed down to the mud again, knocking both of them aside with its second death. Both women lay still, breathing hard as a cool voice reached them over the channel.

"Overwatch is clear," Zero said as though nothing of note had just happened.

Brandt shoved the enormous dead weight of the animal's lifeless lower jaw from her armored leg and stood. She looked at the dead creature before following the line of sight back toward the outpost. Through the smallest gap in the foliage, about the size of a dinner plate, she saw Zero lower his rifle. Even though his visor was down, she could have sworn she'd seen him smirk.

The *Hammer* appeared on the sensor feed of the *Vengeance* a split second after the active display screen registered a dull flash. An unlit patch of space darkened. The hull of the ship, undamaged and intact courtesy of their overpowered shields, blocked out the light of distant stars to create a kind of negative space effect.

"Captain, *Hammer* reports no damage. She took a rail cannon strike from the surface, but their sensors show that the gun position has been destroyed by return fire."

"Good," Halstead said hurriedly. "Did they pick up the distress beacon?"

A pause as the information was relayed via the data link established between the frigates.

"Negative," the comm officer replied. "Captain Hayes recommends a jump back to the fleet."

"Agreed," Halstead answered. "Plot the jump, send coordinates to the *Hammer* and do it."

The two frigates appeared almost simultaneously on the screens of the fleet, having jumped inside the defensive screen of gun barges undocked from the *Indomitable*. Both sent out 'all clear' hails on the fleet-wide ship channel. In unison, the captains of both frigates handed over control of their bridges to senior crew and went to their quarters, where a joint comm link was established, and waited for the admiral to join them. They didn't discuss what they had just been through. Neither had the patience to repeat themselves.

"Captains," Dassiova said as he activated his own screen and sat down, leaning forward in eager anticipation of their news.

"Sir," Halstead said in a clipped, efficient tone. "Emergency beacon detected on the moon of the habitable planet near the largest star of the twin suns. No details of their disposition or location on the surface, but we have to assume enemy hostility, given the events."

"By '*events*' I presume you mean the reason for the *Hammer*'s shields climbing back up from sixty percent?" Dassiova asked, glancing up to look at the right side of his screen where Hayes's face remained neutral.

"Yes, sir," he said in a flat tone. "What appears to be, or should I say *have* been, an orbital rail cannon emplacement on the surface registered an energy spike. We detected it, evaded the shell, and returned fire with an energy weapon salvo to destroy the gun." His report was clipped, efficient, and he knew as well as Dassiova did that he was leaving out a lot more information than he had included.

"Only one shot?" the admiral enquired in a tone of contemplation. "Only one gun battery?"

"Yes, sir."

"So, one shot took you down to sixty percent shields, and you're calling that a one hundred percent win, instead of dumb luck you're still in one piece? Captain… come on…"

Hayes relaxed his face a little, defeated by the lull of the admiral's fatherly tone. "It took us to fifty percent," he admitted, "and the shot was only a glancing blow to the forward shields. A plumb hit would've been a helluva lot worse."

"And no other guns detected?" Dassiova asked.

"None, sir. I can only assume their recharge time was too long or they had some kind of malfunction. Either way, we were lucky. Our sweeps didn't detect the gun until the energy signature flashed up, otherwise we'd have been on the other side of the planet."

Dassiova's face turned to the other side of the screen. "And the distress beacon? Any indication at all about the *Tanto*?"

"No, sir, and we didn't pick up anything on the frequency of the ship other than the emergency blast."

"*Dammit*," Dassiova cursed quietly to himself. "Unfortunately, with what we have heading for us, I can't spare you two to go back there just yet, and I'm sure as hell not going to leave more of our crews there without jump capabilities and a lot more firepower."

He paused, sighed, and dropped his head slightly as he thought ahead to the call he would have to make to Torres, who was stranded on the *Anvil* waiting for his ship to be fixed after it took a beating. He was glad the *Ichi* wasn't fit to sail right then, because he was damned sure what he would do if he was in the young captain's shoes.

Sucking in another breath and lifting his steely gaze, he looked at the screen again. "Dock with the *Cortez* and resupply. I need you two fully stocked and ready to roll out in twelve hours; there's a storm coming, and we all have work to do. Get some rest and be ready."

Turning off the connection, Dassiova leaned back and rubbed his face. Massey appeared inside his quarters. He didn't wait for her question, simply gave her the information before she asked.

"Planetary defense cannons, an armada heading our way and our recon ship still out of action," he said somberly. "Add to that, our missing people are alive, and I can't spare the manpower to go get them until we've dealt with the goddamned Va'alen."

"That's not the sum of your problems," she said without humor. "The algorithm missed a subspace transmission an hour ago. Somehow it embedded itself alongside a ship-to-ship comm and I only found it on a routine review."

Dassiova groaned out loud, wanting the galaxy to stop spinning for just a few hours so he could catch his breath.

"Where from?" he asked her. "Could you trace the source?"

"Oddly yes, this time," Massey said with a small smile. "It came from the *Anvil*."

He stared at her, daring her to make the same implied accusation as before. She did.

"You know, sir," she said with mock melodrama, "I could've sworn the *Ichi* is docked there right now…"

"Yes, Admiral," Torres replied woodenly, "and no, sir, I understand…"

He kept his face intentionally devoid of information until the fleet commander dismissed him and the screen went black. Torres dropped his shoulders and relaxed his expression, the visual equivalent of no longer using his telephone voice. Behind the screen, hidden from the admiral's view and fighting to keep her breathing undetectable in the cramped quarters onboard the fleet's forge ship, Amare Eze let out a breath and fired questions at him as though she hadn't just heard the same conversation.

"Are they all alive? Is the *Tanto* able to fly? Are th—"

"You realize I know as much as you do, right?" he asked wearily.

She stopped talking and rose from where she was hiding behind the data terminal to walk over the only small section of floor not taken up by furniture. Torres saw how the emergency lighting in the dark cabin caught the muscled lines of her body as she moved without shame. Equally without shame, he leaned back and watched her pull on underwear, doing that curious thing with her thumbs as she nestled the waistband onto her hips just right, and added the flight suit, which she intentionally left unzipped to expose cleavage and betray that she had known all along he was watching her.

"So, what are you going to do?" she asked simply.

"Get our ship fixed and go get them, obviously." She said nothing, just leaned over and kissed him before she shuffled to the door and opened it to peer into the tight corridor. The coast must have been clear, because she slipped out to return to her own cabin. Torres stretched, groaned, and launched himself from the small bed. He had to do the same curious shuffle maneuver to get to the bathroom cubicle, which was designed with as much comfort as the rest of the cabin. He turned on the shower, chiding himself for his ingratitude. He knew that one deck down, where the enlisted crew of the *Ichi* were berthed, there were four seaman per cabin this size and still only one bathroom.

The temporary accommodation aboard the *Anvil* wasn't designed for comfort, it was designed to safely house the full crews of any ship in the fleet requiring essential or emergency maintenance and rebuilding. Their ship, battered and venting atmosphere from half a dozen hull breaches, was still suspended by the big repulser docks in a hangar. She was being worked on day and night to bring her back to readiness. The *Ichi* was not a warship, not by any standards, considering the size and sheer destructive capabilities of the two frigates or the eight small gun barges ordinarily docked to the carrier flagship, but she still packed a punch, despite her forte being stealth reconnaissance. Torres's mind wandered briefly, imagining what it would be like to command a much larger instrument of war. He shook that thought away, recalling how lucky he was to still be in command of the ship he had. The captain focused instead on figuring out how he could get himself excused from fleet duties to rescue his people.

CHAPTER 21

Unnamed Moon Surface

Aq D'marath was a warrior capable of bravery only when the person he was challenging was separated from him by either distance or by other warriors braver than him. He had been in a state of near constant panic since the two ships had arrived bearing a transport pod for a Hive Lord. He could not answer why the hundred ships ordered there by the Supreme Commander had not arrived.

He had shown his dominance when the human ships appeared in orbit, and Aq D'marath was ready to accept the praise of his entourage, as well as that of the Hive Lord, when all hell broke loose in his reinforced command center.

"Aq, the human ship has returned fire on our rail gun," a female Va'alen shouted from her position at the sensor array controls. "One has jumped away—"

"Impossible," D'marath snarled, glancing nervously into the shadows at the rear of the room. The Hive Lord hung motionless in the air. "Our shot should have destroyed them easily. They were weak and could not have survived a—"

"Perhaps," interrupted Fal K'rath, the ranking Va'alen of the small escort dedicated to the Hive Lord's personal safety. Although a rank below the Aq, his presence and casual air of dominance threatened D'marath, who recognized a warrior far more capable than he could ever hope to be.

"Perhaps *what?*" D'marath asked dangerously. He knew he was risking a challenge by a warrior who seemed unfazed knowing the young commander was well connected.

He had seen a rapid reduction in the respect shown to him since the humans had destroyed the Va'alen's gateway device and cut them off from the rest of the alliance. Those disrespectful warriors believed they would not gain the safety of their home systems again.

"Perhaps," K'rath said unwaveringly, "the humans are more dangerous now than they were before. Perhaps their previous encounters with the *mighty Va'alen* have taught them how to fight."

Murmurs of agreement rippled around the room as other warriors growled their support of the Fal. Aq D'marath glanced around him for his own support. When he saw none, he tried to answer politically.

"Our Supreme Commander," he whined, "tells us how the humans will be driven from this system. He says—"

"Have *you* encountered any humans, Aq D'marath?" K'rath asked, giving a bow of respect to soften the overt challenge in his words. The disrespect in his voice was palpable, but as he accompanied the words with a gesture of supplication, any challenge would appear unjustified.

"No, I… I have not yet had the honor of killing a human in battle."

"We fought with them," K'rath said as he spread the arms on his left side out to encompass his mate and the pair crewing the other two ships of the escort. "They have new weapons we did not see when we fought them the last time, and their ships do not break like they did before. I believe they *have* learned from our previous battles."

D'marath knew that the junior officer had fought the humans before and escaped with a few remnants of an attacking force. It had proved to be too few in number to beat the invaders. The humans had been reinforced just in time to drive the Va'alen's swarms of ships away.

They had blamed the arrival of more warships for that defeat, and the supreme commander had accepted that reason for their loss and retreat. However, instead of punishing them, he had rewarded K'rath with a reputational promotion, by placing him in command of a Hive Lord's personal guard. Aq D'marath glanced at the Hive Lord, who levitated in silence, head shrouded. The Hive Lord didn't speak; they never had to as they silently commanded the Va'alen around them to speak for them. But the presence of its mind at the back of their brains itched them like an infecting prion.

K'rath shook, his back arching slightly as though overcome by a sudden cramp. He fixed the Aq with a direct look and spoke in a voice not his own.

"And why has your gun position not responded? Did you even check to see if the enemy barrage was effective?"

"Our shields should have absorbed anything the humans could have fired at us," D'marath answered peevishly. He realized too late that the Hive Lord was addressing him directly. He bowed his head slightly after speaking. "I will send a detachment there now t—"

"No," K'rath's voice boomed in the confined space. "You will *lead* a detachment there now. Go."

D'marath, defeated, left and signaled for his entourage to follow. K'rath shuddered as the Hive Lord pushed into his brain.

Why did you speak your own words as though they came from me? it asked, the words hissing into his brain with no sound.

He needs to learn to show respect around you, Lord, K'rath thought. He too bowed in respect.

He blames others for failing at tasks he himself is too weak and incompetent to undertake.

No replying thought arrived in his mind, and he didn't know if the Hive Lord was contemplating a response or was simply satisfied with its escort.

"What air transport do we have?" K'rath asked the remaining Va'alen in the command center, as he stood tall once more.

"We have many ships, Fal," a female said with her head bowed, "but flight is not safe on the surface because of the ion storms and the wildlife."

K'rath snorted his derision.

"You are all as weak as your Aq," he snarled. He turned to the Hive Lord to kneel and speak out loud for the benefit of the others. "Lord, I beg your permission to search the planet for the humans shot down before we arrived here."

Silence hung in the room before all of them shuddered with the intrusion into their minds by the hovering Lord.

Go, it said. *Do not fail. Bring me a living human; I want to feel their minds and learn all that they know before they die.*

"New standing order," Brandt said a little breathlessly as her heart rate was still dropping back to normal. "Nobody goes anywhere alone, and everybody stays ready to shoot."

She had replayed the video feed recorded by her suit for the rest of the team via their HUDs, hearing the gasps and Paterson's trademark low whistle as the gray-skinned crocodile-type animal erupted in slow motion from the water. Zero had made no show of pride in his shot, an impossible shot for almost anyone, but Brandt knew him well enough to recognize that he had just chalked up an entry to his personal top-ten most awesome things list.

"The jungle is too dangerous," Horne complained. "You've holed us up in a death trap and it's just a matter of time before something eats us."

"Trust me, asshole," Payne said, still shaken from her narrow escape. She was allowing the stress to infringe on her professionalism. "Anything taking a bite out of you will probably spit you back out on taste alone."

"What's that supposed to mean?" the PMC asked as he tried to draw himself up to her height and square off.

Specter intervened, putting his hand in front of Horne's chest plate. The shorter man walked into it, expecting some give at least, but rebounded half a step and backed off.

"If you'll recall," Brandt said, as though the altercation hadn't happened, "the plains were just as inhospitable, and there was no water supply there. Besides, the temperature doesn't drop to dangerous levels at night under the canopy. We have an obligation to recover and record what we've found here; unless you know of any other abandoned Va'alen outposts?"

Horne said nothing, but his body language made his feelings plain enough as he puffed up his chest and let out a slow expulsion of air from his nose.

"So," Paterson said jokingly, "you prefer killer dinosaur birds and dropship-sized crocs to dog-sized scorpions and pterodactyls?"

"Yes," Brandt said flatly, with no trace of irony. None of the others spoke.

"Anyway," Paterson said, "I need you to look at something." Brandt nodded to Zero, who acknowledged her unspoken order by deploying the team into defensive positions.

She followed Paterson inside, back into the room where the bodies of the predatory bird and the dead Va'alen were. Each was wrapped in a body bag, straining the edges. They were far larger than the plastic coverings designed for humans. Specter followed her, uninvited but unchallenged, and the three of them stood around the slowly spinning, thrumming energy generator. Brandt used the interface on her forearm to retract her helmet, exposing her face as Specter already had. Paterson followed suit and all three muted their microphones to isolate their conversation from the team channel.

"I've got something," Paterson said. He pushed the 'glyph icons on the console below the two opposing metal objects. They were being suspended by physics Brandt, at least, didn't fully understand. In response to his activation, the hum increased in intensity as the elements spun faster.

"The power supply is perpetual. The elements generate their electromagnetic fields to generate power, and that power in turn increases the spin and the power keeps rising. There has to be an upper limit, but I'm not really comfortable testing that. Not here anyway."

Brandt watched, mesmerized as the copper sphere shimmered out of focus so that both metals could be seen clearly and wavered as though in a heat haze. The humming noise wound down again as Paterson hit a second icon to reduce the power.

"Can we tap into it?" Specter asked. "Can we use it to power the mech?"

Their suits were topped up, even if the mech rig wasn't fully restored. Another day spent on the move would reduce them all to siphoning power from Specter's internal singularity source. That would mean only one or two of them would be effective at any time.

"I'm working on it," Paterson replied a little snappily. He was tired and his sudden return to operational soldiering had frayed his softened nerves.

Brandt shot Specter a look, telling him to lay off, and turned back to Paterson to soothe him. Before she could open her mouth, Zero cut in over the channel.

"Aircraft inbound!"

"Everybody under cover now," Brandt barked, forgetting that her microphone was muted. She cursed herself, reactivated it and repeated the order. "Cut power to everything detectable and tuck in."

She ran to the back of the room, back to where the body of the Va'alen lay. Instead of continuing outside, she peered upward through the hole in the roof where the bright-colored bird-osaur thing had attacked. Her helmet folded out from the collar of her suit at the touch of the screen, the HUD springing to life as soon as the visor covered her face. In her ear, the rest of the team reported their positions. She continued to stare skyward through the canopy encroaching on the abandoned outpost. The sky above her darkened in a flash before the bright sunlight returned. Brandt gasped. Her HUD registered the silhouette that accompanied the high-pitched whine of the Va'alen vessel.

"Clear," Zero said in a voice like still water. "Four ships passed overhead. No change to course or speed."

"Trajectory?" Brandt asked in a soft voice, as though the ships could hear her.

"Calculating," Zero responded, then paused. "Crash site is my guess."

"Which means they'll be following our trail," Horne cut in. "A kid could track us in armor and a mech."

Brandt pressed her lips into a thin line to stop herself from shutting the mercenary down. The thought had occurred to her as well. Two pairs of Va'alen warriors heading directly for their crash site couldn't be a coincidence. Her mind buzzed with questions about why their pursuit had taken two days to start, but she stopped herself. Wasting time thinking about it did nothing to stop the clock. She guessed that the time it would take their enemy to reach them would be far less than it had taken her team to get there themselves. The realization struck her that their time was ticking down to discovery and, inevitably, further conflict.

"Screw it," she muttered under her breath. "Commander?" Payne asked. Brandt ignored the question.

"Turner, is Perez good to move?" she asked over the channel.

"I'm good, Commander," Perez answered.

"Commander, I don—" Turner began before their downed trooper cut in.

"I can drive the mech," Perez offered. "Less movement needed."

Two seconds of silence followed, with no argument from the medic.

"Do it," Brandt ordered. "Everyone else, grab everything; whatever we can't take or don't need goes back in the crate."

"And what do we do with the crate?" Horne asked petulantly. He was impossible to please.

"Jamie?" she asked, dropping the professionalism in favor of a little bravado.

"I can work something out," Paterson said.

"Good. Payne? Rig up the sub-space beacon. These assholes will know we're here soon anyway, and I prefer to place a long-distance call now, rather than later."

CHAPTER 22

Unnamed Moon Surface, Tanto Crash Site

Fal K'rath stood in the center of the crater where the *Tanto* had crashed and lost containment of its singularity drive. The resulting blast and implosion had wiped out any trace of their landing. Any search of the area for clues or trails had to begin far outside the blast radius. He ignored the flashing light of the device in his hand—it signaled a radiation warning—and sent the other pair of Va'alen mates. They began their search at opposing sides of the near-circular crater and worked in opposing directions, so that each Va'alen warrior covered a quarter of the radius.

His mate made the call first, calling them from behind the low crest of the higher ground that had not been leveled by the blast.

"Footprints," she said. "Many footprints. They gathered here and went in two directions."

"They split up?" her female counterpart scoffed. "Why would the foolish humans separate their tiny forces?"

"No," K'rath interrupted as he studied the marks in the dust. "Two went this way, one running with long strides and one with short strides. Both came back at the same pace."

"One of the cowards ran away?" his mate asked. K'rath turned cold look on her, which resulted in her head bowing. She had spoken out of turn to offend him. He had been privy to the feeling of fear felt by the Hive Lords. Fear of the humans, despite how weak their bodies were, even in their metal hides. Fear of what their arrival and their cowardly stealth attacks had done to Va'alen forces.

The alliance, and without doubt their particular expedition, was at risk now that these little mammals had discovered the ability to travel further than their own star. Because of this fear he had been forced to feel, K'rath took her derision of them as an offense.

"Do not underestimate our enemy," he growled at them until all their heads bowed in submission. "We may be hunting them, but if more of them come, it will be *us* who are hunted. Chased through the system until we are all eradicated. The Lords know from the signals and probes these humans sent out into the galaxy that they consume everything they touch. They are a disease, a plague on the galaxy, and they will sweep us away if we do not respect that."

"We must… *respect* them, Fal?" the other male warrior asked.

Fal K'rath considered the question for a moment.

"Yes," he replied. "We respect them, and we kill them. Then we kill any more of them we can find until they stop coming here or we are sent home."

Or until we die by their hands, he added privately to himself. A stab of worry hit him—the Hive Lord could still be lingering at the back of his consciousness to monitor their mission. He was saved any further concern on that point by an incoming communication.

"Fal," his mate said, "the Aq has returned from the rail gun battery."

"And?" K'rath demanded.

"And the gun was destroyed by orbital bombardment, it seems," she said, her head bowed deeply to prevent any hostility at the news being redirected at her, "and the bunker also, but by animals, not humans or their weapons."

K'rath's mind boiled over with thoughts and criticisms. Could the animals on this rock be more dangerous than Va'alen warriors? Then he modified his thoughts. The strongest warriors were elsewhere, and some of the Va'alen he had seen appointed to guard the mining base were not much bigger than the offspring of his clan.

"No matter," he said. "We will hunt down these humans and be done here. I want as many of them as possible kept alive for the Hive Lord to pick clean their minds."

They followed the tracks, bounding forwards in pair and taking turns moving while the others kept watch. The maneuver was a simple covering advance and, unknown to the Va'alen, had been adopted by humans for centuries. The art of infantry tactics was a logical conclusion, it seemed to any casual observer. Their pursuit led them to higher ground where the loose, jagged rocks made tracking much harder. Had they not been following the deeper impressions left behind by the mechanized rig, the warriors might have lost the trail, but the heavier and larger footprints might as well have been a trail of breadcrumbs. They wasted time running through the pitch-black of the underground tunnels, finding nothing but the inedible remains of what appeared to be giant insects. This led them to conclude that survival inside the tunnels was an impossibility.

After all, weren't the humans weak outside of their ships?

Fal K'rath ordered his hunters back out into the harsh sunlight where they cast around for signs until one of them found more footprints leading away from the entrance.

Above them, circling like black wedges and calling out in short, sharp shrieks, were bird-like creatures. K'rath watched them, guessing that if the humans were still on the open plain, the scavengers would be marking them out just as they were the four Va'alen. The trail was found, and the two pairs moved rapidly over the rocky, uneven surface.

"Fal," the other male warrior called to him, "should we not return for our ships?"

"The humans do not have a ship," he responded. "We will follow as they are forced to move."

The trail slowed but became easier to follow. Broken branches and deep impressions in softer ground revealed their path toward a small river. Under the canopy, the oppressive heat took on a new element as the humidity increased. Rather than slow down the Va'alen, their carapaces absorbed the moisture and rehydrated them after the dry heat of the plains had baked them.

As one, the group slowed and at a signal from K'rath, they fanned out silently, crouching in the dense foliage where their brown hides blended into the myriad of natural colors. They watched, listening, until eventually their Fal stood and advanced on the abandoned outpost.

Moving in pairs and proceeding with an unnerving silence for bipedal creatures so large, the four aliens emerged into the compound through a fresh gap they made in the perimeter fence. Their approach was monitored by the human's scout drone nestled in a nearby treetop with the four small repulser engines powered down to prevent detection.

It still gave off a small electronic signature as the two-way link to Brandt's suit gave the stranded recon team a bird's eye view of their enemy. Their silence was thicker than the humidity as they all watched via their HUDs.

Two Va'alen took cover and pointed their weapons at the door as the other two stood to either side. Instead of kicking the door in as the humans expected, one of the covering aliens fired a single, huge blast from its weapon directly at the door, missing its own kind by inches. The two on the door seemed to expect this as they slipped through the smoking ruins of the doorway before the metal had stopped arcing from the discharged energy. Brandt wasn't the only one to purse her lips at the knowledge that their enemy had more powerful personal weapons than they could engineer. Their own technology could only be made small enough to be carried by a mechanized rig, and even then, it had a limited number of shots.

The drone, situated high above the building, responded to the commander's controls and rotated the zoom lens to look down through the gap in the low roof. It had been placed there intentionally so that they could gauge how far they had degraded their pursuers; there was no point in forcing a set battle with unknown numbers of a superior force unless they had the upper hand, or unless they had no other choice.

The pair of Va'alen outside was called in, and on their displays the humans watched one of the aliens slip its weapon into a sheath at the base of its back as it crouched down to lift the lid of their supply crate.

A burst of what looked like steam came fractionally before the terrifyingly guttural bellow of rage and pain that floated up to the drone's sensors. The alien who had taken the brunt of Paterson's booby trap fell back as the acid rigged to spray out from the suddenly depressurized container flowed over their equipment and damaged it beyond repair. Screams of agony and more raging bellows of anger echoed. Brandt wasn't the only one able to detect the sounds in stereo; the alien voices carried loudly through the dense jungle to their position. Whatever the roars meant, she interpreted them as 'time to go'.

She disconnected the feed to the drone, using her hands to manipulate the projected controls and put it back into auto mode. The tiny engines fired up, raising it from the treetops to follow the team from above the canopy. It would be useless to them under the cover of the trees, but leaving such a valuable asset behind was out of the question.

"Let's go," Brandt ordered, sending them to the higher ground in the march order she had already established. "That comm burst will be with the admiral now, and all he has to do is decide how many ships to send for us."

"It worked?" Paterson asked hopefully.

"It did," she said, feeling a little uncomfortable in taking pleasure at such horrific injuries. They were, however, necessary for their survival. Making the Va'alen fearful of pursing them could make all the difference. It had meant the loss of precious battery power to help make the acid, but any degradation of their enemy was worth it.

Abandoned Va'alen Outpost

Fal K'rath watched in stunned horror as the other male warrior fell back from the human object. His pulse rifle fell to the ground as all four hands scrabbled desperately at the front of his carapace. The hissing, bubbling noise mixed with his screams of pain, but what affected K'rath was not the sound or the agony his fellow warrior was suffering, but the smell. The smell of dissolving bio-armor seeped into his senses and turned him sour. He could not afford time for personal distaste, as the warrior's mate began to screech and roar her own challenges. K'rath knew that the wounded warrior's mate would be feeling his pain. Not his pain precisely, but the *echo* of his agony; the emotional response attached to pain that was so strong there was no way to distinguish between pain and feelings. For her, it was as real as if her own body were being eaten away by the spray of chemicals.

He reached for the writhing warrior, grasping a limb unaffected by the bubbling substance, and dragged him clear of the human equipment left behind. A glance at his own mate made her intervene and block the other female from rushing to her mate and being affected by the cowardly trap. The equipment, valuable to so many in their expedition and likely worth a high price, disintegrated and melted into a single lump of indistinguishable metal and plastic. Turning away in disgust, he saw his warrior regaining his senses and trying to get up. He failed, falling back and arching his back in pain.

"We must leave him here," Fal K'rath said.

The mate of the fallen Va'alen looked up and crouched into a stance dangerously close to a challenge.

As one, both K'rath and *his* mate drew their curved blades from behind their backs. The body language was clear: a challenge would mean death. The injured warrior's mate shrank away, the blades were sheathed, and the moment of near-cannibalistic rage was over.

"If he lives, we will return for him. If he does not, I swear that you will be released to claim retribution."

The female bowed slightly, grateful that she would be allowed to honor her mate and unleash hell on the humans who had hurt him with such a cheap, cowardly trick.

"We must be close behind them," K'rath's mate said. She dragged the injured warrior to sit with his back against the wall and restored the rifle to the grip on his right hands. "We can hunt them down."

"It is time I called for reinforcements," K'rath told her.

She snapped her body around to face him, anger radiating off her in pulsating waves.

"You would share the honor of killing these humans with an-other?" she asked in a tone that was also dangerously close to a chal-lenge.

K'rath let it go.

"I would accept the honor of being among the first Va'alen to bring a live human to our Hive Lord and giving the gift of taking everything from its mind. *That* is where the honor lies, not in killing these weak bodies who leave these vile tricks behind them."

CHAPTER 23

The Indomitable, Proxima Centauri Orbit

"Admiral, subspace data comm incoming from the other side of sector three," the comm officer in charge of monitoring the channels said. Her tone was designed to make Dassiova sit up and take notice.

"From who?" he shot back.

Whom, the comm officer thought, before remembering that she shouldn't correct people on their grammar. They seemed to dislike her for it. "From Commander Brandt, detailing the location of her team from the *Tanto*. Sir, she says that her team is being pursued by a Va'alen squad and that there is hostile wildlife on the surface... Sir..."

"Spit it out, Lieutenant," Dassiova growled.

"She says they're being hunted by 'roaches and dinosaurs and could do with a frikkin' ride out of there."

"Dinosaurs?" Dassiova began involuntarily before he caught himself and snapped his mouth shut. "Is there a response frequency detailed?"

"Negative, shot in the dark. The whole fleet would have received it."

Dammit, the admiral cursed to himself. *If we've received it, then the Ichi sure as hell has too.*

Sure enough, the other comm officer responsible for the majority of the ship-to-ship comms piped up.

"Sir, incoming hail from the *Anvil*. It's Captain Torres wanting to speak to you personally."

"My compliments to the commander," Dassiova growled. Torres was currently without a ship to command, so he was not technically a captain at that moment. "Advise him that I received the transmission and will deal with it accordingly." He waited as the thinly veiled orders were passed on, but looked back when his thoughts were interrupted again.

"Sir, Commander Torres is insisting that you take his call."

Dassiova, to use a term the Chief had long ago reserved as his signature move, lost his shit entirely. He sat in his chair, tapped at the console to patch in to the open channel with Torres, and let rip with a full broadside for everyone to hear.

"Commander, let me give you a lesson in military command structure. *I* am the admiral. The fleet commander. The fleet which, for the moment at least, you are a part of. *You*, being a commander serving under me and the captain of a ship stuck in dry dock because you couldn't keep it in your pants, have to do what *I* tell you to do. If you do not *like* this natural evolution of how the human race has developed its command structure, then I invite you to resign your goddamned commission on our return to Ear—"

"Sir, if I may?" Torres interrupted.

Dassiova's eyebrows went up so high they would have disappeared if his hairline hadn't receded greatly over the last decade.

"I've detected a signal trace on the *Ichi's* systems. Sir, as much as I hate to admit it, I think the leak is coming from one of my people..." Torres's tone changed to one of questioning confusion. "Wait. Admiral, what transmission are *you* talking about?"

"Yeah, right here," Massey said as she worked her fingertips over the console, "subspace comm data burst relayed through the fleet data link via the *Anvil* to the *Indomitable* and back to Earth."

"Do we know what it says?" Torres asked. The only other people in the room were the admiral and Chief, his troop commander.

"Actually..." Massey said as she typed commands, "I think we might... *Got it!*"

The screen came up with a long sequence of numbers.

"That's our current position," Torres said. "Someone's sending our current position back home. But why?"

"And to whom?" Massey added.

"I care more about the *who* on this end right now," Dassiova said. "Why can you decrypt this transmission and not the others?"

"Whoever it is got sloppy, I guess," Massey said. "The signal definitely originated on the *Ichi*, though. No doubt about it."

"My ship is crawling with engineers from the *Anvil*," Torres interjected, still hoping that treason wasn't being hidden among his own people. "It coul—"

"I've used this data to trace the earlier transmissions," Massey said, almost apologetically, "and they all came from your ship, even when you were on the other side of this sector."

Torres's head dropped as all hope of a mistake left him. "So, who is it?" Chief asked in a threatening rumble. "Working on it," Massey answered. "Oh... oh my..."

All three men standing behind her asked questions at once and cancelled each other out. Massey held up a hand for quiet, then turned the gesture into a pointed finger at a line of code on the screen.

It was a personal security clearance code, masked in all the previous transmissions, but now revealed through their mistake.

"No," Torres said in barely a whisper. "It can't be. It's not possible, I…"

"I think you need to let us handle this one, son," Dassiova said kindly. He turned to Chief and drew himself up formally. "Chief, please take a dropship over to the *Anvil* and detain that traitor for questioning."

Amare Eze had returned to her own quarters, after utilizing her covert skills to sneak into Torres's cabin. As they were waiting for their ship to be repaired, the lack of duties made for a lot more opportunity for intimacy than they were used to. She had showered and changed into PT kit before heading to the ship's small gymnasium. After waiting ten minutes for a free treadmill, she set the pace high and got into the zone. Normally when training, she would have music blasting through earbuds, but onboard ship where warning bells couldn't afford to be ignored, she had to make do with the deep contents of her mind to occupy her.

She was so deep inside her thoughts that the arrival of four armored troops in the gym passed her by. All around her, others were stopping their workouts and leaving the room, or staying back against the wall and keeping their mouths shut. Eventually only Eze was left running. The sudden lack of background noise snapped her concentration to the present. She glanced around, thinking that she had missed a ship-wide alert. She hit the red emergency stop button to stop her treadmill.

It wound down quickly. With shaking legs, she turned and stepped down to be confronted with the chest plate of a large man. She looked up into the scowling black face of the Chief.

"Sir," she said, out of breath and masking the jolt of fear.

He didn't respond, so she went to step around him. He sidestepped to block her path.

"Come with us, Eze," Chief said in a rumbling, ominous tone.

"Why?"

"Because you must," he answered, adding a word that was dripping in unavoidable consequences. "Now."

Stunned, still out of breath and sweating, she followed Chief out of the gym. The other armored troops fell in beside and behind her to create a box-style escort. Crew and officers flattened themselves against the bulkheads to get out of the way of the procession as it wound its way to the nearest shuttle bay. After stepping up the rear ramp of the nearest dropship, she sat and tried to keep her face as neutral as the Chief's had been.

CHAPTER 24

Va'alen Armada

"Aq," the underling called over the radio to the commander of the armada, "it is time to deploy another communications buoy."

The commander nodded, giving his consent for the prototype comm relay to be dumped in deep space. Under the guidance and secret orders of Aq Qa'shal, his clan senior, he had assembled and led the armada to the human fleet, instead of following the orders from their Supreme Commander, Muq Da'kath. His own flight, that of a hundred Va'alen warriors, should have been sent to a small moon where one of the two Hive Lords had been secreted. Instead, clan loyalty had forced him to disobey those orders. All other commanders loyal to Qa'shal's clan had joined him to make a flotilla larger than their enemy could ever hope to destroy. All of them knew the penalty for failure. Death in battle at the hands of their enemy was preferable to execution for treason, and that fact made every last one of the Va'alen in that armada more dangerous than usual.

When he was successful, when the humans were destroyed, Qa'shal could challenge for overall leadership. He would be promoted to the team of senior advisors, thus advancing his career and his clan's standing back on their home worlds.

The comm buoy relay, an invention of Qa'shal's own engineers, accelerated their communications through the series of waypoints. This allowed for greater distances to be covered. That new technology was derived from the wreckage blown clear from their destroyed portal.

The Supreme Commander was obsessed with recreating the human technology, convinced that it was the key to their ability to travel huge distances in almost no time. His own clan senior believed that the device was their communications array and had ordered studies to be conducted. The mash of alien technologies had quickly led to the ability to accelerate their data communications through space at unimaginable speeds. He sent an update to Qa'shal through the most recent buoy the armada had deployed. He informed his commander, calling him *Supreme* commander in his communiqué for added merit points, that they were within days of dealing a fatal blow to the enemy, and that he hoped to inform him of their success soon.

Ahead of him, the chosen sub-leader's own ship near the front of the tightly packed formation, the black expanse of space held a faint red glow in the distance. The red glow, that of the small dwarf planet where the filthy Kuldar had been hiding, signified their journey's end and the impending battle that would elevate his standing and reputation to previously unobtainable heights. He mused that Qa'shal, the offspring of a prominent sire in the second largest clan of their kind and a warrior of small repute but great support, had chosen him for his bravery. In truth, Qa'shal had chosen him for his malleability. He had manipulated him easily with promises of high social and military honors for a successful mission. Promises like that, especially when cut off from their network, were easy to give. The chances of them being paid in full were slim.

As soon as the message was sent, the sub-leader leaned back in his chair and waited, imagining the new title and riches that would fall on him. A bright blue flash ahead of his ship interrupted his contemplation. The lead ships were engulfed in an expanding sphere of arcing electricity, before it collapsed and crushed the vessels from existence in a heartbeat. He roared for the armada to stop, but a report of a second explosion far back to their left flank was shouted at him.

By the time the fifth shrouded singularity mine detonated and the armada had lost thirteen ships, the commander had ordered a course change. This led them on a circuitous route to the human fleet. He lost no more ships, but the lost time was more galling; it added hours to his arrival time. His commander would be waiting impatiently for a battle report on the conflict that would not yet have happened.

"Curse these cowardly humans and their sneak attacks," he roared, abandoning his tactics in rage. "Order the armada to spread out into battle formation and advance on the enemy."

~

"Long range sensors picking up a mine explosion," Hayes's ensign at the tactical station announced. "And another—"

"You hearing this, *Vengeance*?" Hayes asked over the open channel to both Halstead's ship and the fleet flagship.

"On my sensors also," Halstead replied. "Admiral?"

"Go to it, Captains," he ordered. "God speed and stay lucky." He cut the link, removing himself from the conversation, granting permission for his two frigates to go to war.

"Little hand say it's time to rock?" Halstead asked Hayes with a wonky grin.

"Hell, yes, Captain," Hayes said seriously. "Hell, yes."

The Va'alen armada, spread out wide in loose attack waves, moved slowly to try and maintain their stealth profiles. Such large concentrations of cloaking energy fields resonated to create a kind of sensor hum large enough for the humans to detect. That was precisely what happened. Ahead of them, a dull flash, the only indication of something amiss, signified the arrival of one of the enormous warships that had destroyed their portal. The Va'alen commander roared for his ships to attack. He manipulated the controls to surge ahead and high, coming down in a diving attack run. The enemy ship fired a rippling broadside of missiles, which consumed his leading warriors in collapsing explosions. The human ship vanished, another muted flash the only sign of change, and the surviving flights of Va'alen arrived within weapons range, to find that section of black space devoid of enemy to kill.

"Sensors indicate enemy to our right," came the call over the armada's channel. "Another ship is decloa—"

The transmission shut off as though the source had been lost from the universe. The ships on that edge of the formation were spread thinly, and when the *Hammer* appeared only a thousand kilometers away from the nearest enemy ship, it unloaded a broadside of singularity nukes in a wide spread. The human ship then opened up with their energy cannons stitching bright orange bolts across the black expanse.

The answering eruption of sparks denoted three Va'alen ships coming apart like fireworks. Debris spun out in all directions to detonate as flashes in the shields of their comrade ships. Before any guns could respond, the enemy ship disappeared again, only to reappear to the Va'alen's opposite flank and repeat the process.

"Kill it!" the commander roared. "Destroy that ship!"

The complex sequence of jumps performed by both the *Hammer* and the *Vengeance* called for an open communication link between the two ships. They had choreographed their disappearances and arrivals to make it seem as though one single ship tormented the Va'alen armada with impunity. It didn't take long for their enemy to adapt to their tactics, however. As soon as they jumped, they found every weapon of the Va'alen armada within range firing at the emerging energy reading before the ship had even fully arrived in the real space and time where their enemy existed.

Hayes rocked in his command chair as dozens of hits battered their outer shields. The damage report called out to him claimed a ten percent drop in their shields, and that was enough for Hayes.

"Jump us out," he ordered. "*Vengeance*, they're wising up to us. Jump in farther away next time and use nukes instead."

Halstead acknowledged him, but still her next turn to harass the enemy resulted in the ship taking numerous hits to the point where their outer shield emitter failed.

Twice more each, the frigates emerged into real space at the fringes of the armada. With each appearance they fired ordnance, which took one or two or three ships every time.

When both frigates had expended their payload, they jumped farther to appear in the void near to the *Cortez,* which had been on standby to re-arm the pair as soon as they docked.

"Get me a line to the admiral," Hayes ordered. "Captain Halstead, you still on with me?"

"I'm here, Craig," she answered, stunning him briefly with her uncharacteristic use of his given name.

He had no time to dwell on that, as Dassiova's voice boomed over the speakers.

"Report."

"Sir, we've taken a good few out, but they adapted quickly. They've spread out, which has made it hard to concentrate fire on them. We hammered them," he winced at the unintentional pun, "on the first two passes but we're only getting ones and twos now. I think further attempts could result in losses to us."

"Captain Halstead," Dassiova asked, "you concur with that analysis?"

"I do, sir," she said. "We need to bunch them up again if we have any hope of stopping them before they arrive here."

"That'll happen," he assured them. Stopping them with the frigates' marauding tactics was never the entire plan. "Be ready."

Torres was pale. He sat in his command chair in stunned confusion, after learning what had taken place on the *Anvil*. His orders to deploy immediately could not be ignored, though.

He had little to no ground forces aboard, no commander or her sub-commanders, and the damage to his ship had yet to be fully repaired. But his cargo holds and shuttle bay were rammed full of the rapidly manufactured Shroud mines loaded from the forge ship as they fixed the holes in his hull. Dassiova had given Torres orders, let him in on part of the wider plan, and instructed him to put recent events out of his mind. Unusually subdued and humbled by what had taken place on his watch, wounding Torres's pride further was the realization that Amare had got so close to him to further her treasonous endeavors. He was stung into a resolute rage, which he planned to unload in full on the approaching Va'alen armada.

The *Ichi*, jumping in the opposite direction to the returning frigates, shrouded on arrival into real space. It immediately began rapidly deploying mines at irregular intervals along the approach vector of the enemy. The irregularity, the wanton randomness of the mine deployment, was intentional. The Va'alen had proven over and over that they were quick to adapt to any new tactics their human opponents employed.

By the time the *Hammer* and the *Vengeance* returned, his holds were emptied and he exchanged a brief handover to the warships before jumping back to the *Anvil* for the remainder of their stealth mines.

~

"This is easier if you simply tell us what we need to know," Chief said softly, compared to his usual aggressive rumble.

"I don't know anything," Eze snarled. The welt above her right eye was swollen but no longer bleeding. One of her guards had ensured she 'fell' walking down the ramp of the dropship that brought her to the *Indomitable*. "If I knew what you were talking about, don't you think I'd at least have a cover story ready? Think about it. You've done the same covert training I have; why would I just play dumb?"

Chief considered that as he leaned back in the chair opposite where she was restrained. "Perhaps you are using reverse psychology?"

Eze groaned and leaned painfully against the restraints around her wrists. "I'll tell you again," she said in a hoarse voice. "I haven't sent a single goddamned communication outside of this fleet since before we set sail to Mars *the first time.*"

Chief Onyilogwu treated her to his best hard stare and sighed. He would be forced to extract the truth from her the hard way and would take no pleasure from it. Enjoyment or not, that sigh promised, he would do it.

CHAPTER 25

Unnamed Moon Surface

"They're gaining on us," Zero warned. "No two ways about it."

"Dammit," Brandt answered. "Defensive position?"

"Stand by," Zero replied. He took over control of the drone and scouted ahead. "Terrain change in three clicks, rocky ground as the elevation climbs more rapidly. Mountains in the distance and… and what appears to be a larger base with a high-walled perimeter."

"Crap!" Brandt cursed. "Anywhere we can hole up and take these assholes out?"

Zero said nothing as he scanned the ground with his natural hunter's eye.

"Cave," he said with a hint of trepidation. "Ambush position there."

Brandt looked at the display through the drone link and tightened her mouth as she thought.

"Do it," she ordered. "Perez in the mouth of the cave. Turner, Rogers, inside and farther back." Protecting the medic and pilot would be unpopular with them, but rising fear and adrenaline didn't allow her to waste time dwelling on it. "Paterson, with them," she added as an afterthought. "Zero, find yourself a position, and Payne, watch his back. Horne and Specter, with me; ambush position behind the rocky outcrop to the left of the approach."

As far as rapidly made plans went, it was good. But she couldn't help but recall the adage about plans and their contact with the enemy.

The team covered the three kilometers quickly and deployed to their given positions without question.

Paterson was in possession of the biological samples that would be vital to their research and ultimately their weapon and armor development programs. Surviving the planetoid they were trapped on, however, had to be the priority. To that end, recovering the hidden bodies of the Va'alen and the dinosaur-bird-raptor thing was a tertiary goal, given their current danger.

The wait for their hunters was unbearable. Through the team channel, Brandt could hear the rapid, uneven breathing of more than one person as they lay in frightened anticipation of the ambush. A glance at the team's vitals in a sub-menu showed every single one of them, with the exception of Specter, with elevated pulses.

The wait ended suddenly and unexpectedly by their hastily adopted position coming under fire. Instead of the Va'alen falling into their trap, rapid-fire bursts of directed energy bolts poured onto the humans from the tree line. Perez was struck first, taking four or five direct hits to the armored chest of the mech rig. He fired off three heavy weapon discharges back, before falling backward, transmitting a strangled cry over the channel as if he was being electrocuted. A toe-to-toe fight ensued, fire raining on them. The two races slugged it out like brawlers. No clever subterfuge, no overwhelming tactics gave either side the upper hand, and it simply came down to a matter of who could do the most damage the fastest.

With one down already—and that one being in possession of their heaviest weapons—the humans were backed against the wall by the superior firepower of their enemy.

Zero, having only just gained his ideal position in the high branches of the tallest tree, lay along a branch wider than a dropship's loading ramp. He lovingly caressed the safety of his battle rifle and used his HUD to penetrate the layers of thick foliage ahead and below him. The red outline of a Va'alen warrior was unmistakably in a firing position, and Zero lined up a high-powered 12mm shot on a trajectory that would pass straight down through the torso from the place where its neck would be.

Zero squeezed the trigger, the digital outline of his target shuddering and convulsing with the immediate impact. He didn't wait to see the effect on his target. He fired again, three, four, five more rounds pumping the supercharged projectiles through the body until it transitioned from dangerous enemy to falling corpse.

That was when the humans' troubles truly began.

Fal K'rath relished his successful shots as the big mechanical human fell to his fire. His senses were alive as he finally got to fight the humans in personal combat and not across the black void of space. He was spraying the position indiscriminately, forcing the humans to keep their heads down in fear of the destructive power of his pulse rifle. He was searching for a clear target to annihilate when the berserker rage came over him.

He had never experienced it, but from his memory came tales of the Path of Ending. His mind and body shuddered in response to the death of his mate and the severing of their bond.

Reasonable thought processes were like smoke dissipated by a gust of wind, unable to form for more than a second before the rage snatched it away. K'rath no longer thought—he acted on impulse. On instinct. That instinct drove him to a suicidal, frenzied attack.

He burst from the trees, his lead followed by the other female. He charged up the rocky incline with terrifying physical ease. He fired up at the branches where the fatal shots had originated. Wood splinter and debris fell as the gigantic tree was all but cut in half by his shots.

Horne fell, struck in the helmet with three direct shots after he popped up out of cover to aim at the charging alien. The other had lined him up, stopping her advance temporarily as she fired a burst. Horne's head was rocked back with growing force until the energy transferring into his armor was too great for the resistance offered. Such force decapitated the human with the third impact. His headless body fell in Brandt's peripheral vision and despite the animosity between them, she felt the loss of another life under her command keenly.

Two more humans fell, hit in their torsos by the onslaught of fire as the Va'alen charged. Finally, Fal K'rath, enraged by the Path of Ending, swung his rifle in a vicious backhand blow to spin one of the smaller humans around twice. The human's pathetically small weapon flew from his hands. K'rath roared in challenge, dragged the claws of both upper hands across his chest to scratch a weeping X into his torso, and raised a foot to stamp down and crush the visor of his enemy.

K'rath faltered, the rage vanishing, as if his mind had been dropped into a vacuum. The mental whiplash left him staggering and breathless; the pain of his self-inflicted injury stabbed at him.

Bring the human to me alive, the voice invading his thoughts ordered.

K'rath was powerless to resist as the berserker fury partially came back to him. He was still enraged, but with that retuning anger came a control he had never known, as if something else were making his decisions for him. It was tricking his mind into believing he was in control.

He turned his body and threw out a strong leg to thump into the chest of a fast-moving human. It was tall and black in the gloom of the cave. K'rath's impact sent the human flying back in a glow of sudden blue, like it was shielded. The Va'alen fired two more bursts of fire, smashing the weapon out of the hands of another enemy to knock it back down. He turned and bellowed a roar of challenge at the others, daring them to come and be killed. He placed a foot on the chest of the one he had knocked down to signify ownership, just as if he were hunting big game.

Bring it to me! Now! the voice commanded, threatening to take the power from his legs. The mind control fought against K'rath's returning wrath. The voice boomed and echoed painfully inside his mind, forcing him to obey. He snatched up the metallic body of the unconscious human and sprang from the cave, beating down another human as it fled.

"Re—" Brandt coughed horribly as her entire body shook.
Her HUD flickered as her suit powered up. The energy of the alien weapon had surged the operating systems and shut it down before an automatic reboot had reconnected her with the world. Their armor, even being uprated since their last clash,

seemed woefully inefficient against the weapons of the Va'alen. "Report…"

"Commander," Specter said, leaning in front of her visor and shaking her shoulder gently. "Leslie…"

"I'm alright," she said as she pushed him off and stood uncertainly. "Sound off."

"Specter."

"Turner."

"Paterson," he groaned, evidently in pain.

"Payne."

"Sound off!" Brandt snapped again as she tried desperately to reboot the sub menu to see the vitals readouts for her team. She heard Payne calling for Zero, the pain of his silence evident in her words. Payne had been responsible for watching his back. Brandt finally rebooted her suit and brought up the bio-readings for her team. Horne had flatlined, as had Perez in the mech, and two others appeared weak. Zero and Rogers, both giving the pulse profile of being unconscious, caused her worry as she pushed aside the losses.

"Zero's alive," she said. "Find him. And Rogers seems to be unconscious."

She looked down at her empty hands; black scorch marks confused her. After a moment, her brain caught up and reminded her that her weapon had exploded in her hands when struck by an energy discharge from a Va'alen weapon.

She reached down for the pistol on her right thigh and stopped, seeing the discarded pulse rifle of her enemy lying on the rocky ground. She stooped to pick it up and found it to weigh far less than she imagined.

"Who is good to go?" she snapped.

"I am," Specter answered in an instant as he appeared beside her.

"Got a…" Paterson gasped, "got a power drain in my suit…"

"I saw it take Rogers," Payne said. "It went that way." Her HUD flashed a waypoint onto theirs.

"Paterson's hit bad," Turner said as Brandt spun to see the medic helping Paterson to the uneven ground. "The shot took some of his armor away at the ribs. He's bleeding bad."

"Fix him up," Brandt ordered. "Payne, find Zero and get him back here. Watch over them."

"I've found him," Payne answered. "Bastard shot him out the tree."

"Give me his rifle," Specter said.

Payne appeared, dragging the unconscious sniper behind her, and tossed the customized battle rifle to the cyborg.

"We going?" Specter asked Brandt.

She nodded and turned as another roar of animalistic challenge tore the thick, humid air. She spun, seeing the last of their attackers rear up, injured, to charge them. Without thought, she raised the alien rifle and instinctively nestled it into her shoulder. She sighted down the barrel and saw the unfamiliar targeting holo highlight the beast. Brandt squeezed, rattling off a pulsating burst of automatic fire into it, dropping the alien dead. Its momentum made it slew lifelessly over the dirt, coming to rest a dozen paces from the humans.

Satisfied, Brandt lowered her new gun and set off at a run after the kidnapped pilot.

CHAPTER 26

Deep Orbit of Proxima Centauri

"ETA two minutes," the tactical officer called out over the bridge of the *Indomitable*.

"Two minutes to our weapons range or to the gun barges?" Dassiova asked in return.

"The gun barges. Sorry, Admiral."

"It's okay, son," Dassiova said as soothingly as his gravelly growl could manage. "You just keep your eyes on that console. Comm, open up a line to the barges." The comm officer hit some icons, then turned and nodded to the admiral.

"We have incoming, as I'm sure you're well aware. The second they come into range, you let rip with everything you've got. Unload it all, then fall back to a closer defensive position. *Indomitable* out."

"Where do you need us, Admiral?" Halstead's voice came over the speakers.

"Where we discussed, Captain," Dassiova said, "and wait for my mark, that understood?"

Both frigate captains acknowledged his order, despite feeling uneasy about it. Rank was information, Hayes knew. The higher up you got in rank, the more information you had.

He was high up enough to know most things, but the overall battle plan was Dassiova's to run. The ground-pounder played space battle like infantry ambushes, to the point where very few of their

242

mostly space-faring commanders would be capable of catching him out.

Outside the box, he thought. *That's how he thinks and that's why he's in charge.*

"*Ichi* to *Indomitable*." Torres's voice filled the bridge as he hailed them.

"Go for Dassiova," the admiral replied.

"Admiral, all mines laid, and the enemy has only one direct course safely left open for them. The last mines are detectable as you ordered. Permission to join the fight?"

Dassiova, pleased that Torres had done as he was asked and not tried anything heroic and dumb, considered the request.

"Negative, *Ichi*," he said, knowing he was disappointing the captain. "I need you ready to jump ahead to get your people the moment we've dealt with these assholes. Withdraw to the station and protect the rear from anything slipping by. Out." He cut the comm to prevent any time wasted on his orders being questioned.

"Come on, you sons of bitches," he said, "Show me your faces and let me cure you—"

His concentration was broken by a warning message flashing up on his private console.

UNAUTHORIZED SUBSPACE COMMUNICATION

"Massey?" he said, confused. The flight officer didn't respond. An overwhelming sense of suspicion washed down his spine like a trickle of cold water in a shower. The admiral locked eyes with Asha, who seemed to know what he knew in the same instant. He shouted for her again but received only blank looks from his bridge crew.

"Mainframe," he said to the ship's computer interface, "Locate Flight Officer Massey."

"Unable to comply," the computerized voice said annoyingly. "Flight Officer Suranne Massey does not have an active transponder chip."

"What the hell?" Dassiova said. A shout interrupted him.

"Enemy in range! Gun barges opening fire."

The black void of their sector of space, backlit by the dull, red glow of the red dwarf star, erupted in a huge wave of orange bolts and blue trails of streaking nukes. The barrage, shown on screen on the main bridge of every ship in the fleet, took an eternity to reach the enemy. They had already begun to evade the onslaught. Those ships that left their path to miss the incoming fire found themselves trapped in a shrouded minefield into which they had been lured. Bright, electric blue blossoms filled the dark expanse as Va'alen fighters died in droves. But the fight had only just begun.

A returning salvo, equal in size and savagery to the human fleet, streaked back at them. Singularity munitions caught by the energy weapons burst into blooms of darker black tinged with electric arcs. They collapsed and drew other missiles into their death grip. The threshold of destruction erupted as the first wave of untouched enemy fighters burst through and engaged by the cannons of the huge flagship. Streaks of blue and orange flew out at all angles as the gun pods targeted each enemy vessel at a ratio of three to one. More muted explosions punctuated the space around the ships; gun barges steamed back toward their mothership to act as point defense platforms. A few ships, not many, flew past the warships to the vulnerable vessels in the rear, only to be cut down by murderous fire from the new and now fully operational space station.

More ships added their guns to the fight; *Cortez, Venture, Anvil, Ichi,* all unleashed as much personal hell as they could bring to bear and prevented any of the lone pairs from reaching the soft belly of the Ninth Fleet.

Blue bursts appeared on the shields of the fleet carrier, as unpaired Va'alen turned kamikaze and dove their ships in suicide runs to bring down the shields of the behemoth.

"Report," barked the admiral as another twin concussion shook his ship.

"Port side shields down to fifty-nine percent," cried the tactical officer as he regained his feet.

"Helm, spin us around," Dassiova ordered. "Show these bastards our good side."

"Aye aye," Lieutenant Moon chimed back from the pilot's chair.

The ship responded quickly to his commands, and rotated on a horizontal axis to effectively flip them upside down to where they had begun. It was the fastest means of showing their starboard side, and gravity was only relevant in atmosphere.

"Enemy numbers?" Dassiova shouted over the sound of another flurry of impacts.

"Forty percent at my guess," the tactical officer replied. "They just keep coming!"

"Then we just keep goddamned killing them," the admiral snarled back. He tapped the console beside him, opening up the channel to the two frigates he had ready to go.

"Dassiova to *Hammer* and *Vengeance*," he shouted over the percussive sound of battle.

The subspace comm link blinked to life. Both Hayes and Halstead, cringing at having to watch a battle on long-range sensors, had waited as patiently as they could for the order.

"*Now!*" came the admiral's voice over the speakers.

"Activate jump," Hayes cried, holding back whoop of cruel joy.

Both frigates blinked out of existence in the far-off sector of space where they had been sent to hide. When they reappeared in real space, their sensors lit up with a Christmas tree effect.

"All guns, weapons free," he yelled, trusting his people to do their job like the stone-cold professional experts he knew them to be.

The ship shuddered as munitions thumped out of launch tubes to streak death toward the remnants of the Va'alen armada, and the remaining forty percent of attackers halved in under thirty seconds. The two frigates poured fire into the enemy, killing them without mercy and taking very little damage. The enemy's guns had been focused on the gargantuan carrier, as Dassiova had known they would be.

"Dassiova to Torres, you are good to go get your people."

"Thank you, Admiral," Torres replied simply, as the *Ichi* blinked off the sensor grid.

"Remaining flight of enemy have broken off!" Dassiova announced on the fleet-wide comm channel, "Good wor—"

"Admiral!" the tactical officer called out with panic evident in his voice.

Dassiova broke off from claiming victory and looked at the sensor display readings. He saw it before he was told.

"Second wave incoming!"

He read the data, calculated simple numbers in his head, and saw a second attack heading for them.

"ETA twelve minutes," he was told.

"Time to re-arm the frigates?" he asked.

"Err, twenty-six minutes, sir... and that's if they were already docked to the *Cortez*." He had done his best, and still he felt as though he had failed everyone.

"Prepare to fall back to the station," he said gravely. "Every last human fights to their last round."

"Three readings, all very long range, Captain," the ensign informed Torres.

"Good. Helm? Lay in the co-ordinates from the comm burst and get us there, full burn."

"Sir?" Rogers's replacement asked. "Shouldn't we Shroud and travel at half speed?"

"You want the chair, Lieutenant?" Torres asked harshly with a single finger pointed down at the captain's occupied command seat. The pilot shook his head and swallowed, turning to lay in the course and hit the throttle.

To hell with stealth, Torres told himself. *Outrun anything that comes near us. Go fast and go hard; get our people out and get back home.*

"Course laid in, Captain," his new pilot said. "Engaging maximum engine speed."

They were approaching orbit within fifteen minutes, not wanting to jump in too close to the gravity wells of the planets and the large star.

"Get me a full scan of the surface," Torres ordered. He forced himself to stay seated and not pace the bridge. "I don't want to find out about any more orbital-strike capable rail guns *after* they've opened fire. Comm, we got anything?"

"Negative, sir. I'm detecting some chatter on open source in what looks like Va'alen. Nothing from our people."

"Get a fix on their transponders," Torres demanded.

"No can do, Cap," the young ensign said. He instantly regretted his casual words and carried on quickly. "Ion storms in the atmosphere are making it pretty difficult to get anything through. I'll stay on it."

"Good. Comm, I want you to put out intermittent wideband hails on all of our frequencies. Get some hooks in the water and see if we can't catch us a bite."

It took a further half hour before their patience paid off.

"Captain, we have a resonating reading from the surface. It looks... it looks like a singularity collapse crater. But the *Tanto* wasn't equipped with any si— Oh."

"We don't know anything until we know, Ensign," Torres said stoically. His heart sank as he was faced with the irrefutable sensor data that must have been the crash site of their shuttle and the subsequent loss of singularity drive containment. "If nobody survived the crash, who sent us a 'come get me' message?"

"Good point, sir," the ensign replied, still unable to keep the disappointment from his words. "Wait... I'm getting something in a cloud gap... Va'alen base, without a doubt."

"How big?"

"Smaller than a town, easily, no weapons signatures detected."

"Shroud up," Torres barked. "Are we able to reach them with our weapons?"

"Doubtful, Captain," Sarvanto said. "We're geared for ship-to-ship and not orbital bombardment."

"Captain!" the comm officer yelled. "We're getting an incoming comm. It's weak..."

CHAPTER 27

Unnamed Moon Surface

"And we're sure he's in there?" Brandt whispered to Specter over their channel.

"Without a doubt," came the barely synthesized reply. "I have his transponder on line-of-sight link."

"Enemy?"

"Count fifteen," Specter said.

"Can we take them?"

"Only one way to find out," he said. She could hear the smile in his voice. She knew his glee wasn't flippant. It was borne of the cruel satisfaction of a man created for war being given the opportunity to do what he did best.

"On your go," Brandt said over the comm.

Speed was the key to recovering their pilot alive. Far off to her left, near Specter's position, the air boomed with a dull crump. A super-charged projectile was sent through the dry air to cross the open ground. She kept her eyes on the alien optical holo-display projected above the barrel of her newly stolen weapon. Ahead of her, one of the two Va'alen above what looked like the main gate went rigid as an atomized cloud of its internal fluids blossomed into the still air. The alien beside it flinched, watching as the dead warrior toppled over the edge, plummeting downward. It turned its gun out and began firing indiscriminately. The second alien dropped a heartbeat later as the 12mm bullet streaked through the air and punched a hole through it with a perfect center mass kill.

That one fell backward into the walled compound as roars of alarm reverberated out of sight of the two attackers.

"Easier to kill when they aren't fired up and charging at you," Brandt said softly to Specter.

"You think the bravest warriors would be posted here, at the ass end of the galaxy, guarding a wall with no enemy on the planet?" he asked, changing her mindset about their foe.

"Good point," she agreed. "So we've got the weak, lame and lazy to contend with here?"

Before he could respond, a roar sounded from behind the gate as other voices, louder and deeper, joined the one who'd started up the battle cry.

Aq D'marath, despite his unfortunately small stature for a Va'alen, considered himself a brave warrior. His father had retired from active expeditions and was now enjoying a seat on one of the clan high councils. He had returned the proud victor of dozens of forays out into the galaxy. He was perpetually disappointed with his first spawn and had covered the younger one's lack of natural aggression and ability by circumventing the military channels through political ties. He had purchased, threatened, bargained and traded for his son to advance to Aq ahead of any of his peers, but that was as far as wealth and influence could take him. The reward for his appointment to the biggest expedition known to the alliance was for D'marath to be made lord and master of an uninhabited rock, where he was given a detachment no bigger than a palace guard to protect some crystal mineral miners from the local bird population.

D'marath had complained. He had petitioned his father to exert influence once more on his behalf. He pleaded for the next wave of reinforcements through the portal to bring him home, or to bring him a loyal force large enough to make him a leading voice among the Aqs. His father had no mind to do the former and no purse to afford the latter; sending warriors through unsponsored by the allied clans was a costly venture. His response, a simple data comm containing his answer, was to tell his son to find some enemy and bathe in their blood to make the other Aqs respect him. 'It is earned by trial,' his comm had said. 'It is not bought or given freely. Find your own glory.'

D'marath stood at the inside of the gates, after he'd been roused from his relaxation by the return of the scarred and bloodied Fal K'rath. The Fal dragged behind him what appeared to be a dead human still in its metal carapace. D'marath found himself summarily ordered to rouse every warrior and defend the base. His first thought was to challenge the Fal, but as he rose to do so, he saw the crossed wounds to his chest and knew that he must have lost his mate to these humans. The fact that he had not berserked, had not followed the sacrosanct Path of Ending, frightened him into complying.

He roused his guard, led them toward the defenses, and watched in horror as the two warriors posted above the main gate fell to unknown enemy fire. D'marath turned to his warriors, all bigger than he, and none enthused by the prospect of imminent battle.

"We are Va'alen," he cried, seeing as only a few of them stirred. "We. Are. Va'alen!" He bellowed at them. "We fear no enemy, and we seek glorious death in battle!" He leaned back and spread all four of his arms wide as he issued a roar of challenge to the sky. Other warriors took up the call, and the sudden elation that they were following him into battle buoyed his spirits to previously unknown heights.

D'marath was a warrior. He was a leader. He was invincible, and he would tear the enemy limb from limb.

Pushing his way to the gate ahead of his warriors, he ordered it open and made sure he was the first brave and true Va'alen to leave the safety of the compound. As he crossed the threshold, he envisaged with wondrous glory the stories of his bravery echoing throughout the Va'alen empire for eternity.

~

The gate burst open as the roar still filled the air. Brandt, much closer than Specter in his elevated sniper position, saw the smaller alien at the head of the charge and proceeded to riddle his torso with shots from her new weapon. It faltered, dropped to its knees, and was stampeded by the other aliens running behind it as though it were a thing of no significance; weak cannon fodder to be sent out first.

Specter's weapon crunched its unique report over and over as the shots drilled into the tightly packed advance. Any that faltered or tried to break off were stitched with automatic fire from Brandt. Nine of them died within fifty paces of the gate, and only three remained on their feet as the return fire found the rocks near Brandt's position.

Forced to duck and retreat, she slithered to lower ground and sprinted low along the defilade. She counted to ten, then popped up and drilled a handful of bursts into the flank of the attack. She dropped one just as a bullet from Specter blew the shoulder off another. It turned around on the spot, looking for its missing arm, which lay on the dusty ground. Brandt used the hesitation to hit it hard with ten shots to the chest and watched as it writhed on its feet like a landed fish before falling to the ground. The last one standing turned and fired on her, scoring a glancing blow that temporarily shut down the servos in her right arm and forced her to drop the weapon.

She dived for cover, tucking herself small and hiding from the incoming fire as it advanced. Specter's rifle had gone quiet and she called for him over the radio. She heard nothing in response, then the firing stopped suddenly. She emerged from cover to see the wide blade sheathed in the forearm of his armor protruding from the open mouth of the Va'alen fewer than ten paces from her position.

"You good?" he asked her.

She stood, shaking her numb right arm; the neurological feedback had caused a kind of psychosomatic pain response. She bent to pick up the Va'alen rifle as Specter did the same; Zero's rifle on his back and his own pistols on his thighs.

"I'm good," she said. "Let's get our pilot back."

~

"...immediate medevac... KIA...epeat... equesting S.A.R. to th... ordinates... two casualti..."

"Clean that up," Torres ordered with a snap of his fingers at the comm officer.

She bit back an immediate retort that she wasn't a miracle worker. With a sigh that managed to stay mostly internal, she tried to modify the frequency harmonics to 'clean up' the digital broadcast signal going out over a wideband burst through an alien ion storm

253

about a hundred miles below them. To her amazement, the broadcast came through a little more clearly.

"…UN vessel in this sector… is the cr… of the UNS *Tant*… ash landed on moon orbi… anet nearest the larger of the tw… uns… equesting immed… earch and rescue to these coordina… two casualties and three KIA…"

The bridge of the *Ichi* was silent for a moment before Torres broke the deadlock. "Can we get a fix on it?"

"Close enough, sir," the tactical officer announced. "Only problem is getting through the ion storm in one piece. We're pretty banged up still an—"

"God*dammit*, Ensign," Torres erupted unexpectedly. "You're not paid to state the obvious to me every time I give an order."

"Yes, sir," the chided young man said as he ducked his head back to his console.

"So, we have a rough fix on the transmission area, yes?" the captain asked in a more patient tone.

An affirmative, albeit a relatively sulky one, came from tac.

"Good. Comm, get a link up to the fleet and request a frigate with dropship capability. We need a support team on the ground."

"Sir, fleet aren't responding to subspace hails." Torres blinked.

"They what now?"

"The fleet, sir," the comm officer repeated. "They aren't responding to our hails on subspace." As though the same information repeated in a slightly different way was even more confusing, Torres's mind couldn't make the dots connect.

"Sir, I have an idea," the ensign at tactical said.

"All ears, Ensign," Torres said.

"How about a probe? We fire it at the surface and the comm boosters act like a relay from the surface to us up here." "Could that work?" Torres asked Sarvanto, who looked at the ensign and shrugged his agreement.

"Do it."

"I'll need to reconfigure the sensor array to gather all UN frequencies and feed them directly back to us. The ground team won't necessarily know what we've done and wouldn't think to transmit on a narrow-band fr—"

"Ensign," Torres interrupted. "First off, you need to get an internal monologue or you and I will fall out on a permanent basis. Secondly, how long?"

"Probe is launched," he said. "Reconfiguring now. Should be active by the time it lands." He looked around to see the captain's raised eyebrow and added quickly, "Oh, about two and a half minutes."

It was closer to ninety seconds when the probe rigged to act as the tin can on the other end of their piece of string gave them a clear link.

"This is a distress call to any UN ship in this sector. This is the crew of the UNS *Tanto*. We have crash-landed on the small moon orbiting the planet closest to the larger of the two suns. Hostile alien and indigenous life on the planet. We have two currently injured, repeat two casualties and three KIA. Requesting immediate medevac. Send S.A.R. to the coordinates of this transmission."

"*Tanto* ground, this is *Ichi* actual, over," Torres said confidently.

"Captain? Oh, thank God…"

"Identify," Torres instructed.

"Payne, sir, PO2."

"Payne, are you currently under fire, over?" Torres asked clearly and carefully as the transmission hazed out into static.

"Negative, but Specter and the Commander have gone after Rogers."

"Wait. From the beginning, Payne. Where the hell is Rogers and why have Specter and Commander Brandt gone after him?"

"Sir," Payne said as she forced herself to slow down. "We've been stalked by a pack of Va'alen, and they've taken Rogers. Only four of us are still combat effective; one of those is Turner, the medic, who is dealing with two casualties. I'm ordered to provide overwatch for Turner. Specter and the commander are right behind the son of a bitch who snatched our pilot."

Payne didn't have any more details, which made Torres bite back an angry retort—she didn't need the added stress. To add to his worries, there was still no response from the fleet.

He was on his own, with no dropships, no shuttle, almost no troops onboard and was almost out of options.

"Take us into low orbit," he said, "as close as possible to the ion clouds."

"Sir," Sarvanto asked, drawing out the word like an accusation. "What are you thinking?"

"Tac, how intermittent is the storm over their rough position?"

"Err, there are cloud gaps pretty often… but…"

"But what, Ensign?"

"But anyone who jumped a low-orbit insertion through this would be lucky not to get fried by an electrical discharge and burn their suit's systems. Heard the term 'fly like a rock'?"

He raised his hand and lowered it slowly with an accompanying descending whistle, "*Whoooooo…*"

"Thank you, Ensign," Torres said tersely.

"Sir, I must insist that you do not—" Sarvanto said, stopping as Torres stood suddenly.

"You have the bridge, Mister Sarvanto," he announced formally, cutting off the polite flight officer before he could finish his official protest. "Try to establish comms with the fleet and get us some help here."

He turned and left the bridge, leaving the crew stunned at his sudden departure. Some of them knew how affected he had been by the loss of the ground team and the subsequent detention of the fleet's traitor. None of them knew how deeply Eze's betrayal had hurt him on a personal level.

He walked down the corridor from the bridge and into the soldiers' ready room, where the remnant of his ground force was assembled. They stood as he walked in, unsure of what to do when he walked past them to his own armor and opened it up. They stared at him as he stepped inside and powered it up, stepping down from the charging plinth and rolling his shoulders as though flexing tired muscles. Giving away his intentions by unpacking a 'chute and a set of stabilizer repulsers which he attached to his boots, knees and shoulders, he turned to the noises behind him. All three soldiers were loading into their own armor suits and gearing up.

"Planning on going somewhere?" he asked them innocently.

"You really think we're going to hold our heads high when everyone finds out we let the ship's captain jump out of a perfectly good ship when we stayed here with our thumbs up our asses?"

He left the ready room, walking into the next section of the ship where the grizzled old armorer seemed to have anticipated his arrival. He offered up a pistol and a submachine-gun. Torres locked them to his back—he anticipated a near-lethal drop from the lower limits of the void—and watched as the other troops armed themselves.

Torres smiled at them, activated the helmet on his suit and dropped through the tube to the empty shuttle bay.

CHAPTER 28

Unnamed Moon Surface

Rogers came to as he was thrown across a room. He spun after he landed, skidding hard until his helmet clanged off the far wall.

"Ow," he said sarcastically. His suit wasn't the fully armored and war-capable rig that the fighting members of their party wore. His was designed for survival as well as short-term void and atmospheric protection.

"Silence, filthy human," the Va'alen snarled at him from its position pacing angrily by the door.

Having just regained consciousness, Rogers slowly registered the fact that the Va'alen had just spoken to him in English instead of his suit translating the snarls and hisses of its own language.

"You spea— *aargh*!" Rogers didn't finish his question as a gnarled foot shot forward to slam his chest back into the wall a second time. "Ow! *Asshole*!"

The Va'alen roared, so wired that it seemed unable to contain its rage.

As Rogers's wits returned to him fully, he noticed a presence in the room with them. *Notice* wasn't the right word; he *felt* a presence. A floating consciousness at the back of his mind that pressed in on him. It pulsated and surged like powerful electricity running through a cable. A sensation of fear made a sudden assault on his bladder control. He fought it for a moment, then remembered that his suit

258

would deal with it in a second and stopped fighting it. With that pressure and panic subsiding, his mind was free to explore the emotion he felt.

The feeling wasn't his own frightened reaction; it was more that his mind was being forced to imagine fear. Once he realized that, it had no power over him. Another thing, he realized, was that the sensation was exactly the same as when the Kuldar he had met experienced an emotional response.

The enraged, pacing Va'alen monster, who still dripped thick viscera from his self-inflicted wounds, stopped its incessant movement. It arched its back slightly, shuddered, and grew unnaturally still.

"You, human," it said in a quieter, more controlled voice.

"Last time I checked, dude," Rogers said. His first contact protocols would come straight from the cocky sarcasm playbook. The creature shuddered again and paced forward to lean down at him. He remained slumped against the wall as his eyes ran through the sub-menus on his suit.

"You," hissed the alien as it pointed both right hands at him, "should not be here. This is *our* system; we have claimed it as our own."

"Yeah, well," Rogers began, his mind half on the conversation as he flicked through the long list of options on his HUD, "that's the thing about humans. You see, we're not really good at keeping to ourselves, if you know what I mean."

The Va'alen issued another roar as it seemed to fight with itself before growing still once more.

"You will all be," it paused, seeming to stumble on the next word, "*ee-radicatedd.*"

"That's a little harsh, don't you think?" Rogers said back peevishly. "I mean, *sure*, write a strongly worded complaint or something, but genocide? Too far, dude. Too far."

He managed not to cry out with a triumphant *a-ha!* as he located something useful. The suits had built-in features for high-altitude drops. As that option was deemed a combat capability, there were defensive measures available to the driver. Defensive measures in this case meant flares.

"You know what *I* think?" Rogers asked, all sarcasm dropped from his voice. The alien didn't answer. "*I* think you can shove it up your ass."

He activated the flares and clamped his eyes shut, expecting an approximation of Ragnarok to come to the small room in an instant. Nothing happened. He opened one eye tentatively and saw the error message displayed on his HUD.

ERROR: INSUFFICIENT ALTITUDE TO DEPLOY COUNTERMEASURES

The low growl of the Va'alen pierced his panicked thoughts as it stomped forward.

"I didn't mean that!" Rogers tried quickly, but any other words were drowned out. He was picked up and slammed back down repeatedly by the enraged alien.

"Anything?" Brandt asked.

"Two hundred paces, your two o'clock," Specter shot back. He had locked in on Rogers's transponder. Brandt's suit still had intermittent software failures after the glancing blow from the Va'alen energy rifle she now carried.

"I'm seeing no other enemy," she said, nervous that such a large compound would only have a small detachment of defenders.

"Neither am I," Specter replied.

They moved to the low building, constructed of the same material and in the same style as the abandoned outpost they had holed up in, only this was well-maintained and fully intact. Brandt stood to one side of the doorframe and scanned the open area behind them while Specter assessed the lock.

"Screw it," he said after a few seconds.

He took three paces back to raise the alien rifle in his left hand. He gave Brandt a nod to step aside and fired a quick burst of three or four big pulses of directed energy that mangled the prefabricated metal of the building and caved the door inward. He followed up the shots with two long, powerful strides and connected an armored boot to the remnants of the door. It screeched and complained as the tortured metal opened up to allow them access.

"Forty meters," Specter said quietly. He indicated a ten o'clock direction with the blade of his artificial right hand; the weapon was still gripped firmly in his left and tucked into his shoulder.

They moved at a crouch, leap-frogging one another and covering every possible concealed place where an enemy with a weapon could be lying in wait. Brandt, despite the highly irregular situation, took a second to marvel at the thrill of working beside someone so highly skilled, before she snapped herself back to the full reality. Specter stopped, right fist clenched up and away from his weapon, before the fist bladed into a flat hand once more and indicated a door dead ahead.

She hesitated.

Sure would be nice to call in some backup right about now, she thought.

A blood-curdling scream sounded muffled from inside the room, and all hesitation left her mind.

⁓

Nathan Rogers, feeling devoid of bravery following his failed attempt to blind the alien and escape, suffered white-outs in his vision from being hammered off the bulkheads and deck of the small, dark room. That room was his personal hell. A hell where an enraged alien was slamming his body around like a rag doll.

No, he thought. *Scratch that; like one of those apes that used to be endangered. Like it's marking its dominance or something by displaying how strong it was.*

His HUD flashed in and out. Connections were bounced around worse than any crash-landing was expected to cause. But in the moments when it was active, he saw the red health and injury messages pop up like error codes, and each subsequent one seemed to push him closer to unconsciousness and ultimately death.

WARNING: DAMAGE TO INTERNAL ORGANS –
IMPACT TO SPLEEN DETECTED. SEEK MEDICAL
ASSISTANCE IMMEDIATELY.
WARNING: INTERNAL BLEEDING DETECTED. SEEK
MEDICAL ASSISTANCE IMMEDIATELY.
WARNING: FRACTURE TO RIGHT HUMERUS
DETECTED. ISOLATING LIMB. SEEK MEDICAL
ASSISTANCE IMMEDIATELY.

ERROR: UNABLE TO ISOLATE RIGHT ARM DUE TO
SERVO MOTOR MALFUNCTION. SEEK SUIT
ENGINEER ASSISTANCE.
WARNING: FRACTURE TO RIBS DETECTED. SEEK
MEDICAL ASSISTANCE IMMEDIATELY.
WARNING: DISLOCATION OF LEFT KNEE DETECTED.
ISOLATING LIMB. SEEK MEDICAL ASSISTANCE
IMMEDIATELY.

The long feed of error and warning messages stacked up and provided a distraction from the cruel and savage beating he was receiving as his limp body was thrown against the walls repeatedly. The alien bellowed, a guttural, animal noise that spoke more of pain than of rage. It faltered, staggering on its feet and shaking. It froze before resuming its attack. Twice more it seemed to hesitate before the onslaught finally stopped.

"Get out of your metal skin, human," it said.

A human would have been out of breath from the exertion of so savagely beating someone, but the voice showed no indication of being winded. Rogers said nothing, but kept his jaw clamped firmly shut as a tiny pinprick sensation stung the back of his neck.

It was his suit administering pain relief and a stimulant to keep Rogers conscious, now that it been given a few seconds to take stock of his current state. The pilot wished he could turn the function off so that he would be allowed to go off into unconsciousness quickly and not suffer for the extended period he feared would be his last interrogation.

He would have given anything at that point to be back behind the controls of a ship in the safety of the fleet. He cursed his childish need to be at the front of every line when a dangerous mission was on offer. He cursed himself for not undertaking more combat training or learning how to use one of the more complex armor suits that the fighting crew members used.

Then Rogers realized that the feelings of regret and hopelessness and self-blame weren't his feelings. He was again being forced to experience something that didn't originate in his own mind.

"Are you…" he hissed through gritted teeth. The pain racked him despite the drugs. "Are you trying to control my mind?" Said aloud, the question seemed stupid. It wasn't as though he believed the comic book science fiction of his childhood, with its aliens coming to Earth and conquering the population with their mind control devices.

The Va'alen warrior paused again, as though fighting its own body, and shuddered before it became suddenly still.

"I am controlling this body," it said. "Although it is very difficult because this one is experiencing the Path of Ending. The emotions it is feeling are too strong for any of my kind to control for long. Why are you not letting me into your mind, human?"

"Into my *mind*?" Rogers blurted out. "Are you *insane*? Of course I won't let you into my mind!"

"How do you do this?" hissed the still Va'alen. "Does your metal skin protect you?"

Rogers had no idea if the armor prevented the mind control—he still couldn't get away from that imagery—but he was damned if he was going to admit anything. He stalled for time, in the desperate hope that help was on the way.

"No, my metal skin doesn't protect me—you can't penetrate my mind because I am stronger than you are."

Rogers tried to fight through the pain and give a theatrical resonance to his words, but it was too difficult to endure. Plus, he winced in childish anguish at having said the word 'penetrate' and kept himself from giggling. He knew he was starting to be delirious as the pain meds and stress threatened to push him over the edge of reason. The Va'alen growled and shuddered again as it took a forced step toward him. He shuffled back against the wall and cradled his right arm as the forward momentum of his tormentor stopped again. The hulking beast shuddered and went still once more.

"It takes great strength to control this body," it said. "Tell me your secret and I will see to it that you live."

"No," Rogers growled back as he doubled down on his dramatic performance. "Spare my life and surrender, and I will see to it that *you* live."

Silence answered him as though his counter offer was being considered carefully.

"I… cannot control this body any longer… tell me your…" The Va'alen shook uncontrollably. It raked all four long, curved claws across its chest in an X to reopen the scabbed wounds and drip more thick fluid onto the deck. It opened its mouth wide and unleashed the loudest roar Rogers had ever heard. Finally, it dropped its head to look directly at the pilot, coiled its body as it sank down onto powerful legs, and pounced.

~

Such was the volume of the alien roar, Brandt and Specter heard the roar through the metal wall as though it was inside their own helmets. A glance at one another said enough, and Specter strode three paces and slammed a boot into the door where it met the frame.

It didn't budge. He kicked it again and again until some play appeared and the sounds from inside grew louder. Roars and snarls punctuated by metallic noises and muted screams. Screams of pain, torn from the mouth of a human being inside compromised armor.

Specter changed tactics. Instead of trying to kick the door in, he reached over to mag lock the alien gun to his back. It failed to lock and dropped to clatter on the deck. He ignored it, and hooked his gauntleted fingers into the gap created by his kicks. He tore at the door, bending the protesting metal with all of his doubly enhanced strength until a gap appeared large enough to see inside.

"Move!" Brandt yelled.

A Va'alen, the same one who had rushed them with impossible speed and unfettered violence in the nearby cave, attacked Rogers so ferociously that she was sure he was dead. The alien held something in the claws of its left arms that poured liquid onto the poorly lit deck. When Brandt realized in utter horror that it was an arm, still in the armored greave, she aimed her weapon and paused.

The beast froze and began to shake uncontrollably. It went into spasm, arms bending at unnatural angles as it convulsed and fell into a heap on lifeless legs. Even when prone on the deck, with black sludge leaking out in a widening puddle from its corpse, it continued to twitch as though willing any of them to come close enough to its claws, to be torn apart. Specter shoved her aside as he tore at the door again, calling Rogers by name over and over.

He ordered the pilot to stay with him, in a voice so firm yet full of empathy and emotion, that he was almost indistinguishable from the old Jake. Finally forcing the door open, they piled inside, finding Rogers unconscious. Specter hit the commands on the pilot's comm device and breathed a sigh of relief. The automated protocols had saved his life and activated a tourniquet that was built in at strategic points to the limbs of their suits.

"He's alive and stable," Specter said, "but he won't be for long."

"We need to get him back to the fleet," Brandt said, "but he's our only pilot."

"I can fly," Specter said, ignoring the shocked silence of his friend and commander. "We need a ship."

CHAPTER 29

Deep Orbit of Proxima Centauri

Dassiova was speechless as he looked at the display beside his command chair. Everyone in the fleet, from the ratings to the specialist engineers, was doing their duty to the best of their ability. He was certain of that, though he was less certain that he was performing his own duties to the required standard.

"Admiral, *Venture* reports less than fifty percent shields remaining," cried the comm officer over the sound of a sparking, muted explosion in a nearby console.

The second wave of enemy ships was just as large, if not larger than the first. The empty ordnance launch tubes of his fleet could not be cycled fast enough to turn the tide this time.

"Second gun barge destroyed by enemy fire," the tactical officer reported in a flat tone, which hung heavy with accusation.

Dassiova had given it his all, and it hadn't been enough. He racked his brain for anything else he could do; any insane, out of the box plan he could come up with as the *Indomitable* shuddered with each impact of the Va'alen armada's weapons and suicide runs. He reached for the console and the fleet-wide comm channel he had programmed ready. He prepared himself to give the order to abandon the system and everything they had fought for, had bled for. His finger hovered over the icon, fear of failure and a stinging pride making him hesitate, when the tactical officer shouted another warning.

"Multiple ship readings," he cried.

I'm aware of that, Dassiova thought bitterly to himself. *Hell, I could reach out a window and probably slap an enemy ship, there are so goddamned many of them.*

"More jump signatures," the tactical officer said again.

Jump signatures? Plural? Dassiova questioned. *The only fleet asset not here is the* Ichi.

"On screen," he ordered, the battle raging outside temporarily forgotten until another impact shook him in his chair. The viewscreen blinked to life, the display cutting out a couple of times, before the image stabilized and formed a curious mirror of what he imagined their fleet to look like.

"That's..." he said uncertainly, his words trailing off.

"Sir, incoming hail."

"Put it through," he said, pausing until he got the nod from his comm officer.

"Unidentified vessels, this is Admiral Dassiova of the UNS *Indomitable*. We are under attack by a fleet of hostile aliens and request immediate assistance."

Silence.

"Unidentified vessels—" Dassiova began again angrily before being cut off.

"Admiral Dassiova," came the crooning and unmistakably human response, "what would you offer for our assistance?"

Dassiova frowned, nodding at the comm officer, who activated the video link. The image of multiple ships was replaced by an Arabic-looking man in his fifties, wearing a black uniform and sitting in a command chair almost identical to the admiral's own.

"Identify yourself," Dassiova demanded.

"I," the man said with a smug arrogance as he placed a flat hand on the chest of his uniform, "am the General Chakour of the Middle

Eastern Alliance. My fleet is willing to engage the enemy if you give your word that we will enter into negotiations in good faith. Alternatively, I could order my fleet to withdraw and return to finish off the Va'alen when they have destroyed you."

So many questions boiled up inside Dassiova that he could barely corral them to arrive out of his mouth in any semblance of order. He wanted to know who the hell the Middle Eastern Alliance was, what they were doing with a fleet that looked almost identical to his, why the man called himself a general when that rank had been abandoned worldwide generations before. Most of all, however, he wanted to know what he would be agreeing to if he accepted the help. A series of heavy impacts rocked him in his chair as he wasted precious seconds thinking, before a scream from an injured bridge officer forced him to respond.

"Very well, General," he said. He tried to ignore the sinking feeling that he was about to whip back the covers and jump into bed with the devil himself. "You have my word that we will have discussions in good faith when we are all safe. Dassiova out."

He turned to his comm officer who had already severed the link. His face was an unreadable mask as he ordered someone to get the injured female officer to the medical bay. She was clutching her face tightly, with blood seeping between her fingers. He sat down, tapped the fleet-wide comm icon, and growled his brief orders to all ships and the space station.

"Ninth Fleet, this is the Admiral," he began, feeling defensive of his crown as another bull had entered the field. "An additional human fleet has entered this sector. We have a truce with them until the Va'alen are defeated… hold your nerves, people, and we will see this thing through to the end."

He felt a surge of pride as the enemy attack lessened. The new ships joined the fight, attacking from all flanks with their energy weapon cannons and doubling the rate of enemy destruction in moments. After a moment, he realized that the pride hadn't originated with him, but had come from the small alien smiling at him from the observer's chair to his right. Asha was radiating the feeling that Dassiova had just saved them all.

"Don't get too excited just yet," he said quietly to the Kuldar ambassador. "I get the feeling that we're in for a rough ride before things get straightened out."

The Va'alen armada's commander watched the progress of his attack with satisfaction. He was under orders to command the second wave and not die in glorious battle with the first attack. Having waited for what felt like an eternity, as he and hundreds of other warriors moved slowly under the safety of their cloaks, they felt that mirroring the cowardly tactics of their human enemy lacked the honor of a direct assault. When their first wave was all but destroyed, the commander gave them their wish and ordered them to attack.

The humans, damaged and degraded by the Va'alen in the first wave, had spent all of their heavy ammunition, as he had hoped. The mines they had left were gone, allowing the Va'alen free rein to move and swarm over the lumbering ships as they tore into them with their cannons.

The commander was already celebrating his victory, already imagining welcoming his Aq to the space station they would capture. He pictured himself presenting him with high-ranking prisoners to be recycled and consumed in honor of his glorious leader and their victory. He imagined being elevated to become the second-in-command of the expedition; the Gan-Ch'aal or Second Warrior and relished the thought of standing beside his Aq as the formal challenge for leadership was made. He knew that their Hive Lords never intervened in such matters, preferring to allow the Va'alen to organize their structure and leadership as they felt best. They must have known what Aq Qa'shal had planned to do, and they must have felt the presence of many Va'alen leaving the sector to begin their long journey to destroy the humans after they brought a second fleet to the system.

That daydreaming was interrupted by the sensor display in his ship bursting into life. A warning sound fired off multiple times. Each shriek of electronic alert indicated a jump signature detection, and for a moment he was worried that the humans were escaping and abandoning the space to them.

A glance at the display told him quite the opposite.

Eight more ships showed on the readout, and all of them humming with detectable weapon signatures. The numbers of his own ships decreased at an alarming rate only moments later as these new ships joined the fight. Knowing the battle was lost and the mission a failure, the commander faced a choice. He could either retreat, fly the long and torturous journey back to his people, where he would be executed for treason and failure, or he could report the failure via the communications relay and die in battle. Such was what any true Va'alen should wish to do.

The sub-leader was no politician. He had no family connections of worthy reputation that could stave off retribution for his actions. Instead he sent the report back to Aq Qa'shal and opened a channel to his mate in her ship. He called a Va'alen mantra to her, telling her that their bond was breakable only through death. That death would spark the Path of Ending and transform them to the next world. She roared back in unison with him as both ramped their engines up to full pitch and set a direct course for the nearest enemy.

~

"What killed it?" Specter asked as they carried Rogers carefully from the room they had found him in. His severed forearm rested on his chest as he stayed still and silent in his medically induced rest.

"Not me," Brandt said. "I never got a shot off before it had... I don't know, a heart attack or something."

I ended the life of the Va'alen, because I could not control the rage it felt through the Path of Ending, a voice said inside their heads. It sounded pained, as though barely holding on. *I have a proposal for you, humans.*

They stopped, almost dropping Rogers. Brandt hefted her new weapon and scanned a full three-sixty.

"Who the hell is that?" she called out.

Her head snapped around to the shadows behind her. Specter looked the same way. Something had caught their senses, but not their sight or sound or smell. Something *tickled* their consciousness like low-voltage electricity. Thin arms came into view ahead of a large skull and dark skin.

Big eyes without pupils contracted as it stepped into the light to protect its vision. It looked like a Kuldar, only different.

"You're Kuldar?" Specter asked.

No, it said, *we are something different. The Kuldar, like the Va'alen, were once our children.*

"Okay," Brandt said. "I call bullshit. We're taking you back to fleet where someone else can decide what to do with you."

NO!

The voice was suddenly stronger and reverberated like an echo.

I cannot leave this place, but I will give you everything you need in return for information.

"What information?" Brandt asked suspiciously.

I need to see the mind of a human who knows how you move between the stars without a portal.

"You want a Fold Drive?" she asked. "Is that it?"

We, it said as it slid back toward the shadows again, revealing that it was actually hovering, *simply want to return home without more lives being lost.*

Brandt didn't believe it, but she saw little choice.

CHAPTER 30

Deep Orbit of Proxima Centauri

"*Venture, Cortez,*" Dassiova said into the comm, "Are you jump-capable?"

They were. It was a risky strategy, but it both removed two vulnerable ships from the fight and got support to Torres and the *Ichi*, without losing a fighting ship.

"Do it. God speed," he ordered.

The two ships' icons blinked out on his sensors as he looked at the arrayed warships facing them.

"Talk to me, tactical," he said.

"Sir, they er… they're pretty much the same design and layout as we are. Same weapons, same multiple-layer shield emitters, same Fold Drive resonance…"

"Same shield harmonics?" he asked, thinking ahead.

"Can't tell, Admiral. Should I rotate our shield harmonics?"

Dassiova gave him a long, expectant stare until he did it.

"Incoming hail, Admiral." He nodded and stood in front of the viewscreen.

"Elias," the woman on the other end said. She smiled at him, a smile of triumphant evil.

"Massey…" Dassiova began, about to question her when the penny dropped.

A strangled noise from his tactical officer caught his attention. The admiral was glad that the young officer knew to keep his mouth shut when the comm was active to the enemy. Dassiova looked down at the console, identifying the reason for the noise. The ships were giving off a radiological warning.

"You goddamn—"

"No need for all that," she cut him off with a dismissive wave. "I just wanted to strongly suggest you listen carefully to what General Chakour of the M.E.A. says. Things could get... *messy*, otherwise."

"It was you all along," Dassiova stated. "Those ships. Designed from our schematics you sent from Mars?"

"Down to the last bolt and weld," she replied. "Only stronger and more heavily armed. You see, you're really not in a position to make any demands. That's why we are offering the UN a truce. A ceasefire, both here and on Earth, until we can agree on the best way to divide up the spoils of war."

Dassiova stared at her for a long time before glancing down and nodding. The link cut, leaving the screen in darkness.

"Chief, this is the admiral," he said into the comm device beside him. "Release Lieutenant-Commander Eze with my deepest apologies and escort her to the bridge." He walked away toward his quarters. "Anyone needs me, I'll be on the horn back home. Stay tight people. Like that bitch said: this could get messy."

~

"Ready?" Torres asked. The team was ready, and as the *Ichi* was brought to a low

geo-stationary orbit, he hit the override control to open the lower section of the shuttle bay ramp. The bay had already been depressurized when they broke the very upper limits of the atmosphere to allow them to jump and not be fried to a crisp.

The captain stepped up to peer over the edge, seeing thick clouds arcing with purple electrical discharge far below him.

"We wait for a gap, and we drop," he said, feigning a confidence he didn't truly possess. He'd had grown into command enough to know how to make it sound good.

"Jumping in three, two, o—"

"Bridge to Torres!" The captain faltered as he arrested his step to the abyss.

"Torres here," he said, a slight crack in his voice, which he coughed to disguise.

"Sir, two ships just jumped into this sector. We're being hailed by the *Cortez*. The *Venture* is also broadcasting ident codes."

The Venture, he thought. *She's got dropships and ground troops.*

"Give me a direct line," he said, slapping a shaking hand at the control panel to shut the ramp and re-pressurize the empty shuttle bay.

~

The arrival of the dropships filled with troops created a comm network as soon as they broke through the thin cloud cover where the storm was weakest. Chatter and hails filled their comms. One by one, the surviving members of Brandt's team sounded off. She called a medevac to her location first, then requested the ranking officer meet her to deal with the first contact situation. The alien allowed itself to be taken into custody; Brandt had to admit that she was happy it was someone else's problem and not her own.

Rogers was placed into a field stasis device—affectionately known as a coffin—capable of stabilizing him for the flight back to the *Venture*. There he would undergo emergency surgery. His arm was lost, that much was certain. She had only ever seen clean-cut limbs reattached and not messy wounds like his. She felt for him, knowing that a pilot of his skill level was uncommon. Brandt hoped that he could get the medical help he needed to do his job again. She said as much to Specter, who smiled.

"I know a guy who is good with prosthetics," he said. Brandt furrowed her brow.

"Did you just make a joke?"

"Yeah," he replied. "What of it?"

"Nothing," she said quickly. "Just … for a second there you just seemed like… well, *you* again."

"I've always been *me*," he said, "but I get your meaning. I'm back now. I'm sure of it."

"You mean you're Jake again?"

"You make it sound like I'm Doctor Jekyll or something."

"I didn't mean it like that," she explained. "I just…"

"I get it," Jake said. "It's okay." Brandt hesitated before asking the question on her mind.

"What are Hyper going to do with you? When we get back, I mean?" Jake shrugged.

"They can let me go or I can transmit their tech secrets to the whole UN."

"You'll blackmail them?" she asked, her eyebrows going up so high they risked altitude sickness.

"I'm sure I won't have to," he said. "Besides, something tells me they'll have their hands full mining all these crystals and other minerals. Who knows what's on the main planet, too?"

They turned as a long file of captured Va'alen came through, all of them much smaller than the others of their species Brandt and Specter had seen. So much smaller that they were the equivalent height of an adult human. These Va'alen had been found hiding in the mineshafts that the base protected. Crate upon crate of bright crystal had been harvested from deep inside the rock. None of humans yet knew what it was, only that it must be valuable.

Brandt was reunited with her team, what was left of it, and apart from Rogers and Paterson who needed medical treatment, she kept them on the surface to recover the bodies of their team. With the help of a squad from the *Venture,* they returned to the caves where they had encountered the large scorpion things, and there they found the bones of McMarrow.

The commander of the troops remained on the surface to conduct the defense and inventory of the base, which they were ordered to defend. Meanwhile, Brandt was shuttled up to the *Ichi* to rejoin her crew. She had delegated two troops from her escort to carry the heavy bag she wanted kept with her. The second she set foot through the airlock, she was summoned to the bridge. Deciding against stripping off the armor and letting out the smell, she went as she was dressed, including the alien rifle she had intentionally forgotten to surrender and catalogue.

"Good to see you," Torres said emphatically but distractedly as she entered.

She nodded to him and remained standing behind his chair.

"What's going on?" she asked. The atmosphere on the bridge was anything but relaxed.

"Another human fleet arrived and helped us defeat the Va'alen attack," Torres explained, forgetting that she hadn't even known about the armada heading to destroy them.

"What atta—"

"In a minute," he interrupted. "Looks like since we left home the first time, parts of other territories on Earth have splintered and formed a separatist alliance."

"Against the UN?" Brandt asked in shock.

"Not so much *against* us as *apart* from us. They want independence."

"Let them have it, then," she shrugged. Her casual throwing out of political opinions was a direct side effect of exhaustion. As a commander, she would otherwise know better than to give her true opinion.

"Yeah, well there's a little standoff going on right now, and I don't want to miss it. Helm, jump us back."

The *Ichi* blinked back into real space as a small and insignificant blip on the sensors of the leviathans facing off. The *Indomitable*, as damaged as she was, could hold her own against almost anything. The separatist fleet had twice the number of frigates and a fully armed carrier, but experience worked wonders over technology.

Countless numbers of soldiers in new gear had died on countless battlefields throughout the history of the human race.

"What now?" Brandt asked.

"Shh," Torres chided her as he tapped at icons to link into the channel.

"…sure you don't want to reconsider?" a voice Brandt didn't recognize asked with cruel threat echoing the words.

"Nah," Dassiova's voice shot back. "I'm good. You have a *lovely* day, though."

The comm channel cut and Brandt looked down at Torres. He didn't respond, just watched the sensors.

Brandt hit her comm device to bring up the ship-wide channel. "All hands, battle stations, gunners to pods, standby to defen—"

"Belay that order," Torres said. "All hands stand down." He looked at Brandt kindly.

"Just watch."

"Sir, Alliance fleet is powering up weapons and moving to flank positions."

"Awesome," Torres said flippantly. "Aaaany second now…"

Before the tactical officer could contain his squeaking excitement and get the words out, the display screen showed a dozen dull flashes at three-second intervals, as new ships filled the black expanse.

"Say hello to my li—" Torres began in an extravagant accent.

"Don't," Brandt said. "Don't embarrass yourself, *sir*." Torres took her point.

"Ladies and gentlemen of the Ninth Fleet," the captain announced gleefully, "meet the Tenth Fleet, all new and shiny."

CHAPTER 31

UN Base, Los Angeles, Earth

"Like it or not," Dassiova said to the assembled captains and senior crew of the fleet, "this is how it is now."

The room was quiet. The thought of the Earth being split again, of territories observing a wary ceasefire but always being ready to go to war, was sobering at best. At worst, it was the most dangerous state that any of them had ever known. The United Nations and the Middle Eastern Alliance had formed a hasty peace treaty. Their joint effort in the Centauri system had seen their defeated enemy confined to a single planet. Ships capable of orbital bombardment kept a careful eye on them until such time as a decision was made on what to do with them.

In the fleet's absence, the entire Middle East, most of Africa, and half of the Asian sub-continent, had declared themselves separate entities and cut themselves off from the UN. Half a dozen other smaller countries fell in with them for the promise of new technology. This greed, further driven by the promise of new materials and entire planets to colonize in the far reaches of the galaxy, plunged the Earth into uncertainty at a time when they had already been through hell. The Ninth Fleet had naïvely expected a healthy dose of world peace on their return.

The sudden and unexpected arrival of the separatist fleet in the Centauri system had put that foolish notion out to pasture.

"We have to stay tuned-in," Dassiova went on, "and accept the accords made generations ago about other planets being joint property of all territories. We can't claim a planet as belonging to our territory, nor can we occupy it for the UN. Whatever we discover out here belongs to all of humanity... that's what I've been told to tell you, anyway." He added the last words with a half-smile devoid of any humor. "We bled for this space. Our people died to take it, our ships were damaged defending it and *our* lives were on the line against the goddamned Va'alen..."

"It's progress, Admiral," Halstead offered. "The troops go in and secure the new territories, then the governments give all the land away to the politicians and civilians who don't know what it's worth and who haven't paid the true price for it."

Nobody answered her. All were deep in their own thoughts, after reading the mandate sent from Earth.

Colony ships were being constructed; the Ninth Fleet would be responsible for escorting them back to the Centauri system, where mining and farming colonies would be constructed. The next wave would be to populate the worlds made safe by the UN detachments there—ever alert for any returning Va'alen and keeping the civilians safe from the murderous wildlife. The thought of those natural dangers made Brandt shudder involuntarily.

"Good news is that we all have a month of shore leave," Dassiova went on in an attempt to change the dark mood. "Well... *you* do, at least. Use it well, because I want each and every one of you back with the fleet and fully charged for our next tour."

The fleet had docked their ships at Mars, trusting them to the suddenly far bigger contingent working the shipyards. The maintenance teams there promised to bring the ships all back to the standard they had first left in. The crews had taken a new transport back to Earth, fitted with a Fold Drive. Their next tour, limited to nine months, promised to be full of guard duty and dangerous safari-type expeditions protecting civilian, UN and company scientists. Those types would likely bumble around the alien world like the danger wasn't real. Brandt hoped that her team, Torres's crew of the *Ichi*, would be exempt from such boredom, because why have an elite recon vessel, crewed by elite personnel, and not use them for that role?

The gathered officers all groaned a little when their admiral, still their fleet commander/father figure/personal deity, advised that all departments and key personnel would be required to submit to a video debrief before shore leave would be granted. This would consist of sitting in front of a console with a live camera feed and being subjected to dumbass questions thought up by a civilian whose biggest danger ever faced was crossing the road. Said civilian invariably thought up the questions from the safety of their comfortable, security-controlled office, unrelated to the actual experiences of the crew. They wanted to hear that the weapons and armor were fit for purpose and that, if anything, they could do with slightly less protection and less firepower.

A report of that nature would mean a reduction in overall unit costs and, in turn, would represent a significant overall credit value to be found in the next fiscal year's budget for repurposing.

Certainly, it was a priority to demand that ground pounders deployed to the most dangerous zones were issued with uprated armor. Arguing that *everyone* needed the upgrade, with the astronomically expensive micro-singularity power sources and personal shield emitters, was likely to fall on deaf ears. Or at least ears that were still ringing with white noise, after hearing the credit tag value attached to each prototype unit.

Whatever they said, whatever they asked for, they knew they wouldn't get. The biggest threat had vanished when the Va'alen were removed from the system. They could safely go back to being armed and protected by the lowest bidder, as all the planet's resources went in to mining and colonization budgets.

"All we can do," Torres said quietly to Brandt as they filed out, "is keep doing our job…"

"…and hope we survive to take the pension," Brandt finished for him.

Torres chuckled; she had known exactly what he was going to say.

"You want to grab a bite with me and Amare later on?" he asked her, now open about their relationship after half of the crew had witnessed their reunion after her detention. The treachery of Dassiova's flight officer still stung all of them deeply, none more than Dassiova himself who felt that he should have seen it coming.

"Sure," Brandt said, eager to make up any good grace to her second-in-command.

"You hanging around base, or heading back home to see family?"

Brandt let out a mirthless chuckle. She hadn't seen what remained of her family in years and had no burning desire to start now. She ignored half the question and responded.

"Hanging around with Jake for a while. You know, try to reintegrate him to society and all that. They kept him locked up like a robot for so long that he's forgotten a lot of his social graces."

"Like the grunt had many *before* they got to work on him?" Torres joked as they walked toward the dropship hangar.

"True," Brandt agreed, "but he needs time, and some familiar faces to help him along the way. Paterson's wife is coming down to stay on base with us, and after that it might be time I went back to NYC for a week of real R-and-R."

Torres said nothing, but she was sure he was thinking something he found funny. To his credit, or at least his sense of self-preservation, he kept his mouth shut.

"He said what he wants to do yet? Now that he's a person again and not company property?"

"He wants to stay on," Brandt said. "Keep serving. It's kinda *literally* what he's built for."

"Under you?" Torres asked.

"We'll see," Brandt mused. "We'll see."

Agoura Hills, California, Earth

The transport settled down on the empty roadside. The driver powered down the electric turbines and let out a breath in the sudden silence left by the absence of engine noise.

"You good?" she asked.

Her passenger took his turn to sigh, and only his expulsion of breath carried a hint of electronic synthesis. "I'm good," Jake said. "I'm just…"

"Want me to go first?" Brandt asked. "Smooth the way for you?" Jake said nothing, but his scarred face looked back at her wearing an expression of deep panic. "I'll go talk to her. You stay put." She patted his knee. She knew that what she patted wasn't *him*, but that he could feel it. She exited the plain gray transport and zipped up her civilian jacket against the unseasonal chill in the air. Brandt was amazed how quickly her body adapted to any change of environment; on board the *Ichi* she was either too hot or uncomfortably

286

cold, as with the surface of the moon they were stranded on, only less extreme. Now she'd been back on Earth for a little over two weeks, the last five days of that in California with her friends, building up to this moment.

She stepped up the curb and reached down, automatically looking for the grip of the pistol that usually sat there; her unconscious gesture betrayed how nervous she felt at being unarmed, out of uniform and not stomping around in her armor. She didn't know whether it was the lack of uniform or the lack of weapons that made her feel more vulnerable. Less elite. More anonymous.

Stopping at the threshold, she reached up, squeezed her hand into a fist until her knuckles shone white, and let out another breath. Before she could knock, the door opened. She found herself looking down into the suspicious face of a teenage boy who resembled Jake Santana when she had first met him over a decade before.

She was so caught up in the familiarity that she just stood there; hand up, ready to knock, and mouth open.

"Yeah?" the kid asked.

"Hey," she said as she recovered herself and dropped her hand back down. "Your mom in?"

"Maybe," he said, "depends who's asking."

Brandt opened her mouth again to introduce herself. To invest her rank with pride, having truly felt that she had earned it. A rapid-fire burst of Spanish from further inside the house wiped the cocky look off the teenager's face in an instant and he replied so fast that Brandt didn't catch a single word. The teenager retreated, and the dark doorway was occupied seamlessly by a short woman, olive skinned, with kind eyes set between deep lines of crow's feet that were partly caused by laughter and partly by tears. She wore a simple apron and was drying her hands on a dishcloth.

"*Si?*" she asked. "*¿Puedo ayudarte?*"

"Mrs. Santana?" Brandt asked formally, her tone unfortunately screaming government business.

A resultant look of blank hostility descended over the woman's face.

"Listen to me," she began, fire in her eyes and an angry finger pointed at Brandt.

"You go tell them that I pay them the credits on time this month. I no behind on mortgage payment again. *Adiòs.*"

She stepped back to shut the door on Brandt who involuntarily stepped forward ready to shove her boot in the way. Then she remembered that she wasn't there with a squad of UN troops to search and seize; she used her words instead.

"I'm here about your son," she said. The door stopped mid-swing and opened a crack more.

"Thomas?" she asked, with worry affecting her voice.

"No, no, I'm sure Thomas is fine," Brandt said hurriedly to try and ward off any hysterics. "I'm here about Jake."

Maria Santana's face softened. A deep sadness mixed with fond memories washed over her in an emotional tide, transforming her from head to toe. Her voice changed, her shoulders sagged, and she seemed to grow a little older and more tired.

"You knew my Jake?" she asked.

"I've been here before with him…. a long time ago. My name's Leslie Brandt. Jake and I… we joined the UN together and were stationed together on…"

"I remember you," Maria said. "You got hurt by those people who took my boy from me." She crossed herself quickly, something Brandt guessed she did maybe fifty times a day.

"That's right," she said, lost for words until her inner self told her to get a grip. "Mrs. Santana, I—"

"You call me Maria, okay?" Maria said, opening the door and gesturing for Brandt to step inside. "I appreciate that one of Jake's friends came to visit me. I keep all his things, in storage."

Brandt didn't know why she was babbling about Jake's things, but her eyes strayed to the low table in the hallway. A framed picture of Jake in his dress uniform, surrounded by candles and with the posthumous medals the UN had awarded him to complete their lies, still boxed in their velvet-lined cases.

Brandt choked at seeing it but didn't know how to tell the still grieving mother.

Get a grip, she told herself.

"Mrs. Sant— Maria. Please can we sit? I need to tell you something."

Maria's face dropped, but she pulled out a chair from the kitchen table and sat.

"There's no easy way to say this," Brandt started, "but Jake is… Jake is alive."

Maria's face didn't change. It stayed frozen still as though she was expecting the punch line to a terrible joke. She said nothing, just stared until Brandt said her piece.

"Jake was badly wounded. He technically died a few times… I didn't even know he was on the same shuttle as I was… it was over seven years before…" Brandt stopped, closed her eyes and took another breath. "Seven years I thought he was dead too, but he isn't. He isn't exactly who he was before, but he's still here."

"How do you say this to me?" Maria whispered. "All this time I grieve for my first boy, for my baby, and *now* you say this to me?"

She stayed sitting down, didn't move, but her hostility was radiating from her.

"I'm sorry. I'm doing this all wrong," Brandt apologized in a pained voice. She was saved any further attempt by a long, drawn-out noise from the hallway. It was the universal sound of a teenager calling their mother. Maria sprang to her feet, sidestepped Brandt in the doorway with a speed and grace that made her realize where Jake got his natural ability, and she winced as the woman let out a scream.

Brandt spun around; the tall form of Jake 'Specter' Santana blocked the open front door.

Even without his prototype armor, even without the array of weaponry he usually carried, his tall frame appeared muscular in the rubbery exo-suit covering his prosthetic arms and legs, giving him the athletic body type of a pro swimmer.

The civilian shirt, cargo pants and boots looked more alien on him than her own plain clothing did.

"Jake?' Maria asked in a whisper.

"Mama…" he replied, the synthesized edge cracking in his voice.

"Jake… my Jake…" Maria descended into flowing, wailing Spanish as her second language could never even begin to explain the emotions she was experiencing. She flew at him, hugging her son before pushing him back to see him better and then hugging him tightly again. She stroked his face, kissing him and pressing his cheeks together roughly as she spoke.

Brandt walked past them as other doors opened in the house and two more of Jake's siblings joined the tearful reunion. She stepped outside, closed the door softly behind her and walked back to the transport with a satisfied smile on her face. She climbed back behind the controls and pulled up her sleeve to tap out a quick text comm into her forearm device. The message, which she knew would appear in her friend's brain with the built-in HUD, simply told him to call Paterson when he needed a ride.

She cycled up the engines, set a nav waypoint far to the northeast and piloted the transport up to cruise altitude. She hit the autopilot controls and leaned back. Her next priority was to place a call to her favorite steakhouse in her favorite city, reserving their best booth table for ten o'clock that night. Her status at that restaurant was already high, but the worldwide news of the crew's adventures had elevated her standing to a whole new level. She marveled at how quickly her recent disgrace had been forgotten. She guessed there might have been a worldwide UN-imposed media ban on anything negative. The next call she placed went through on video to Paterson, who was with his wife on the UN base.

"Yo," he said, as he sat back in view of the datapad he was using and took a long pull on a bottle of what looked like European lager. "How'd it go?"

"Emotional, dude. Emotional. I've told him to hit you up for a ride when he needs one, that cool with you?"

"Sure," Paterson answered. "You're not coming back here?"

"Nah," Brandt said as she leaned the seat back and put her boots on the sticker reminding UN personnel not to eat or drink in the transport's cockpit. "Got a dinner reservation in Manhattan."

"Eating alone?" Paterson asked, drawing out the words in a theatrical accusation, which he deployed in unison with rapidly moving eyebrows.

Brandt smiled. "I may have to call a lawyer before I answer that."

EPILOGUE

"If you'll observe, I'm about to begin," the German scientist, Professor Schulz said.

The autopsy was being witnessed live and via video link in a dozen other countries in all of the world's territories. By invitation, a team of scientists from the newly formed and highly distrusted Middle Eastern Alliance was there, although behind plexiglass and escorted by a small team of CP operators from the European territory.

"Notice the tough carapace is difficult to penetrate using traditional edged tools," the pathologist went on, performing the autopsy on the dead Va'alen. He worked a scalpel down a ridged seam before giving up, setting aside the small implement and lifting a small laser cutting torch. "So, I will carefully open up what appears to be a growth line between two parts of the hard exterior." Silence reigned; few of the spectators breathed when the tiny surgical tool sliced a path through the unbroken shell of the hostile alien's corpse.

"As you will see from the redacted reports," he went on as he worked, "this subject was killed by another alien capable of telekinesis and other, as yet, unknown abilities." How he would love to get his hands on one of those specimens and pick apart its brain. He cherished the hope of recreating the alien's ability to unlock the potential of the human mind.

He kept such thoughts private and concentrated on his task. He finished a cut with a theatrical flourish, before beginning another.

"Note the humanoid somatotype, yet with clearly insectoid influences, such as the enlarged body encased inside a shell-like carapace and, of course, the additional pair of limbs to make this creature six-legged. Spreaders, please." This last he added as an aside to his assistant, an American doctor of similar qualifications and experience in their field of xenopathology. He had less renown, however. The American had yet to earn a prize for his research papers. He placed the edges of the spreaders forcefully inside the cut made down the center of the alien's chest and activated the small motor that cranked them open. As it moved bit by bit, he made additional, small cuts with the laser torch to ease the way until, with a sinuous crack, the chest popped open.

The American scientist let out a noise like a weak yelp and stepped groggily away from the operating table to steady himself against the wall.

"*Hhrrrrgh,*" he let out, trying to stop the contents of his stomach appearing on the eternal record of the first alien autopsy. "*Hhhrrrrrgh!*"

"Control yourself, please, Herr Carter," the German doctor said peevishly. "If you cannot control yourself, please kindly leave my operating room in order that you do not contaminate the specimen."

"*Hhhrrrrrrrrrrrugh...*" Doctor Carter replied as he fled the room.

Schülz surreptitiously swallowed the sudden influx of saliva in his mouth as he heard the faint sound of splashing out in the corridor.

"As I was saying," he went on, "oh... oh, um, I er... *cut the feed. Turn off the cameras now!*" His was face pale and his words breathless.

Outrage erupted from the speakers and the live audience until the plug was pulled and the plexiglass whited out to blind anyone not inside the operating theater from the specimen on the table.

"What is it, doc?" an American soldier in armor asked with concern, one hand on the butt of his pistol.

"You won't need that," Schulz said as he recovered himself, "but I'm not sure our new friends have told us the truth."

The soldier was confused, but he leaned over and looked anyway. His own stomach flipped at the stale, rotten, ammonia smell of the alien's insides. He blinked away the tears in his eyes and looked inside.

Instead of the internal organs that he was expecting to see, he saw a small, and very dead Kuldar.

END OF BOOK THREE

Remember to sign up for my emailing list at **www. devoncford.com**
Follow me on social media for cover reveals, release information and general shenanigans:
Facebook: @devoncfordofficial
Instagram: @dcf_actual

Also by Devon C Ford
The *After It Happened* series:
(Also on Audible)
1 – Survival (Performed by R.C Bray)
2 – Humanity (Performed by R.C Bray)
3 – Society (Performed by R.C Bray)
4 – Hope (Performed by R.C Bray)
5 – Sanctuary (Performed by R.C Bray)
6 – Rebellion (Performed by R.C Bray)
7 – Andorra (The Leah Chronicles, performed by Kate Reading)
8 – Piracy (The Leah Chronicles, performed by Kate Reading)
9 – Home (Performed by R.C Bray)

The *New Earth* series:
(Also on Audible Performed by Marc Vietor)
1 – ARC
2 – SWARM (with Chris Harris)

The *Burning Skies* Multi-Author series:
(Also on Audible read by Neil Hellegers)
1 – The Fall
2 – Fallout (by Jacqueline Druga)
3 – Uprising (by Chris Harris)

www.ingramcontent.com/pod-product-compliance
Lightning Source LLC
Chambersburg PA
CBHW020300200626
46814CB00006BA/2016